I0452967

Bitter Vintage

* * * * *

Riona Kelly

Praise for Bitter Vintage:

Riona Kelly takes us on a tour in her latest fast moving, hard hitting romance of the grapes in BITTER VINTAGE. A page turner from start to finish involving a modern woman drawn into a past filled with passion.

M.L. Weatherington, author of FOR ELEVEN MILLION REASONS

Copyright © 2015 Riona Kelly

All rights reserved.

This book edition is published by:

Pynhavyn Press

First Edition: December, 2015

http://www.pynhavyn.com

This novel is a work of fiction. Names, characters, businesses, places, events and incidents are either the products of the author's imagination or used in a fictitious manner. Any resemblance to actual persons, living or dead, or actual events is purely coincidental.

All rights reserved. Quotations and short excerpts may be used for review; otherwise no part of this work may be reproduced in whole or in part, by any means, without written permission from the publisher or the author.

Cover Art by Angie Alaya

ACKNOWLEDGMENTS

Thank you to my Aunt Emilie, who was a second grade school teacher in Redondo Beach, California and was the first person to critique my first book back in 1965.

Thank you to my various beta readers, who offered encouragement and great feedback through each revision, and my editors for sound advice and invaluable assistance. Without your input this book might never have been published.

A special thank you to my collaborator on this, who shares the credit for the book. Patricia Kelly contributed in so many ways and is an integral part of the writing.

A big thank you to Angie Ayala for the striking cover.

CONTENTS

Chapter One

Monday, April 13, 1964

*T*he golden orange of the sun dropping behind the hills formed a breathtaking panorama as I came to the rise above the valley. A well of unexpected emotions bubbled up inside me threatening to break into a flood of tears at the once familiar sight. I pulled my car off the road onto the shoulder, switched off the engine, and gave into the sobs that escaped. As I reached for the tissues I had on the seat of my car to wipe at my eyes, I surrendered to the grief that I'd denied ever since my father's foreman had called in the early hours of the morning to deliver tragic news.

Still bawling like a child, I got out and walked the few yards ahead to where the road descended into the sheltered San Martino Valley. Our valley... the place where my brother and I had grown up on our parents' land, Claremont Vineyards. It was the largest vineyard in the valley and the only one with a full-fledged winery on it. I'd left this place almost seven years earlier to go to college, then on to San Francisco where I started my career as a journalist. My mother had passed on, my brother would inherit the winery, and there was nothing here for me, so I hadn't come back. Then that phone call had come just before daybreak this morning. Standing here, gazing into the past, I recalled those unbelievable moments.

"Martinique, *c'est Jacques ici*. I am so sorry. There has been a terrible accident." Although I hadn't heard his voice in close to four years, I recognized it as Jacques Boucher, who was the foreman at my father's winery.

"My father—?" I'd asked at once.

"Mais non. Not your father." His voice faltered. "It is Philip. His car went off the road. He is... He is gone. Your papa would like you to come home."

The shock of it shot through me. My brother dead? After a long pause, I found my voice. "Of course. I need to make arrangements here, but I'll be there by evening at the latest. How is my father holding up?"

"He is distraught, shaken by this, as we all are here. It is tragic. Please take care coming home."

"Yes, I will." I'd held the phone for another moment or so as the connection ended. Dropping back into my bed, I'd replayed the conversation in my mind, still not believing what I'd heard. Then I tried to plan what I would need to do to get away by as early as mid-afternoon. I had responsibilities, a job to attend, and arrangements to make.

I'd been practical, getting everything taken care of at home, arranging for a neighbor to watch my apartment while I was gone, getting clothes packed, and the newspaper stopped. A friend had agreed to take my dog, Freyda, a dachshund, in until I got back. I'd gone to the office, arranged for the leave of absence, and managed to get on the road by 3 p.m. Then I had driven straight into heavy traffic, so it had taken longer to get to this junction that was just north of Sonoma than I had expected.

I wiped my eyes, blew my nose and gazed across the valley. Beneath me stretched the hollow of land bordering on the Napa and Sonoma counties of California. From this vantage, it looked to be a low forest of deep green created by the acres of grape vines. Nestled among them, neat country houses squatted and sprawled with gardens and pools while the smooth blacktop of the road threaded through it. Beyond the next hill was the junction that would connect this road to the highway to Sonoma.

The expansive acreage of grape vines that comprised Claremont Vineyards sat towards the end of the valley with its back pressing against the tree-covered foothills. Although the house and the winery weren't visible from here, I knew exactly where they were. They had been my home for over eighteen years until I'd abandoned them for college and a career.

Now, of course, I wished that I had maintained a closer tie to my brother. But I always thought that there would be time to rebuild our bond later on.

What could I say? We always knew he would become the master of Claremont Vineyards, so even as a freshman in high school, I had made my plans to separate my life from this wine producing valley. Now it seems I had separated a little too much. I felt the guilt one often feels when one loses a member of the family not seen in a long time. Oh, I was a busy young woman, but not so busy that I couldn't have come here for an occasional weekend. I could feel the tears welling up in my eyes again and I bit my lower lip to stop it from trembling.

With the sun below the hills, the darkness was settling in and I still had quite a few more miles to go before I passed under the arched entryway to the house. I turned back to my car, the coveted, sky-blue MG my father had given me for graduation. Getting in, I pulled out another tissue to wipe my eyes.

As I glanced in the rear-view mirror, I caught a partial reflection of my tired face. My gray-blue eyes look black from the makeup smudged around them. My father had always said my eyes were enormous. When I was little, I was all eyes, like pictures of the wide-eyed children, but now with the makeup and red rims, they look sunken and somewhat grotesque. I felt as if I hadn't slept in a week. I resigned myself to the fact that no amount of makeup would help and wiped off the remaining traces of eyeliner. Pulling my long, honey blond hair back into a twist, I secured it with a couple of bobby pins, then I started the car and began the descent into the valley.

Down next to the vineyards, the leaves were no longer a mass of solid green. Here, the neatly-staked rows of grape vines marched in long lines as far as the eye could see. From their supports off the ground, heavy branches, like arching tendrils, hung to the earth. The vines, some still flowering, were just beginning to produce their fruit.

By the time I pulled the car between the stone arches at Claremont Vineyards, it was quite dark. It was a moonless night and I was thankful I still remembered the road so well as it curved through the eucalyptus-lined path to the main house. This was a French-style country house built by my great-great grandfather. Although he was building a life in the New World, he wanted to feel as if he was still in France. I stopped the car in front of the house and slid out from behind the wheel. As I took my suitcase out of the trunk, I heard the front door open.

"Marti! Thank goodness you've come. We were beginning to get worried."

Startled, I looked up as a stout woman came down the walk towards me. "Hello, Elaine," I said as she approached. "I wasn't expecting to see you here." She and my father hadn't always been on good terms.

"You should keep in touch, sister. I've been here almost a year." She took the suitcase from my hands. "Let me take that. You'll be in your old room. No one has used it since you left."

I followed her to the house, feeling more like a guest than a family member. Weariness settled on me and seeing Elaine had not helped ease my anxiety. I had never been especially close to my half-sister, nor she to me. She was nearly eight years older than I, the product of my mother's first marriage.

"How is Papa?" I asked.

"He's not doing too well. I am glad you've come, Marti. He's been asking for you since Philip... Since the accident." She opened the door and I followed her inside.

Even this had not changed. The same heavily padded furniture occupied the same spots they had when I'd last seen them. It was a cool night and the fireplace crackled as it sent warmth and the scent of a campfire into the room. Jacques rose to greet me. He was small, but sturdy, and dark-haired with sprinkles of gray through it. His face was tanned and showed a few wrinkles although I knew he was in his late fifties. Clear gray eyes above a thick hawk-like nose welcomed me more than the sad smile he offered.

"Martinique! *Ma petite*, it is well that you have come home." He opened his arms to embrace me. "If only circumstances were better..." He paused, looked as if he were going to add to it, then did not continue. I nodded, unable to say any words myself.

Elaine watched us and from the corner of my eye, I glimpsed the narrow-eyed, hostile expression on her angular face. As usual she resented the older man's affection toward me. She always had. I suspected it was due to the lack of similar expression in her life. In some ways, I felt sorry for her; however, Elaine never allowed herself to weaken, as she considered it, to closeness with anyone.

Jacques raised his eyes and his lips moved to say something else, but Elaine spoke first. "Come along, Marti. I'll take your bag to your room, then you'd probably like something to eat. Madame Boucher has made a quite delicious bouillabaisse. I remember it used to be a favorite of yours."

"Yes." I resented the condescending tone of her voice as if I was still the baby sister. "Yes, it is my favorite. But I'd like to see Papa before I eat. And I can find my own room." My voice was a little more sarcastic than I'd intended, but if it bothered Elaine, she gave no indication. She merely nodded.

"As you wish. Your father is in his room. Try not to tire him. I'll tell Madame Boucher to expect you in about thirty minutes." With that she turned then crossed the room to open one side of the French doors that led to the dining room and the kitchen beyond that.

For a few moments, I watched my mother's other daughter and thought she'd grown plainer, if that were possible, in the last seven years. Her shortly cropped hair was a dull brown, looking greasy, and the little weak curls were limp against her scalp. Her face, unremarkable except for the broad flat-tipped nose inherited from her father, was deeply tanned by the warm California sun and almost matched her hair. Her eyes were gray, not very large and huddled next to her unplucked eyebrows.

As I recalled, her father was a stocky German and she resembled him quite closely. At least, she did not resemble our mother, who had fine, delicate features. I thought she could be more attractive if she'd use make-up and style her hair, but she had never shown any desire to improve her appearance. Although the sweater and pants she wore were expensive, their ill-fit conveyed the impression of shabbiness.

I turned back to Jacques, who was watching me and no doubt, deducing what I was thinking. He gave his head a shake. "Ah, she is not *tres charmant*, your sister." He looked sad and weary as if he had been battling something a long time. "In many ways, I believe she is the cause of many headaches around here. But enough! Go see your papa, *ma petite*. He is waiting."

Although I wanted to know more about what headaches my half-sister caused, I knew Jacques would say no more now and I was anxious to be with my father. Telling him we would talk later, I grabbed my suitcase and went through the doorway to the right, which led to the hallway and staircase.

My bedroom was the first one across from the bathroom on the left-hand side of the stairs. Four bedrooms and three baths were on this side of the staircase; the master bedroom with its private bath suite was on the other side.

The house, a two-storied rectangle, had a one story extension off the kitchen that provided living quarters for the household help. About fifty yards from the house was the square building where the field workers slept. The tasting room was a separate building adjacent to the right side of the house and the winery was back closer to the right side of the barn. Beyond all of this were the acres of grape vines that ran across the valley and up the lower elevations of the hills.

As I entered my bedroom, I realized that it was just as I'd left it. Nothing had been touched, except to dust, and the room was spotless. The lovely rose pink bedspread I'd chosen when I was ten still covered the white wooden double bed. Behind it extended a high padded headboard covered with rose-colored velvet. With a small smile, I recalled how delighted I'd been to discover a bedspread that matched the color of the headboard so closely. Across the window were rose-tinted frilly curtains that allowed pink sunlight into the room. Even the wallpaper on the window wall cascaded with hundreds of pink roses.

I could still hear Mama's voice as she decorated my room. "Oh, Marti, darling. I think pink is just about the prettiest color there is for a young girl. Don't you think so, angel?"

In complete agreement, my hopeful, younger self had thought that it made the room seem like a fairyland. Now it seemed too sweet for anyone past the age of sixteen, although I'd kept it that way until I'd left home. I think I did it mostly because it reminded me of my mother.

I shook myself out of these distant thoughts, then went across the hallway to the bathroom. I refused to see my father until I'd refreshed some. This was the blue bathroom–lavatory, Mama had called it– blue with gold accents. I washed my face in the pale blue marble basin, then brushed my hair to smooth it out.

For a few moments, I regarded my face that was so unlike Elaine's. Sweeping dark brown lashes framed my eyes while my eyebrows arched just enough. Like my mother, I had a heart-shaped face with a straight, Patrician nose that tilted up slightly at the tip. I was almost a duplicate of my mother, I thought. Even our height was the same, five-feet-two-inches.

While a complete re-do of my make-up might alleviate some of the signs of exhaustion, I decided not to take the time. My father would be expecting me and I'd dallied around long enough as it was. I ran my hand down the front of my dress to smooth it, then turned to go to my father's room.

Chapter Two

"Entrez."

My father's voice answered my knock. Nervously, I opened the door. Even though my father loved me deeply, it had been several years since I'd last seen him and I was uneasy. A dull light greeted me from a small lamp on the table by the chair.

Unlike the furnishings of my bedroom, this chamber contained heavy Mediterranean furniture, much of it antiques. A massive carved desk squatted before the window that over-looked the tasting rooms, positioned to give my father a view of the activity there. In front of it was a carved high back chair with a gold and green brocade seat cover. The huge mahogany bed occupied the center of the back wall where its eight-foot carved headboard rose almost to the high ceiling. The green bedspread was neatly tucked in behind the exquisitely carved sideboards and footboard so that none of the superb craftsmanship should be hidden.

On the wall, next to the hallway, a matching armoire with three drawers faced the bed. The crowning piece of the set, an eight-foot dresser with double mirrors and an Italian marble top, dominated the opposite wall.

But all of this I was aware of from long familiarity with the room for my eyes rested immediately upon the old man who sat hunched in the arm chair. A newspaper laid across his lap where he'd just put it down. The sunken eyes gazed across the dimly lit room to me.

"Martinique! Welcome home, my daughter. Welcome home. Come in. Sit where I can see you." His voice sounded old and worn, but there was strength still behind it.

In obedience, I got the high-backed chair from behind the desk and sat facing my father. I was shocked by the changes in his appearance. Even when I was a child, he had not been young, but he'd never looked as old as he did now. He was nearing seventy-five, but the tired, wrinkled face gave the impression of ninety. In fact, it was difficult to believe he could have aged so in a few years.

"Don't you have a kiss for your father anymore?" he asked. With a start, I realized that I had failed to greet him at all. I had been too stunned by his appearance.

"I'm sorry, Papa." I hugged and kissed him, feeling his still strong arms pressing me to him for a moment. I stood back. "You've changed so. I hardly recognized you."

The wrinkled old face split into a half-smile to reveal his aging teeth were still even although slightly yellowed. "Time, the persistent witch, caught up with me all at once. Now I'm a broken old man and you, my dear, are my only surviving child. Incredible!" He laughed bitterly. "I've outlived them all—two wives and three sons. But I still have my daughter."

His faded blue eyes grew tender and his leathery fingers touched my cheek. "My lovely daughter... You're so like your mother. Now, tell me what you've been doing these past few years and why you've not come to visit your family?"

This was one of those moments I'd dreaded, but now that it was here, it didn't seem half as hard as I'd expected it to be. The familiar ease I'd always had with my father returned as I sat back and told him all about my work at the West Coast News periodical. "WCN, that's what we call the magazine for short, is controversial, presenting all sides to a story. We try to cover anything of interest to people, from politics to arts, so long as it appeals to the general public. My editor, Paul Thorpe, has been described by Business World Weekly as a 'young, dynamic genius who pulls everything together and puts out this widely read glossy.' Their words, of course, but still very true."

"Young genius, eh?" Papa said, picking up on the one thing that interested him. "Is he married?"

I smiled a little at that. "No, he's not married... or living with anyone. We've gone out a few times, but it's nothing really." I underplayed my relationship with Paul, which was more than I let on. No point in getting into that right now.

Papa nodded his head thoughtfully. "Hmm, he can't be much of a genius if he's let you pass by him."

"I didn't say it couldn't be something. We just aren't ready for it. Anyway, he really has his hands full and so do I. This magazine is the most exciting thing I've been associated with and it sort of consumes my life. I'm afraid the idea of coming for a visit didn't even cross my mind."

My father pushed forward a little in his chair. "What about vacations? Doesn't this Paul-fellow allow you vacations?"

"Guilty again. I had vacations, but I spent them researching ideas I had for articles. For instance, did you know that there's a small group of people, brilliant people—doctors, lawyers, politicians—in Oregon who've been fighting personal income tax as being unconstitutional? When I heard about it, I had to investigate. I ended up spending my whole vacation talking with these people and finding out just what they were doing. I followed them all over the state, attended meetings, talked to lawyers preparing court battles, and really got to know them and why they were doing this. It turned out to be a great article. But it took my whole vacation."

I stared down at my hands, small with thin long fingers, folded in my lap. My college ring was the only ornament that dressed them. Unlike Mama, I almost never wore jewelry. I wasn't captivated by the glitter and they got in the way when I was working. I kept my fingernails trimmed to a short, straight line which was practical for typing and office work.

In the past few years, this house had ceased to be the image of "home" to me. That had become the apartment off Geary Boulevard that connected to the word. "Of course, now I'm sorry I didn't come back here. I never expected anything to happen to Philip and it never occurred to me before that you could die. I guess I thought there was plenty of time. I always thought you'd be here like you are as much a part of the land as the vineyard itself. Dumb of me, wasn't it?"

"Perhaps a little naïve, but it's forgivable. I sometimes wonder myself if the vineyard will not die before me." His voice was sad and his eyes seemed distant as if they weren't looking at me at all.

"Why do you say that? Has there been trouble? The vines look perfect—"

He raised his right hand. "No, no! Nothing is wrong with the grapes or the vineyard. We've had no serious problems since 1885 when the root louse destroyed all the grapes and my great-grandfather had to start all over again. No, I was speaking figuratively. I've had three heirs to this vineyard, three fine boys, and all three have died before me. Is there a curse on it, daughter?"

"You don't believe in curses," I answered at once. "In spite of your French education, you are a modern American and American vineyards don't get cursed. Cussed maybe, but not cursed." It was an old family joke.

He laughed a little at that. "Oh well, it's a good thing that you don't believe, then, because you are the next heir to Claremont Vineyards."

I don't think I really took in what he said at first, then I gaped at him, stunned. For some reason, it hadn't consciously occurred to me that he would leave the vineyard to me, but perhaps it had been in the back of my mind since I'd told Paul I didn't know how long my leave would be. Still, I objected. "But, Papa, I never planned for this. I know nothing about growing grapes. I don't really want a vineyard! I have my own life—"

"Wait, Martinique! Don't get all excited. I'm not dead yet; however, you are still my only living relative unless you get married and produce some more heirs, then this vineyard will be yours one day." His voice had that ring of finality as if there was nothing more to be said.

"You could leave it to Elaine," I suggested without any real conviction. Papa wasn't deeply impressed with his step-daughter. "She's always liked the vineyard..." I broke off my sentence as I saw the glower on Papa's face. Even through the folds and crinkles of it, there was disgust and what surely must be hate.

"Elaine!" He spit the name out when he was finally able to speak. "I won't even see her! Why your brother tolerated her here, I couldn't say. I think... I think she is responsible for Philip's death!"

Chilled by these words, I could feel an uncertain fear taking hold and I swallowed hard. "I—I thought it was an accident. Surely you can't be serious. I mean, it's— Well, it's just not possible!"

"Not directly, no. But still responsible. She—" Suddenly, he began to gasp. "On the desk... my pills... hurry!"

I was half-way to the desk before he finished speaking. His face had reddened with his anger, then blanched as he made a grab for his chest. I'd never seen anyone look so pale and I was frightened. I found the small vial of pills and my hands shook as I handed one to him with a glass of water he'd had on the table next to the armchair. After he swallowed the pill, he leaned back and closed his eyes, his shaky hand still clutched against his chest. After a few tense moments, his breathing became easier and I relaxed a bit.

I sat down again and watched him. What was it Elaine has said? *Try not to tire him.* That was hardly adequate warning for this. It seemed evident that my father had a heart condition. Why hadn't I been told? At last, he opened his eyes again.

"Are you all right, Papa?" I asked, anxiety straining my voice a little.

He nodded, then spoke slowly. "I'm sorry if I frightened you. I'm all right now, but I am quite tired. I think we had better talk again later."

I agreed with him, then kissed him good night. At the bedroom door, I paused for another backward look at him. When I turned away, I realized my eyes were moist.

As I started downstairs, I was amazed to discover how weak I felt. Between not eating and the shock in my father's room, I moved at a slower pace than normal. My knees felt spongy and I wavered a little, feeling lightheaded. Well, a good meal would certainly take care of that, I surmised. I crossed the living room and dining room without encountering a soul. When I entered the kitchen, I was relieved to find only Madame Boucher there.

"*Bon soir*, Martinique." She greeted me in French. Even though she'd been in the United States for twenty years, she still spoke only French. "It's about time you came to dinner." Then she hugged me. "This house is not the same without you, Bon-Bon".

I smiled at the use of my childhood nickname. Madame Boucher had called me that ever since she came to the vineyard with her new husband and discovered that the little daughter of the household had a passion for bonbons. For that matter, I still loved the light, sweet confection.

"It's good to see you again, Madame," I replied in French, then stepped back to look at her. "You haven't changed a bit!"

Emilie Boucher was only slightly taller than me, very thin, with fine, dark brown hair that curled obediently around her face. Her skin was fair and her dark brown eyes seemed to sparkle. If her small, narrow lips weren't actually smiling, they gave the impression that she was constantly frowning. At first, this had frightened me until I discovered what a delightful person she was under that sober exterior.

Sitting at the large wooden table, I soaked in the welcoming ambiance of the room. It had always been my favorite, but, of course, I loved food. Definitely a French kitchen with dozens of spices and herbs filling the room with enticing fragrances. The bay window behind the table overflowed with hanging planters and pots where sage, parsley, bay, chives, and thyme grew abundantly. Outside, where the kitchen and the servants' wing met in a ninety-degree angle, was the vegetable garden, which Madame attended herself.

Across from the table, the cooking island, complete with six gas burners and two huge ovens, dominated the center of the room. Along with the refrigerator and dishwasher, the appliances were installed about ten years ago. The island was covered by a layer of red brick except on top where red and white tiles and chopping boards filled in the areas not used by the range. The walls were painted off-white, contrasting with the fruitwood finish of the cabinets. It was a homey kitchen where you felt at ease with a cup of tea and a croissant in the afternoon or a late night sandwich.

A large, cast-iron pot simmered on one of the burners. I didn't need to be told it contained the promised bouillabaisse. The delightful, tangy aroma was as familiar to me as the scent of a rose. My mouth watered and I could almost taste the tender shrimp and succulent bass. From this, Madame ladled out a large bowl of the steaming stew and placed it in front of me along with a plate of freshly-baked French bread and creamy butter. For the final touch, she produced a bottle of our own Sauvignon Blanc wine. Eagerly, I devoured the feast.

When I pushed the bowl away, I thanked Madame profusely and complimented her cooking, as was expected. We spoke a few minutes about the food and the garden before I asked the question that had been on my mind ever since I'd left my father's room. "Madame, has my father been ill lately?"

She paused in wiping the counter, a puzzled look on her face. "Ill? No, Bon-Bon, not really ill. Sick at heart, perhaps, with all that has happened and the death of your brother. But who is not sick over that?"

"So, he has nothing wrong with his heart?"

She looked amazed that I would ask that. "But, no! He is in perfect health for a man his age. Whatever made you think that?"

"He has pills—?"

"Of course! But it is not his heart. The doctor says it is a nervous condition. When he gets upset, the whole chest tightens up and he can't breathe. It is nothing to worry about." She smiled at me in assurance.

But I'd caught something else in what she'd said. "What else has happened besides my brother's death?"

"Why, nothing!" She answered at once, looking away at the spot she had been wiping on the counter.

"You said, 'with all that has happened'. I thought maybe something else had occurred."

"That is just my way, you know. One event... one tragedy... It creates so much grief." Her voice faded, touched by sadness.

I accepted that and with relief from my worries came exhaustion. It had been a long, tiring day. "*Bon soir*," I said, bidding her good night and went straight up to my bedroom.

For a moment, I wondered where Elaine was, but I really didn't care so long as she was out of my way. Still, the question Papa had introduced plagued me. In what way did Elaine contribute to my brother's death? Did they quarrel? Did he leave in anger, driving recklessly to his demise? That really puzzled me. That and Jacques' statement about Elaine causing headaches. But the answers would have to wait. I was much too tired to think about them now.

Back in my room, I unpacked my suitcase, putting my gray pin-striped pantsuit and an evening dress on hangers in the closet, then hanging my shirts and blouses next to them. I'd brought the gown as a precaution since I knew my father often liked more formal dress for dinner.

I crossed to the delicate French provincial, white chest of drawers. I opened a drawer to put away my folded jeans and found a black knit shirt, along with a pair of black stretch stirrup pants, in it that I'd left behind. A smile tugged at my lips as I recalled wearing them to school and the bonfire rallies.

Then my eyes moved to the matching dressing table where a gold-framed oval mirror held court. A porcelain ballerina on a music box was the only object on the dressing table. Tears stung my eyes as I picked up the box and the little tinkling notes plucked out the "Dance of the Sugar Plum Fairy" from the "Nutcracker Suite". As it played, the smiling ballerina figure, dressed as the titular character, rotated in a dance on the pedestal. The music box had been a Christmas present from my mother just two months before she'd died of a brain tumor.

At Thanksgiving, Mama had taken Elaine and me to San Francisco to see the "Nutcracker Suite" performed by the city's renowned Ballet. Actually, Elaine, at twenty-two, couldn't have cared about seeing the ballet, but had gone because she wanted to shop. I'd been captivated with the whole performance, especially the beautiful fairy. In my mind's eye, I could visualize Mama's laughing hazel eyes delighting in her young daughter's enchantment. Then she'd found this music box for me to remind me always of those beautiful days. I think she knew even then that she was dying.

The music dwindled to nothing and the mists of memory faded from my eyes as I set it down. The depression I'd felt since Jacques had called settled like a weight on me now and manifested itself in a tightness in my chest that threatened to choke me. Going to the window, I threw it open to the cool night air.

Was this just depression? Perhaps it was something else. An uneasiness touched me. Something out of place... I was being silly! Of course, it was just depression. After all, who wouldn't feel very low returning home for a funeral and then being reminded so vividly of another deeply loved person long dead?

I'd already snuggled into bed when I realized that my bedroom window was still open. My first thought was to leave it, then I recalled how chilly mornings were here. With reluctance, I shoved the covers back, crawled out of bed and, leaving the light off, crossed to the window. As I reached out to shut it, a shadow detached itself from the servants' wing. Although it was dark, I knew the shape of that black figure. It could only be Elaine.

As she ran across the opening toward the workers' barn, another figure stepped out from behind the building to meet her. Obviously, it was a man, for the person was tall and appeared to be broad-shouldered, but not too heavy. He greeted her with a kiss and, arms around each other, they strolled toward the fields.

"Well, well," I murmured to myself. "Plain Elaine has an *amour*." I suppressed a grin. Who would have thought it? For a moment, I wondered at the relationship, then decided it was none of my business and went back to bed. Once again, I snuggled under the covers and fell at once into a deep sleep.

Chapter Three

*W*hoever said things will look better in the morning had obviously never awakened to a dull, gray, overcast day with a funeral to attend. I stared out my bedroom window and thought I'd never seen a gloomier morning. Heavy clouds hung overhead promising rain before the day was over. A fitting day to bury my brother, I reflected.

I dressed in the most somber clothes I owned, the gray pin-striped suit I'd brought, with a plain white blouse and went downstairs to breakfast. Now, in the somewhat subdued light of this new day, the events of the previous evening disturbed me even more and the question of why my father suggested Elaine had anything to do with my brother's death nagged at me. There was something going on here and I hadn't been clued in on it. The reporter in me was determined to find out exactly what. If Elaine had, in any way, caused or contributed to Philip's death, I wanted to know about it. I considered the whole idea preposterous, yet my father wouldn't have made that statement if there wasn't some truth behind it.

Again, I was fortunate enough to miss Elaine at breakfast–she'd eaten and gone out nearly an hour before I came down, I was told– and I had a quiet, light meal alone. My father, according to Madame Boucher, no longer came down to breakfast or lunch and, less and less frequently, to dinner.

Following breakfast, I had time for a walk around the grounds. Near the house and along the left side of the curved entry road was a magnificent garden. My great-great-grandparents had planted it and built the stone walls around it themselves. Inside were hundreds of roses, irises, tulips and dozens of other flowers. Beautiful old oak trees offered shade while a few willow trees draped the large pond in the center. Always a favorite place for ducks, the green-tinged water rippled with the movement of several of them now. I went to my special place, a stone bench under one of the oaks where I'd carved my initials in the bark to mark it my spot. This was my retreat for solitude and serious thought where I'd spent many of my teenage days.

I sat down on the bench, feeling the cool roughness of it with my hands. On sunny summer days, the oak provided welcome shade, but now it only added to the general gloom of the day. I gazed around, letting the serenity of the garden calm me.

For a while, I thought about the great-great-grandparents who had built this house and garden when they settled this land. Martin Claremont had been among the first settlers to begin a vineyard in California. The thriving winery that bore his seal now was built up painstakingly into the profitable business it had become. That first American Claremont had crossed the ocean and a whole continent to start a vineyard like the one he'd left behind in France.

He was the youngest of eight boys, but he was ambitious enough to want his own land. Traveling with a few other French and a number of Germans, he'd come to America to fulfill his dreams. I tried to picture this area in those days. It was not too difficult if one could imagine only the green plains and valleys without the grape vines and with mostly oak trees dominating the landscape. He and his young wife worked long hours to plow this land and plant it while they built their home here. What a lot of courage that took. I sometimes wondered if my contemporaries had the strength or courage to match that achievement.

This vineyard he'd labored to build was handed from father to eldest son through the generations. Only once was there any real problem for my family–that was what my father had mentioned–the root louse in 1885 that nearly destroyed all the grape vines. Of course, this affected a great many other vineyards, not only in the

United States but in Europe as well. It was a serious problem. I recalled Papa telling me about it. He said that a different variety of grape, a native American plant, was almost completely resistant to root louse and was grafted to the European grape varieties they were growing to produce a strong, resistant wine grape. This combination plant still grew in our vineyard.

Our vineyard–I hadn't thought about it that way in years.

My father was the fourth Martin Claremont to own it. My brother would have been the first Claremont not named Martin to inherit. That was because we were my father's second family. There had been a Martin Claremont the Fifth, as well as another son, Alain, whom my father had by his first wife. Alain and his mother were killed in a train accident when he was fourteen and the elder boy, the heir, died in World War II, towards the end. My father had already married again and Philip had been born before his other son's death. I was named after my father and I doubt any child could have been more loved and cherished, but Philip was his pride and joy, another Claremont to continue the line. His death must have been a terribly bitter blow to my father. To lose three sons is a very heavy burden for a man to bear. And now, he wanted to pass the vineyard to me, his only surviving child.

I tried to look at this objectively. I don't think I ever really wanted it although there had been a time when I was jealous that my brother should get it simply because he was the older and the son. I think it hurt even more when I realized he would have gotten it even if he had been younger. But I'd grown up with the knowledge that it would not be mine and I never entertained the idea. Then there was this strange twist of fate.

To face it now was a whole different thing. I wasn't prepared for it and I tried to think if it would be possible for me to run this business. I suppose I would have Jacques and his wife to help me, but there was so much to it that I knew nothing about. Of course, my father was right; there would be plenty of time to prepare for it.

I glanced at my watch again—nine-twenty. Soon it would be time to leave for the chapel. As I gazed around the quiet place once more, my eyes rested on the ducks bobbing in the water and for a few more moments, I let happier memories recharge my spirits.

As I left the garden, I spotted Elaine, who approached from across the driveway. When she noticed me, she raised her hand in greeting and broke into a slow trot. She was dressed in a somber black pantsuit that suited her perfectly.

"I was just looking for you," she said, sounding out of breath.

"At the end of the drive?"

She shot a glance at me, but her expression remained neutral.

"I'd thought maybe you'd gone to the Kellog place. It used to be a second home to you, as I recall. Didn't you go to school with Beth Kellog? So I thought you might have gone over there and I went to check when I couldn't find you. We'll be leaving in a few minutes. The services start at ten-thirty, you know. I do hope it doesn't rain during the funeral." She paused to look up at the gray sky. "It certainly looks discouraging, doesn't it?"

I nodded, thinking it was unusual for Elaine to be prattling on in this manner. She sounded as if she was trying to hide something and once again I thought about my father's accusation and wondered exactly what Elaine had done.

I rode with my father to the nearby town where the services were being held in the small chapel that served the whole community. The town was little more than a junction. The few buildings housed a general store, a post office branch, a bar and grill, the church, and a gas station. For anything more, the people of our valley went to St. Helena or the city of Napa. The cemetery on the hill was the final resting place for all of the American Claremont family, so far—from the first Martin and his wife through to my father's wives and his sons.

The limousine turned into the church parking lot where a fair number of vehicles were already parked. My father spoke little during this ride and I didn't press it when he barely acknowledged my presence. Mostly he stared blankly out the windows as if only his body was in the car and his mind was somewhere else entirely. I couldn't even begin to guess his thoughts, but frankly, my mind was occupied with my own remembrances.

The funeral itself was a dreary affair and I felt as though it was happening to someone else. Due to the extent of the injuries, my brother was buried with a closed casket, which only added to the unreality of the whole morning. The family was in a side box, away from the general mourners where they could have privacy during the service. It also afforded me the opportunity to look at the gathered friends and acquaintances who'd come to bid farewell to Philip. I recognized many of them and some were employees and part-time help at the vineyard.

About mid-way up the aisle, I noticed a young woman with dark brown hair, who wiped at her eyes often with a handkerchief as she attempted to cry unnoticed. Who was this? She displayed more grief than a casual friend would, so she must have been close to Philip. I wanted to find out more about her and how she knew my brother.

One of Philip's college friends and a fraternity brother, Edward Solano, rose from the pew to the left of us and went to the podium to give the eulogy. His voice cracked as he recalled the good times the two of them had shared throughout college and beyond. Once his voice caught in an emotional sob, but he managed to control it and ended the tribute with a wonderful memory from a recent fishing trip he and Philip had taken.

A few other friends from both high school and college spoke for a few minutes, although there was one very close buddy who appeared to be missing. One who should have been doing the eulogy. I didn't understand why he hadn't and I looked for his face in the mourners, not spotting him. Then the Reverend started the final prayer.

The long procession of cars followed the hearse with the grim black box to the cemetery where six pallbearers carried it to the grave site. I recognized them all–Jacques, Edward, two more of Philip's college buddies and two of our neighbors, although not the one I had expected. A light rain began to fall as we said the final prayers. For a long time, I stood staring at the box as if I might find some answers there.

This is it, I thought, the end of all life, the ultimate goal from birth, to be laid within the earth in a box. *One day that will be me in a similar box...* I shivered involuntarily. I don't believe I'd ever really thought about death before and I was shocked by this revelation.

I turned to look at my father, who was leaning most of his weight on his cane as he accepted the condolences of friends and business acquaintances with the same graciousness he always displayed for those outside the family. His grief was private. To all appearances, he was holding up well, but I was concerned that he might have another attack such as he'd had the previous evening.

The same could not be said for Madame Boucher. She was crying fiercely on her husband's shoulder. Jacques patted her back and shoulders as you would comfort a child. She had loved Philip, and me, as her own children, the ones she could never have.

I looked for the weeping girl from the service, but I couldn't see her. Perhaps she'd not come to the grave site. Not everyone did.

"Marti?"

I heard the soft, deep voice behind me, but it seemed distant in this setting. It was a voice that belonged to days long past, to high school proms and country picnics, yet the voice of the man I had expected to see here. Slowly, I turned to face the speaker, not sure if I'd really heard him or only imagined it. He wasn't the same as I remembered him. The seven years since I'd last seen him had made a big difference. He was heavier now, not overweight, but not the scrawny teenager who'd taken me to the prom. His long chestnut hair had been replaced with a shorter, neatly styled cut that accented his face. The warm brown eyes hadn't changed though and they still held affection for me. This was my other brother and Philip's best friend,

Lee Kellog.

"Hello, Lee." I hesitated a moment, then I hugged him and the awkward moment was over. I felt his arms close around my shoulders, strong and comforting as he held me to him.

"I'm so sorry, Marti. I never dreamed that when I saw you again it would be like this."

For a few moments, I thought I was going to start crying, only this time the tears wouldn't be for Philip. I'd been so glad to see Lee that I hadn't realized I'd missed him until then. His right hand caressed my hair with a light touch, then he pulled back and looked at me, his eyes meeting mine and holding them as they always had. I wondered how much he might think I'd changed.

"I have to talk to you. When can we get together? Perhaps I could take you to dinner?"

I shook my head. "I don't think dinner would be a good idea under the circumstances. At least, not for a couple of days yet. I'll meet you in my garden tonight at seven-thirty. My favorite place. Do you remember it?"

He nodded. "I'll be there." He held my hand, his fingers caressing my thumb, a moment more then left with as much stealth as he'd arrived. I wondered then why he hadn't said anything to my father and why he hadn't been inside at the service. Later, I would have to ask, but I had to surmise that some kind of falling out had occurred between him and Philip.

With a touch of reluctance, I returned to my father's side. As we made our way back to the car, the light rain turned into a downpour. The tears that I'd held back did start then, a steady trickle down my cheek just as the raindrops cascaded down the car's windshield. Pulling out my handkerchief, I wiped my eyes. Such a damn depressing day to bury him...

* * * *

$\mathcal{I}$ tapped on my father's door before entering. He'd asked me to join him for a late luncheon in his suite, foregoing the large spread that Emilie had set out for the stream of visitors who came by to pay their respects and offer condolences. I'd greeted as many as I could before excusing myself and leaving the task to Jacques and Elaine. We made excuses for Papa, citing his health as an issue and that he was upstairs resting.

When I entered the room, I found that Madame Boucher had already delivered a tray of sandwiches and the silver coffee service. My father sat behind his desk facing the window where the rain rivers still flooded down the pane. He did not seem the tired old man at this moment. Some of the old vitality showed–the same vitality he'd passed on to his children.

"Papa?" I spoke softly, not wishing to intrude upon his thoughts. As he turned to face me, I felt as if his eyes looked through me, not at me. For a brief moment he seemed not to recognize me, then he bent his head and gestured toward the tray of sandwiches.

"Enough for five of us," he said wryly. "Pour the coffee and we will talk while we eat."

I poured two cups, then set one and the sandwiches in the middle of Papa's desk. My hand hovered over the tray, selected a chicken salad sandwich from the assortment, then I sat down in the side chair facing my father.

"Have you thought about our conversation last night?" He plucked up a sandwich, indifferent to the type.

"Yes, I have. I don't really know if I want this place. I don't know anything about the wine business although I suppose that Jacques could run it for me."

"My daughter, there is no one else to inherit the place. I could never leave it to Elaine. When I married your mother, I tried to treat Elaine as if she was my own daughter, but she was always aloof, rejecting me. In short time, first your brother, then you were born, children of my own blood. Claremont Vineyards will belong to

Claremonts as long as one lives to own it. When there are no more Claremonts, there will be no more Claremont Vineyards.

I looked up in surprise. "What do you mean, Papa? Why won't there be?"

"Because I put a clause in the business contract that if the business is ever sold, the name will not be transferred with it. Of course, any children you might have would still be considered Claremonts as far as the business is concerned." He paused, sipped his coffee and watched me with an expression that did not seem pleased. "Incidentally, I saw you speaking with Leland Kellog today. About six months ago, James Kellog approached your brother and me about selling them our vineyard."

I almost choked on my sandwich. That couldn't be right! Everyone knew my brother was devoted to this land.

"Of course, we said no. Then for a while Beth Kellog was here frequently to see Philip. I think she was hoping for some kind of romantic involvement to marry into the vineyard. But when nothing happened, she left for New York."

By now I was sitting up with a stiff back and staring at him. I had the feeling my father must have imagined this. What he was saying just wasn't possible. I'd known the Kellogs all my life and they weren't the kind of people who would do that. They knew my brother would never sell Claremont Vineyards, not to them or anybody else. And Beth was not the kind of girl to throw herself at my brother or any man.

The disbelief must have shown clearly on my face, for my father gave me a sad smile and continued. "I can see you don't believe me, but it is true. You can ask Leland about it when you see him." Papa's perceptive eyes must have caught an unconscious reaction to this remark. "Oh yes, I know you're going to meet him. When I saw him talking to you, it wasn't hard to conclude that he would want to see you. You're a much better catch than Elaine, my beautiful daughter, and you were always good friends, weren't you?"

I didn't answer him, but I could feel my face flush. So Papa went on talking about the vineyard and the way he wanted his will changed when his lawyer came in the morning, but I wasn't really listening. Although my mind rejected Elaine and Lee as a couple, it was dawning on me that he could very easily have been the man she'd met last night. He was the right height and build. A man could change a lot in seven years. It was possible Lee had but still unbelievable. Once the seed of suspicion is sown, it propagates rapidly and I was already beginning to allow myself to believe the worst of the Kellogs. Thinking back, I realized that although Elaine had come from the Kellogs this morning claiming to have been looking for me, she could have just left Lee.

I forced my mind back to my father's voice. He was still talking about the business and what his plans were. "Papa, why did you say Elaine helped kill Philip? What happened between them? What exactly happened in this accident? No one has given me any details."

"I was upset with Elaine. Forget I said anything about it. As to your brother's accident, it was just that—a terrible car accident." He waved an arm as if it would dismiss the subject.

"You wouldn't have said it just because you were upset," I said, firm in that conviction. "It's not like you to make accusations. What are you trying to hide from me and why? Was there something unusual about Philip's death other than he was so mangled that it was a closed casket?"

"I said forget it, Martinique!" He spoke sharply, a hard edge on his voice. "There's nothing more to be said."

I bit my lower lip as I felt my anger rising. I didn't like the sharp tone of his voice nor the way he dismissed my questions. I wasn't a child anymore. I was more convinced than ever that something was irregular about Philip's accident. I stood up. "I think there is more to be said. Much more. And if you won't tell me, I'll find out on my own."

Turning, I left his room, walking rapidly. Although I could feel his eyes on my back, he said nothing more.

In my room, I paced and allowed my nerves to calm a little. I was trembling with my anger. I hadn't had cross words with my father very often and it always upset me when I did. It was still drizzling outside, so I grabbed my raincoat and boots. Rain or not, I had to get outside and walk. Within ten or so minutes, I was sloshing through the rows of grape vines.

Walking to hash out my thoughts was a habit I'd started in Berkeley while I was attending the University. I found it helpful to get out into the fresh air. Of course in Berkeley, and later in San Francisco, a cool breeze generally blew across the Bay, which made it a pleasant walk. There were quite a few shops near the University and I loved to browse through them. In San Francisco I enjoyed walking down to Fisherman's Wharf and strolling through some of the import shops and sampling the variety of fish offered.

But here, in this vineyard with the steady tapping of the rain, it was peaceful. All around me were the dark green leaves of the vines that had been a constant part of my childhood. Here and there, tiny bunches of grapes were just beginning to develop. For the first time since I'd been here, I truly missed my brother. Philip wasn't in the house; his spirit was here in these fields where he loved to be. I felt almost as if I could turn and see him bending over a vine inspecting the young fruit.

He had loved this vineyard, just as Lee Kellog loved his family's. Both boys had accepted their responsibilities at an early age and had gone to work in the fields. When my father had sent Philip to Europe for a summer to study European vineyards, Lee had gone with him. It seemed incredible that the Kellogs had seriously believed they could buy our property. Yet my father wouldn't lie about it.

I'd known Lee all my life, but how well did I really know him? He was a couple of years older than me and a year younger than Philip and they'd been best friends. Beth Kellog and I were the same age and naturally enough, I had practically "lived" with the Kellog family half the time. By the same right, Lee and Philip had been almost inseparable.

As I grew older, Lee became friendlier to me and all through high school, he was my big brother, friend, and frequent date for school functions. Once in a while, I would go with boys in my class, but I'd preferred Lee's company and I'd felt secure in our friendship.

But what was really in Lee's mind? What made him tick? No matter how much I thought about it, I had to admit that in very many ways, Lee Kellog was a stranger. We'd never really talked about him, about what he wanted. He'd just always been my big brother, more than Philip even. The one "little Marti" could tell all her problems to, the shoulder to cry on, the instant escort. But I was never the sympathetic sister to listen to his problems or even his thoughts. Funny, Philip talked to me a lot, but not Lee. Was I just too caught up in my own little school dramas that I never gave him the chance to confide in me? Could he really be the kind of person who would use Elaine to get what he wanted?

Then there was Beth, my best friend. Surely I knew her well enough to know that she wouldn't try to use Philip? She'd idolized him when we were younger. What girl wouldn't? He was Adonis, beautiful and shining, envied and adored. But that was it. Beth was a level-headed girl and she was honest, especially with her emotions. As a matter of fact, I was sure I'd gotten a letter from her at Christmas telling me about her new boyfriend and that they were thinking about getting an apartment together near Central Park. She was an illustrator and from what I gathered from her letters, doing very well.

Which brought me to another point. Why was the Kellog family keen on acquiring our vineyard? Certainly they didn't need it. Their own vineyard was almost as large as ours and they made an excellent profit off it, plus they had income from other sources. It didn't make sense. I felt like I'd been handed a thousand-piece puzzle to put together only to find all of the key pieces missing.

Back to Philip, I instructed myself, and I mentally pictured my brother. Slender, medium height, always smiling, Philip was fun-loving and well-liked in the community. He'd always had a fondness for alcohol and not just wine, but he was a good drinker. That is, he held his liquor well. When I thought of Philip, one of two pictures came to mind—either the handsome, laughing young man with a mug of beer in his hand or the blue-eyed young Adonis standing among the grape vines as if he'd sprung from the earth as much as the grapes. It was the latter picture I preferred to remember.

Suddenly, I sensed I was not alone although I'd heard no sound except that of the rain tapping the earth and splashing into puddles. I turned and was startled to see a figure about ten yards from me bending over one of the vines. For a disoriented moment, I imagined it was Philip. Then the figure straightened and I realized it was Elaine. Had she been following me? She waved her right arm in a wide sweep and approached, stepping carefully over the puddles between the rows.

"What are you doing out in this rain?" she asked as soon as she was within hearing distance. "I saw you from the house and I thought you were going somewhere, but then you just stood here. Is something wrong?"

"I wanted to walk. It's a habit of mine."

"In the rain?" she questioned, disbelief evident in her voice.

"I don't mind the rain. In fact, I find it rather soothing."

"Oh." So much conveyed in that simple, flat oh, that said she didn't quite believe me. "Well, I wanted to talk to you."

I raised an eyebrow. Must be my day for unexpected conversations. I resumed walking at my leisurely pace as Elaine fell in beside me.

"You told Madame Boucher you would be staying for a couple of weeks."

I turned my head to see her. She was looking down, side-stepping puddles. "That's right."

"Why?"

I stopped and turned to study her expression. The dark eyes glittered at me and for the first time, I sensed that she was actually hostile toward me. Granted, we didn't share any affection, but I never thought she disliked me.

"Why? Why have you decided to stay now? I thought you'd leave right after the services. What about your job? I mean, you said you had a hard time getting away to even come in time for the funeral. Don't you have to go back?"

"I have leave. After seeing Papa, I decided to stay a little while. In case you forgot, my brother just died and my father may need me here. He seems a bit fragile at the moment. I want to stay until I'm sure he's okay."

A frown compressed her face and she looked like she was about to explode. "So you're staying because Papa needs you. Why should he need you after all these years that you haven't bothered to come here at all? Is that the only reason, Martinique?"

"I don't see where it would concern you. If I choose to stay here, that's my business. Mine and my father's. Now I prefer to walk alone, if you don't mind." That was telling her. I was a bit surprised at the forcefulness of my own voice.

Her face reddened and when she spoke again, her voice was brittle. "I have one more thing to say, Miss Martinique Claremont. I've been here, you haven't. See that it stays that way."

"Is that a threat?" I managed to stay somewhat calm, even though I was seething inside. How dare she?

"If you want to look at it that way." She turned abruptly and scurried back to the house. She was not so careful of the puddles on the return trip.

I watched her progress to the house for a few minutes, then realized I was shaking. She was openly telling me she wanted Claremont Vineyards! She, who had no real claim, was defying my right to it. Maybe I hadn't wanted it before, but I wouldn't let this go unchallenged. I was still a Claremont.

Chapter Four

*L*ee was waiting in front of the duck pond. I could see him as I hurried up the path, a tall, dark figure pacing back and forth, then leaning against a tree. I was late. A small voice within me asked if I'd ever been on time anywhere. Silently, I admitted I had not, but this time it hadn't been my fault. My father had chosen dinner time to deliver a long-winded eulogy about Philip. I thought he must have drunk too much wine in the afternoon for he rattled on quite a lot and he usually organized his thoughts better. When I had finally been able to escape, I was already fifteen minutes late.

He heard me coming and started down the path to meet me. His voice seemed loud in the quiet of the garden.

"Marti! I'd almost given up. Did you have trouble getting away?"

"Only an unexpectedly long dinner. I'm so sorry. Today has been a terribly hard day for my father."

Lee reached out for me, grasping my right hand and pulling me closer to him. The drizzle had stopped, but it was still a little chilly and I welcomed the warmth of his body against mine. His free hand brushed my hair and I tilted my face up to see him. His eyes sparkled with the same affection they'd shown this morning. He could be a coldly remote man at times, but he'd always been gentle with me. Suddenly, he kissed me with an unexpected fierceness. I responded to his kiss, lifting my left hand to cup around his neck, pulling him closer, and a burning warmth sprang to life deep within me.

His mouth pulled away, but his forehead remained pressed against mine as he held me tightly. "I wrote to you so many times. Why didn't you answer my letters?"

"I thought it was better not to write." I replied with the response I had resolved many years earlier. "We were both so young and our lives had different patterns. It seemed best to end it there."

As I saw the pained look in his eyes, the memories of all those years flooded into my mind. He'd written at least a dozen letters to me when he'd gone to college, but I hadn't answered them. Our parting then had been difficult. I knew he loved me, but I couldn't regard him any way other than as a brother. I hadn't wanted to encourage him and I couldn't find the nerve to tell him outright. When I refused to write to him, I recalled that Philip and I had a terrible row over it and didn't speak for a few weeks. And what about now? Now, with what my father had told me still ringing in my mind?

"Our lives weren't really that different. You could have stayed here. You could have married me." His voice held a sadness I wouldn't have believed possible.

I looked down. I had never wanted to hurt him. I still didn't. "I wasn't in love with you, Lee." Then before he got the wrong impression, I added, "That is, I didn't love you in that way. You were like a brother and it was obvious you wanted more. I guess that's why I didn't want to write."

"So you wanted to spare my feelings." He kissed me again, gently this time. As his arms pulled me even closer, I began to tremble from his touch, aware of the feelings that conflicted with my perception.

"What about now? Do you still think of me as a brother?"

"I— I don't know." I turned away from him and walked to the duck pond. The emotions I was experiencing were totally new to me. I felt as if I'd been kissed for the first time in my life. Could I really be so drawn to Lee? But I was unsure. I mustn't love him, at least not until I knew the truth of what was happening here. I sat on the edge of the pond wall and stared, without seeing, at the water.

Without saying a word, he sat beside me. A couple of minutes passed and he didn't speak, just watched my face, then he asked, "Are you okay?"

I nodded. "It's been a very difficult day and I'm confused. So much has happened." I paused, wondering how much I should say to him before I plunged ahead. "Lee, how did my brother die?"

His eyes reflected his puzzlement. "What do you mean? There was a car accident. Didn't they tell you?"

"I mean the details. I know there was an accident and he's dead, but that's all I know. What exactly happened?"

He looked down. His right hand traced a circle on the stone as he silently thought about what he would say.

"Please tell me. I want to know. I need to know and no one seems to want to tell me."

Taking a deep breath, his eyes came up to mine and there was pain behind them. "There are some things that it's better you don't know. Let's just leave it at that."

"No! I can't leave it! Everyone is avoiding telling me. What dark secret are you all hiding?"

"It's not a 'dark secret'. I just don't want to upset you."

I didn't move, didn't speak, only stared at him with every ounce of my being willing him to tell me about it. After a minute or so, he swallowed nervously and continued.

"Phil had been drinking that night, more than usual. He lost control of the car on the curve above the pass."

I knew the place he meant. It was on the opposite side of the valley from the way I'd come from San Francisco.

"The car plunged down the side, rolling a few times. Phil was trapped inside and he was crushed. The coroner said he died instantly. We didn't find him until early the next morning, around six a.m."

"You found him?"

"Jacques and I. When he didn't come back here, Jacques came to get me and we went looking for him." He broke off. His voice was strained and I could see it hurt him to talk about it. I'd somehow forgotten he was Philip's best friend. Or had I thought he was no longer a friend because of what my father had said?

"Philip usually could control his drinking," I said quietly. "It's hard to believe he was drunk enough to go off a road he knew so well."

He shook his head, a sign of his own disbelief. "I know. I've thought about that night a lot. There's one thing that still bothers me, Marti. It was raining and the dirt on the shoulder was pretty muddy. Where the car left the highway and went over, the tracks in the mud were smooth and straight. I would have expected to see skid marks or something to indicate he slid."

I shook slightly as a chill went up my spine. "Maybe he couldn't see through the rain and thought the road continued instead of turning. If he was disoriented... What did the sheriff say?"

"What you just said. That the rain was heavy and he was probably too drunk to realize that he'd left the road. But Phil had been on these roads all his life; he knew them forward and backward. He would have put on the brakes if he'd taken that curve too fast. I'm sure he knew the curve was there."

"What are you suggesting?" I was unnerved by his words. They were true and I knew it. Philip did know the roads too well. Even I still remembered them clearly, every curve.

"I don't know exactly. I only know something is not right." He noticed me shaking and pulled me to him. "Now I've frightened you. I'm sorry, honey. I didn't mean to tell you any of this. It's just my suspicions, nothing to prove anything."

As I clung to him, my arms shook. "I'm glad you told me, even if I don't understand it. There are so many things that aren't making sense right now."

"For instance?"

Was now the time to bring up my father's accusation? I hesitated, then thought if not now, then when? I blurted it out. "For instance, why did your father try to buy Claremont Vineyards? For instance, are you seeing Elaine? Did Beth—"

"Did your father tell you this?" His face registered alarm.

I nodded affirmatively.

"How much do you know about what's been happening here?"

"Not much. Just what my father's told me."

Lee pursed his lips in thought, then reassured me. "I can't tell you everything right now. Yes, my father tried to buy your place, but I won't tell you why. I have seen Elaine a few times, but there's no romantic involvement. I haven't loved any girl since you left here. No one. All I can tell you is that there's a good reason behind it all and you'll have to trust me for now."

"There seems to be a lot going on around here that people don't want to tell me about," I said, my voice rasping a little.

He squeezed my hand. "Believe me, there is a good reason. Please trust me for now, Marti."

This time I said nothing and we were both silent, lost for a bit in our own thoughts. In the stillness, birds chirped a cheerful evening song as they began to settle for the night. Somewhere in the garden a frog croaked, calling for a mate. It was so peaceful, yet I was uneasy. How much could I trust Lee?

At one time, I would have trusted him with my life. Strange how a few words could create so much doubt about a person that you'd been sure you knew. I felt a sudden resentment of my father for saying anything and causing so much turmoil. Logic cast aside, I hated my brother for dying and bringing me back to this confusion. I regretted that thought as soon as it entered my head. It was just so damn hard. I would rather have been absorbing the serenity in the garden than waging a battle in my mind. And I had to cope with this unexpected change of emotion toward Lee.

"How long are you staying?"

His words startled me and I jerked my head up, drawn back from my thoughts. "Oh, I don't know exactly. A couple of weeks maybe." I pushed back my hair and smiled wanly. "It depends on how my father is doing."

Standing, I pulled my light weight jacket about me a little tighter as if it would keep me warmer. Now that the sun was below the hills, the air began to chill and we'd sat motionless for too long. As I thought about what Lee had said, I resolved one thing. "I'd like to go to the pass where the car went over. Will you go with me tomorrow?"

"Sure. I can get away about ten. Will that work?" He sounded tired and I got the distinct impression he wasn't eager to go.

"That would be fine. Thanks." I slid my hand over his and laced my fingers between his for a moment. I wanted him to know that I appreciated it.

A small smile touched his lips, not the warm engaging one that lit up his face, but a sad, wistful curve that was barely there. Then he took my arm to walk me out of the garden.

As I turned to go up the path to the house, I paused. "I'll go on from here alone." I anticipated that my father would be watching from his window.

Lee was hesitant. "Are you sure you'll be okay?"

"Yes. I'm sure. I'd rather no one in the house saw me with you. I'm sure you understand."

"Until tomorrow then—" He pulled me in and planted a quick kiss on my lips, then released me.

As I hurried away, I turned once to see him still standing at the path's edge, a shadow in the darkness. I ran the rest of the way to the house.

No one was in the living room when I came in, but the fireplace radiated a welcome warmth. Grateful to whoever started it, I sat in the nearest chair to soak in the heat. After a few minutes, I slipped off my jacket and relaxed completely. As I stretched my arms and thrust my legs out toward the fire, I realized I was drained. It had been a long, emotion-charged day and although I was used to the pressures of the magazine, they were nothing like this.

Right now, the idea of a steaming hot bath appealed to me and I pictured myself slipping into a tub full of lilac-scented bubbles. But imagine was all I could do. My tired muscles didn't want to budge from this comfortable position.

Eyelids half-closed, I watched the flames dancing. I was always fascinated by the rhythms of fire. I used to think they were magical. They brought to mind a different fireplace, one at the Squaw Valley lodge where Beth, Lee, Philip and I had gone for the weekend to celebrate my seventeenth birthday. There was a late March snowstorm that left the mountains covered with glistening, fresh snow. It was all so beautiful and it couldn't have been more perfect for me. I recalled falling flat on my rear in the snow when I'd tried to ski the first time and I could hear Philip's laughter echoing across the valley.

Lee had given me a locket with a diamond set in it for my birthday. Although I didn't wear it much, I still had it tucked away in my jewelry box. That was the first time he'd told me he loved me. I'd laughed it off, thinking it was just a casual thing, but later I'd realized how serious he was. I was positive then that I didn't love him. Now I wasn't so sure.

I closed my eyes and thought about Paul Thorpe, picturing him easily in my mind. Of medium height, he was thin with a lean, oval face and a strong jaw covered with a jet-black beard that was always impeccably trimmed. Impeccable. That was the word for Paul. Although he was English-born, he'd spent the majority of his life in the United States. He retained his English accent more for show than anything else. His hair, almost as black as his beard, was worn long and combed straight back from his forehead. His eyes were a bright blue with fine lines around them from frequent squinting. I was extremely fond of Paul. Up until a short time ago, I had believed that I loved him.

My thoughts were interrupted as the door squeaked open. My eyes flew open and I turned to see Jacques closing the door. His mouth broke into a huge grin when he saw me.

"Ah, Martinique, there you are. A gentleman called from San Francisco for you. He sounded English, but he didn't leave a message. He said he would call back tomorrow."

"That would be my boss." I straightened up, smiling back.

"Ah, of course. Would you like some hot cocoa? I'm going to have Emilie prepare some for me."

"That sounds wonderful, Jacques. I would love some. Thank you."

Paul had called. Just my luck to miss him. With the mention of him calling, I suddenly felt that I needed to talk to him. At least he would be one person I could tell my concerns without worrying about what I was saying. I picked up the phone and dialed Paul's San Francisco apartment. No answer. He might be working late, so I tried his office, but that number switched to the answering machine.

"Hi, Paul. It's about 9:30 and I just got the message that you called. I'd like to talk to you and I'll call back tomorrow morning."

I guessed that Paul was checking on me. I had brought some work with me from the office. A couple of articles I was working on for the next issue of the magazine were about half-done and I figured I would have some time to complete them. He hadn't been thrilled that I wanted to take two weeks. While I knew some of his reluctance was because he counted on me to handle a good part of the editorial work at the office as well as writing articles, I also thought it was because of our personal connection. At least, I hoped that was part of it.

Jacques returned with a tray carrying two steaming hot mugs of cocoa and a plate of assorted French pastries. He placed them on the table between us and offered the plate for the first selection. I reached for a delicious-looking raspberry tart as I thanked him again. I'd always been at ease around Jacques and now he seemed to be at least one person I could trust here.

"What is going on, Jacques? Everything seems so different, so off balance. It's not just my brother's death."

Jacques took a big bite out of a cream puff, washed it down with a gulp of cocoa, then leaned forward. His quiet voice still carried a French accent. "I don't know what has happened, *ma petite*, but you are right. Something has changed. It began about six months ago.

Your brother always confided in me, but then something began to trouble him and he quit talking to me. Your papa also did not call me into his conferences as he always did before. He did not interfere in the way I ran the vineyard, but I felt he was hiding things from me. Elaine kept arguing with Philip about something, but I could never hear what it was. Whenever I came into the room, they stopped."

"Is that why you said that Elaine was causing headaches?"

"*Oui.*" He sighed and shook his head before taking another sip of his cocoa. "She is nothing but trouble, that one. She argues with everyone. She even argues with Emilie! You know my Emilie's no trouble. She loves everyone. She is just a simple country girl who does not like to get involved in quarrels."

Hearing the annoyance in his voice, I could readily understand it. Emilie was the last person anyone would want to argue with, especially Elaine, who spoke outrageous French. It was an almost comical image.

"No, there is something wrong here, but I don't know what it is."

We sat quietly, sipping our cocoa, savoring the warmth and the quiet company. After a bit, I asked, "Was there anything else that was different about my brother? Did he have a new girlfriend or anything like that? Was there something that would have upset him?"

Jacques rubbed at his chin with his long, sun-browned fingers. "He seemed worried. He was not himself. You know what I mean? He began to look very tired as if he was not sleeping well. And he drank a little more than he usually did. That is all I observed."

I absorbed this and tried to fit it into my puzzle. Jacques lit a cigarette and before I realized it, I'd asked him for one. As he passed it to me, I felt a stab of guilt. I hadn't smoked in six months and poof! Just like that, I couldn't function without a cigarette. I pulled in a deep draw and almost choked. After a couple of coughs, it got easier.

"I talked to Lee Kellog today," I said, trying to gauge how much I should say to Jacques. He solved that dilemma quickly enough.

"Oh, yes. He is a good man." His eyes saddened and watered. I wondered if he was thinking about the morning he and Lee found Philip. "He was very distressed at your brother's death. It was almost as if he blamed himself."

"Was there a reason why he would?"

He shrugged his shoulders. "Not that I know. Philip did not talk to him much in the past few months. Like most of us here, he cut him out. When Beth was home from New York for a couple of weeks, she spent a lot of time with Philip, but Lee was not around often."

So much for Beth and her departure. A simple vacation visit with family and friends. Why had my father twisted it? I wanted to ask Jacques if Lee had been dating Elaine, but I couldn't bring myself to ask the question. Not yet. I knew Jacques would tell me the truth and I was afraid to know. I guess I wanted Lee's version to be true.

Our conversation drifted to other subjects—my job, my apartment, my love-life, such as it was. I told him a little about Paul while stressing that we were not really a couple, then asked myself why I kept doing that. As the clock chimed the half-hour past ten, I decided it was time for that hot bubble bath and said good night.

On a hunch, I hesitated to turn on the lights in my bedroom. Instead, I pulled back and crossed the room to the window. Sure enough, there was Elaine stationed by the servants' wing again. Now that I knew where to look, it was easy to spot her against the light-colored building.

My mouth went dry and my heart jumped as the tall figure strode toward her from the workers' barn. She'd already stepped away from the wall and had started out to meet him. I realized it could be Lee and my mind raced for an explanation. If it was, he had to have come up from the road and circled around the grape fields to behind the barn. Why this odd meeting and what were they planning?

I made my decision. I had to find out.

Chapter Five

S till in the dark, I stepped across the room to the small lamp by my bed. It wouldn't be as obvious a light from outside as the overhead one. Next, I rummaged through the dresser and pulled out the black stretch pants and black knit top that I'd found. Standing well away from the window, I wriggled into them, delighted that they stretched enough to fit my slightly fuller figure, then with a quick pair of twists, pulled my fair hair back and covered it with a black scarf wrapped into a turban. It wasn't the neatest job, but it would do.

As I grabbed my jacket again, I stole across to the window, pressing myself flat against the wall, then I peered out. They were still out there, walking arm and arm toward the winery. I left the small lamp on and slipped out as quietly as possible. If they spotted the light, they might think I was in my room reading or even taking the hot bath I'd promised myself.

The fatigue had disappeared now and I was alert and cautious as I went downstairs. Taking care to not alert anyone, I let myself out the back door. For a few seconds, I stood near the house and let my eyes adjust to the blackness, then I moved toward the trees. With the new moon barely visible, the sky was filled with stars, but they didn't help illuminate the way any.

Although I tried to go as quietly as I could, to my own ears I seemed to be making too much noise and prayed that no one else heard me. I ducked in behind the nearest tree and paused for a quick reconnaissance of the area.

Looking toward the house, I could see the light shining through the window of my room, but it wasn't the only beacon in the darkness. With a shock, I realized that the last room down the hall also had a light burning. That room was Philip's! As I watched, the window winked out as if the house had shut one eye. Someone had just been in Philip's room.

But who? Elaine was here in the back fields with Lee. There was no way either of them could have circled back to the house in this short a time. My father? Perhaps, but not likely. I was sure he was sleeping soundly by now. That left Jacques and his wife. My eyes flew to the servant's wing. I could just see a glow from one of the windows that told me the Bouchers were watching television—or at least one of them was. Although Madame didn't speak English, she understood some and enjoyed watching the shows. I was certain it was not she who was in Philip's room. But what would Jacques be doing there at this hour? I was very curious, but I wouldn't be able to catch whoever it was now and I still had to follow Elaine and Lee. I needed to know exactly what was going on between them.

Gazing toward the winery, I saw no sign of them now, but I knew they'd gone that way. I ran across the open field as quickly as possible, not liking the exposure one bit, and stopped next to the nearest end of the long building to catch my breath and listen for any noises or voices that might suggest their location. It was quiet. Too quiet. I had no idea where they were or what they were doing. If the man was Lee, I didn't want him to discover I was following him.

A small, rustling noise sounded near me and I stiffened. Only when a field mouse passed me did I begin to breathe again. I wouldn't have known it was a mouse at all if he hadn't squeaked a couple of times as he scurried past me. In the silence of the night, he'd sounded far louder than I expected. My cowardly half began wishing I hadn't come at all. Mustering what little courage I had, I told myself that I'd come this far and I was going to find out what was happening.

As I pressed my back to the wall—if anyone approached, I wanted to know about it—I side-stepped my way around the corner of the building. When I'd passed the crushing equipment and was facing the house again, I realized I'd gone completely around the building without seeing anyone at all! I made my way back to the door and tried to open it, but it was locked as I'd expected it to be.

The only thing to do now was to try the worker's quarters nearby. I raced across the ten or so yards to the building and repeated the procedure there. The results were also a repeat. I cursed silently. I couldn't have lost them! Then I spotted the tool shed. It was more of a barn than a shed, built to house the plows, tractors, truck, gondolas and other farming equipment. Perhaps they'd gone in there.

I estimated the distance at about seventy-five feet with only muddy ground in between. I'd have to move over the mud with caution so I'd be exposed for a few minutes. At least there were no windows in the shed so if they were in there, they wouldn't see me unless they came out while I was traversing the open ground. I bit my lower lip, then decided to try it. I said a hasty, silent prayer that they wouldn't see me and started across.

The mud wasn't as bad as I'd feared it would be, but I still made slow progress. Once or twice, I almost slipped and I was grateful I had good balance. After what seemed like a long time, but was only a few cautious minutes, I stepped into the darkness next to the building. I leaned against the wall and strained to hear. There was no sound. Inching my way up to the door, I listened again. Nothing. Not even a hint of noise. Very slowly, I pushed the door open and slipped through it into the shed.

The inside was pitch black and totally quiet. I was disappointed. Leaning back to rest against the wall, I tried to think of any other place they might have gone. Then I heard something outside. I couldn't tell what it was, but I moved away from the door. My hands groped for the tractor or whatever the nearest piece of equipment might be before I ran headlong into it. As I touched the metal and identified the shape, I crouched down beside it. There was no light in the shed and if whoever approached had a flashlight or lamp, I had ample time to slide under it before I was spotted.

Barely breathing, I knelt and listened again for the noise. Silence. I waited a few more minutes, but nothing stirred. Discouraged, I stood up to retreat back to the door. No point in staying in this dark shed any longer. But something held me and I realized my jeans must have caught on the tractor. Kneeling again, I ran my fingers over the material until I felt where a piece of metal held it.

As I fumbled with it, the edge of my hand brushed against the floor and something slid on the concrete surface. I paused and groped around, feeling the area where my hand had touched. My questing fingertips found the object, a chain of some sort. As I explored it by touch, I felt an engraved medallion of some kind at the end of it. I wished I'd brought a small flashlight with me or even a pack of matches. Thrusting the chain into my pocket, I turned back to the snagged material. After struggling with it for a few more minutes, I finally freed my pants leg, tearing it in the process, then felt along the wall, and intervening farm machines, to reach the door.

Still cautious, even though I heard no sounds outside, I pushed the door open a crack and gazed out. Everything appeared to be normal. As I stepped out, a large white cat ran across the opening, no doubt searching for a field mouse feast. I hoped the little entrée I'd seen earlier would escape.

Once again, I surveyed the area. The only place left where Elaine and Lee could have gone was the small shack fifteen feet away. Philip built that when he was twelve and nobody ever bothered to tear it down. It was about eight feet square and looked as if a rank amateur had built it. One of the corners wasn't quite a right angle and it was lopsided. I wondered if it was even safe. While anything was possible, I doubted they were there. I started to check it out when I caught a motion out of the corner of my eye.

I stepped back against the shed and peered across the clearing. For a few seconds, I wondered if it was only the white cat I'd seen, then a figure moved away from the crushing equipment. I immediately recognized Elaine's stocky figure. She was talking to someone, her hands gesturing constantly. Although I couldn't see him, I assumed it was Lee. I wished I could hear what they were saying, but they were too far away and there was nothing between us to offer me concealment so that I could move closer.

While I was pondering where they'd been, the other figure stepped out next to Elaine. For a few minutes more, he remained beside her, then he took her into his arms and kissed her. I suppose it would be called a passionate kiss and I reflected miserably that he'd never kissed me like that. With that thought came the realization that I was jealous. I could barely continue watching, yet I couldn't force myself to look away.

The couple embraced again, then Elaine turned and strode toward the house. He disappeared into the darkness of the winery. Time went by slowly as I watched and waited, not daring to move until I knew where he was. In the stillness, every thump of my heart sounded like an amplified drum beat. I worried I would be discovered. If they had known I was there, Elaine wouldn't have just walked back to the house, or at least, I didn't think she would. But I couldn't be sure. Elaine should be at the house by now and still there was no movement from the long building.

Then he emerged from the far side of the building, walking quickly, but with an easy, swinging gate. He came across the clearing, heading—not toward the tool shed where I pressed even harder against the wall–but toward Philip's shack.

Perhaps it was something about the way he walked or even something I sensed as he neared me, but before I could even see him clearly, I knew that it wasn't Lee. A wave of relief washed over me.

As he came within a couple of yards, I held my breath, afraid that in the stillness of the night he would hear me. It was too dark to see his face clearly. His build was almost the same as Lee's although I could now tell he was heavier and a little shorter. He stopped and looked back in the direction of the house, his head cocked slightly to one side as if he was listening.

A tingle of fear ran up my spine. What if he spotted me here? It wasn't just that I was spying on him and Elaine, but I was inexplicably afraid of him. Keep on moving, I urged silently.

He looked around as if searching for something.

God, please don't let him discover me, I prayed.

Abruptly, the white cat leaped out from the branches of a nearby oak tree and dashed toward the shack. The man visibly relaxed, apparently satisfied, then turned again to resume his journey to the lop-sided structure.

Only after he'd gone inside did my muscles relax and I could breathe deeply. I couldn't explain the sense of terror I'd felt. It was illogical. Although I was relieved that Elaine's boyfriend wasn't Lee, I felt unbalanced by this unknown element thrown into my puzzle to confuse me.

Now that I could gather my wits together a little bit, more questions flew into my mind. Who was that man and what was he doing in Philip's shack? Obviously, he and Elaine were holding their night time rendezvous there. Why? What was his connection with Elaine? Was he just the passionate lover or was there something more? My father often hired migrant workers and he could be one of those. If he was, it was too early to be hired for the grape harvest. That wouldn't happen until fall. But if he was a regular worker, he would have one of the rooms in the workers' quarters or a place in town. There was no need to stay in the shed.

Very curious, I thought. A line from "Alice's Adventures in Wonderland" popped into my mind. I was beginning to feel like the little girl who fell down the rabbit hole. More strange things appeared to be happening in my childhood home than I would have thought possible.

Although I wanted to know more about the stranger who was living in Philip's shack, I knew I would not discover any more tonight. The shack was dark now. Satisfied that the stranger would not emerge again, I started back toward the house, walking as fast as

I dared on the slippery mud. I was almost across it, when my foot slipped and I went down, coating my pants and arms with very wet, cold mud. I scrambled back to my feet, sliding again before reaching the grass. I ran to the cover of the nearest tree, then made my way more cautiously to the house, kicking off as much mud as possible before slipping my shoes off so I wouldn't tracked any inside.

Back in the security of my bedroom, I stripped off the muddy clothes and ran hot water for the bath, a necessity now rather than a luxury. As I slipped into the soothing bubbles, I thought more about everything I'd seen tonight, but I couldn't piece it together. Was any of it even connected to Philip? Then I remembered the chain I'd stuffed in my pocket. I retrieved it as soon as I'd dried off and put on my pajamas, then sat on the bed to study it.

A shiver scampered up my spine as I recognized it. It was the St. Christopher's medal that my mother gave to Philip on his tenth birthday. He always wore it. The chain was broken and where the links separated, the pulled metal looked as if it had been torn apart. Possibly Philip had caught it on something and it ripped off. Or someone had yanked it off him.

I laid the medal on the bedspread and stared at it, willing it to reveal its story. The implications of my last thought were terrible. If the chain had been accidentally pulled off him, he would have noticed and retrieved it. If he'd fought with someone and that person had jerked it from his neck, he still would have recovered it, unless he was unable to because he was unconscious or dead. Surely what I was thinking couldn't be.

I rose and went to the window, opened it to let in air and I breathed deeply to clear my head. I had to consider this rationally. Just because I found a St. Christopher's medal didn't mean it was Philip's. A lot of people had them. But even if had been my brother's that didn't mean he couldn't have lost it. Maybe he was so involved in what he was doing that he didn't miss it. On the other hand, if someone fought with him, then it might mean his death wasn't an accident. And if it wasn't an accident, then someone here was a murderer.

I went back to the bed and picked up the chain again. Engraved on the back was a prayer for safety in French. It could have been the one my mother gave him. I had never seen the back of it. As I shifted it from one hand to the other, I considered the possible people who might want to harm Philip. Elaine? My father accused her, but refused to give voice to his suspicions. I didn't think he meant she actually did it. Jacques said she was arguing with everybody and it was possible that she could have gotten into a fight with Philip, but I didn't think she could kill him. Still, if she had confronted him, it could have led to the accident.

Could the stranger have anything to do with it? Possibly. Who was he and did he have any dealings with my brother? How did he fit into all this?

Then there was Lee. I forced myself to consider him. What motive would he have? His family wanted our vineyard, but murder wouldn't bring that about. Why did he want the vineyard? I was back to that question, the one he wouldn't answer. No, Lee wouldn't murder for the vineyard. He was Philip's best friend, but it appeared they might have fallen out recently. Lee had secrets and that made him suspect.

Who else was there? Jacques? Emilie? My father? Impossible! None of them could have done such a thing. It was back to Elaine, the stranger or Lee. Or, I realized as the thought of the light in my brother's bedroom came to mind, whoever was in Philip's room tonight.

Incredibly, I'd almost forgotten about it. Why had someone gone there? What was he, or she, looking for in room or was it to cover up something? I glanced at the clock. Twelve forty-four. Everyone in the house should be asleep by now. With slow, cautious movements, I opened my door and peered up and down the hallway. No light escaped from under any doors. Elaine's room was across from Philip's and I hoped she was sleeping soundly.

Walking as lightly as I could, I slipped down the hallway to the end and turned the knob. It didn't open, so I pushed and turned harder but the door wouldn't budge. Disbelief kept my hand turning in vain a few more times. I was sure the light came from this room. Finally, I stepped back and accepted that it was locked. Whoever was in the room earlier had the key.

I was shaking again and I felt truly frightened. It wasn't just the locked door. It was everything that had happened. I scurried back to my room and locked the door behind me. I wished for a cigarette to help calm my nerves.

Marti, get out of here. Go back to Paul and forget any of what's going on here, said my more rational brain. But the other part, the part that made me a good reporter, kept telling me I had to stay. I had to follow this story.

I dropped onto the bed and picked up the St. Christopher's medal once more. As I stared at it, willing it to tell me something, the gold blended together to form a solid blob and I realized there were tears in my eyes. Angrily, I shook myself. "Stop being a ninny, Martinique Claremont," I scolded in a low whisper. "You're blowing this out of proportion, jumping to conclusions without a shred of evidence except a broken chain. What kind of journalist are you? If Philip was murdered, the autopsy would show it."

Autopsy? I needed to see the autopsy. Tomorrow.

After a few minutes of breathing deeply and slowly, I began to calm. I dropped the medal into my jewelry box and crawled into bed. I was tired but still unsettled and I left the light on. I kept tossing, trying to locate a relaxed position but my mind kept trying to rehash everything that had happened in spite of my efforts to distract it with thoughts of Paul and my work in San Francisco.

When at last I dropped off the sleep, it was fitful and haunted by dreams of a car going over a cliff—a slow motion picture, but one without an end. I never saw it hit. Then I would see my brother laughing, the chain of gold shining around his neck.

Chapter Six

*T*he Land Rover bounced and jerked over the dirt road Lee chose to take as a shortcut. He sat ramrod straight behind the wheel, large gray sunglasses covering his eyes and half his face. Apart from a quick "good morning", we hadn't spoken at all in the past twenty minutes. His mind seemed to be somewhere else while I was still trying to wake up, wishing for another cup of coffee.

Unlike yesterday, the only clouds in the sky this morning were a few fluffy white ones. I tried to recall what type they were, but my usually good memory failed me. I had to content myself with the obvious knowledge they weren't rain clouds. In truth, the cloud identification exercise was only an attempt to keep my mind off the previous night. I turned my head to study Lee's posture. He was absorbed in the road, both hands grasping the steering wheel. If he was aware of my gaze, he didn't show it.

I'd awakened late and it was the sheer determination that I was not going to be tardy that got me dressed, make-up on and downstairs in time to grab that single cup of coffee before I set off down the road to meet Lee. I'd even taken a couple of minutes to try Paul's office, but the line was busy. I was almost to the end of the road when Lee, highly visible in his bright yellow Land Rover, turned down it. When he'd tried to kiss me a good morning, I'd pulled away from him. He started to say something, but he evidently read my cool expression correctly for he said nothing more and left me to my own thoughts.

They were muddled thoughts. With nothing in the way of evidence to point to my brother's accident being any more than a tragic event,

I still sensed there was a mystery here and I was determined to get to the bottom of it. Yet I felt my heart jump every time I looked at Lee and it was disconcerting. *You mustn't give in*, I told myself. *You need your head and heart free to solve this puzzle.*

Here I was, sitting next to a man I didn't want to love and feeling butterflies in my stomach. Even with all that had happened, I was undeniably attracted to him in a way that I had never been before. "Do you have a cigarette?" I asked, both wanting one and needing to break the silence.

He glanced at me, a curious look, then he pulled his cigarettes and lighter out of his pocket and handed them to me. Tapping one out, I handed the pack back. As our fingers touched, a thread of pleasurable warmth ran through and made my skin tingle.

"Thanks," I said a bit hoarsely. He nodded. Taking a long draw, I leaned my head back, exhaled and gazed out the window. "Now if I just had a cup of coffee..."

"There's a thermos in the back. Would you like some?"

"Absolutely. You do think of everything, don't you?"

He laughed. "I don't leave home without it in the morning." He pulled over to the side of the road.

As he got out and went to the rear of the Rover, I leaned back again and enjoyed the panorama of the countryside. It was a rich, green valley shining in the morning light with touches of gold dancing on the leaves. Ever since I was a child I'd thought the world was more vibrant after a rain. The earth was washed clean and smelled fresh and new, somehow restored. Even the tiniest of leaves and flowers stretched a little taller, reaching for the sun.

The roadway was lined with vineyards, some newer than others, but all producing the varieties of grapes that went into wines. In this hollow, nearly all the grapes raised went to Claremont Vineyards since ours was the only winery nearby. The next closest ones were at St. Helena or Kenwood. Except the Kellog crop. They always sold theirs to a winery in Sonoma.

Our winery was small. Unlike Mondavi, Sebastiani or Christian Brothers, we produced very small quantities of four wines only: Mountain Chablis and Chenin Blanc, two fine white beverages; Cabernet Sauvignon, a rich red wine; and a golden cream sherry for which the recipe was a long guarded Claremont family secret. Consequently, the majority of grapes grown in this area were of the varieties that made those wines. Not that I could identify them. The vines all looked the same to me except when the grapes were mature and I, along with any other visitor to the valley, could readily identify a red grape from a white grape.

Clustered on the hillside we'd soon be driving up were hundreds of oak trees, including, I'd learned from an uncomfortable experience in my childhood, poison oak. Light green spring grass covered the hillsides and wound around the trees like a luxurious shag carpet. It was California wine country at its finest. I could almost forget my troubled thoughts. Almost, but not quite.

For one thing, a small golden medallion on a fine matching chain still rested in my jewel box. Even in the reassuring light of day, I was convinced it was Philip's and that something terrible had happened to separate him from it.

As Lee handed me a cup of coffee, I accepted it, took a welcome sip and smiled my thanks with a contented sigh. The second cup was the one that usually cleared my mind. This was strong, but delicious, without even a hint of bitterness. Better than the coffeehouse stuff I usually grabbed on the way to the office. Lee stared intently toward the end of the valley, lost in his own thoughts. His right hand held the thermos on his knee.

Within me, a warmth rose, not entirely from the coffee, and a feeling of security enveloped me. It was difficult to believe the way I felt with this man. When I was away from him, I could tell myself he was suspect and nurse doubts. When I was here, sitting next to him, I felt I could trust him with anything and that everything would be fine.

My eyes traced the sharp line of his jaw, strong and firm. He was always a man to fight for what he believed. So different from Philip. For all his arrogance and independence, my brother was a follower. Not so this man. Lee Kellog was a leader.

He swiveled his head to meet my gaze. "How's the coffee?"

"Terrific. What were you thinking about?"

"Oh, a lot of things." His hand fidgeted with the thermos, fingers tapping it. "Mostly what I might have done differently a few years ago to change what happened. I hate to think of all those wasted years."

"You couldn't have changed what happened. It would have been the same, no matter what you did. I didn't love you. Not the way you wanted."

He was silent and I began to feel uncomfortable. I could guess what was going through his mind. I knew what mine kept asking; *How do you feel about him now?* The answer wasn't clear.

Some moments, like now, I felt that I could love him. Obviously, there was a deep physical attraction, one I hadn't felt when I was sixteen. It's always difficult for a young girl to accept a brother image as anything more. I grew up with Lee and had never considered him romantically, not even when he thought of me that way. Even now, I rebelled against it. He'd always occupied a special place in my heart and part of me was unwilling to move him to a new place. There was a risk in that. If I accepted him in the new role and it failed, I could lose him as the dear friend I treasured.

Then there was Paul. Until I saw Lee again yesterday, I fancied that I loved him and that it would lead somewhere. Paul was like Lee in many ways—strong, determined, an individualist. But Paul was all business. I understood, but sometimes I was jealous of the magazine. Whenever we went to dinner, the topic was the WCN, what we were publishing, how the sales were doing or something else related to it. Yet, I admired Paul, loved him for so many different reasons and wanted to share his life. Yes, even his magazine. I admitted I loved that slave-driving goddess, too. But I wondered if I would have loved it so much if it hadn't been for Paul.

We were both lost in our own thoughts for a few minutes, not saying anything. It was time to break the silence. "Listen, is anyone staying in that little shack that Philip built?"

He twisted his head toward me and I could tell I'd startled him out of his thoughts. It took a moment before he responded. "What?"

"Philip's old shack behind the house. Is anyone staying in it?"

He laughed outright. "You mean that rickety box he built when he got angry at your father and decided he needed a sanctuary?" He shook his head. "No one in his right mind would stay there. Why?"

"Oh, I was just wondering. I thought I saw someone near there last night." It was better not to tell him what I'd seen. Not yet, anyway.

"Who?" The question was casual, the tone suggesting only curiosity. There was nothing to indicate that he knew anything about it.

"I don't know. No one, maybe. My eyes may have just been playing tricks. Let's go on. I really want to get to the bluff."

"Why, Marti?"

"Why what?"

"Why do you want to go up there? There's nothing to see. It's the same bluff it always was."

I looked down, not wanting to answer that. Finally, I replied. "I have to go. I can't tell you why. I'm not sure I even know, but it's something I have to do. Please understand."

He nodded, then started the Land Rover.

* * * * *

*A*s he said, the cliff was the same as it had always been. It was not straight down, but more of a rough slope. The road was smooth, well-marked, and I thought, too obvious to just drive off. Nothing showed in the dirt beside the road, not even tire tracks. Of course, the rain could have washed them away. But if Philip had braked hard, there would have been skid marks, even after the rain.

I got out and walked to the edge. The drop went down about three hundred and fifty feet. A few wildflowers dotted the ground. At the bottom was a cluster of oak trees and one had a scrape where something had hit it recently. A few digs in the dirt indicated that the truck rolled and bounced its way down the decline toward that tree. Looking at it, I thought that you could almost drive down the slope. It seemed amazing that it could kill anyone.

The sweet smell of the damp grass and earth filled my nostrils and a cool breeze swept my hair away from my face. My ears tingled with the slight chill. Closing my eyes, I tried to imagine what happened that night.

Against my shut eyelids, I could see Philip's truck coming along the road too fast, his hands furiously turning the wheel, then the vehicle starting to slide over the edge, out of control. There should have been skid marks. The slide should have been recorded in the dirt along the edge of the shoulder. I couldn't quite picture him driving over the edge without trying to brake.

Suddenly, strong hands pressed hard against my arms. I screamed as I struggled to stop them from pushing. Someone was trying to toss me over the bluff!

Chapter Seven

*A*s I twisted around to face my attacker, I stared into Lee's face. His arms were locked firmly around me. I'd been pushing and shoving, trying to break away from him, to get free of what was holding me.

"It's all right, honey." His voice seemed distant. "You were swaying. I thought you were going to fall, but it's okay now. I have you."

I realized then that I must have begun to rock as I imagined the accident. Thinking I was going to tumble over, Lee had grabbed me, not pushed me as I'd believed in that short moment before I'd turned to face him. Seeing the deep concern on his face, I relaxed, glad for the security and comfort of his arms.

"I'm okay now. We might as well go back. There's not much else to see here."

He clung to me, reluctant to release his hold, then he leaned forward until his lips met mine. He pulled me in tighter, deepening the kiss. The pleasure of that contact rolled through me in rising waves. When our lips parted, I was trembling, wanting more. But he released me, slid his left arm around my shoulder and I clung to his waist as we strolled back to the Jeep.

Noticing that a side road wound down below the bluff, I asked Lee to take it. Some intuition or impalpable reason urged me to see the bottom where Philip's truck actually crashed.

"There's nothing there," Lee informed me. "I already checked it thoroughly."

"Why?"

"I was looking for something, Phil's St. Christopher medal. He wasn't wearing it when..." He paused, swallowed hard and looked away for a moment. "...when we found him. I went all through the cab thinking it must have somehow come off, but I couldn't find it."

"The sheriff didn't have it?" I managed to ask through the sudden dryness in my mouth. So, Lee had looked for the medal. Now I was certain that the one I had belonged to Philip. I debated whether to tell Lee or not, then decided against it. At least, for now. If I told him I'd found it and where, it would undoubtedly lead to more questions and I wasn't ready to answer those.

"No. I asked about it and he checked everything they had in evidence from the crash, but there was no sign of it. I even went to the wreckage yard to go through the truck. I was sure he wanted to be buried with it. It was such a mess, though."

"Oh, no. That must have been awful. It is odd because Philip always wore it."

Lee nodded. "I know. He treasured that ever since your mom gave it to him. It was hers, you know."

That surprised me. "No, I didn't know. Neither of them ever told me."

He half-smiled at that as if he had something up on me. "I thought it had to be some place near the accident or in the truck, but I never found it. What are you looking for, Marti?"

I shrugged. He waited a little longer, but when I didn't answer, he ushered me into the passenger's side, then took the road down to the bottom and stopped just off the road.

"I've been wondering something..." My voice seemed to rasp in the quiet after the engine quit. "How did the coroner say my brother died? I know you said it was instant, but what was the exact cause?"

He stared at me, his dark eyes boring into mine and they seemed to ask if I was serious. But he answered in a gentle, compassionate tone. "He was killed by a blow to the head. Honey, he was mutilated in the accident. I barely recognized him." I could see the pain in his eyes as he spoke. His words came slowly, with difficulty. "The coroner seemed pretty sure he struck his head against the door."

"How could he have been so badly torn up? I don't see how coming down that slope could do it."

"I don't know. He wasn't wearing his seatbelt. I just don't know how or why. It happened, that's all. The way the truck hit and rolled, it looked like it caught the front and flipped it over three times on the way down. The metal was twisted and torn like a giant took it and reshaped it." He rubbed his eyes in an attempt to obliterate the mental image.

I phrased my next question carefully. "Is it possible he was dead before the accident?"

His eyes narrowed as he frowned, then he turned away from me. After a moment or two, he pushed out his side, came around the front and opened my door, offering his hand. Without another word, I got out, fitting my hand in his and we started to stroll toward the damaged tree. To anyone watching, we must have appeared to be one of the thousands of young couples in the world taking advantage of a beautiful spring day and a free morning to be together.

But tension was there; I could feel it in the way his hand pressed mine. He didn't need to answer me now. I already had my answer. A simple "no" wouldn't have caused this much distress. The pace he set was slow and easy, a casual stroll while he thought. When he finally spoke, his voice was low as if the trees might overhear us.

"Why do you ask that? Do you think he was murdered?"

"Don't you? You indicated that yesterday, didn't you?"

"I only suggested that something didn't seem quite right about it— that there could be more to it."

"In what way?" I stopped and he turned to face me. "If there was more to it, couldn't it be that he was dead before he went over the bluff? Lee, I want to know everything that happened that night. Every detail."

"Marti, don't!" His voice was still low, but it carried a stern warning. "Don't get involved. Can't you see that if what you're suggesting might be true, then you'd be putting yourself in danger?"

"Is it true?"

He shrugged.

"Who should I fear? You?"

"No, not me." He sighed. "I don't know. It had occurred to me that it could be murder, along with a dozen other unlikely theories of what happened. But there's nothing to confirm or deny any theory other than the obvious... that he was drunk and went off the road."

But I had something more. I had the small gold medal. How did it come to be on the floor of the tool shed? Who was my brother struggling with? Perhaps there was another clue there. I resolved to visit the shed again–with my flashlight this time.

"Look, let's just drop this. I brought along a picnic lunch–fried chicken and freshly baked rolls. We can get it from the car and sit under one of the trees." He started to tug me back toward the Rover.

"All right. I'll drop it. For now, but I assure you I'm not through yet. I still want my questions answered."

He shook his head. "You are the stubbornness darn woman."

I grinned as I followed him.

Over the lunch that followed, it was easy to be just two picnickers and drop the earlier conversation. We'd chosen a tree well away from the accident area and sat facing out toward the valley rather than toward the bluff.

But I didn't forget anything and dozens of thoughts flitted through my mind as I carried on a pleasant conversation with Lee. I answered his questions about my work and managed to throw in a couple of amusing tales about interviews that I'd done.

The inner voice, my reporter's voice, was more insistent than ever to know all the events that had lead to Philip's death. I was sure there was more than the obvious to this story. So, when we'd finished eating and Lee has settled himself comfortably against the tree trunk with a second cup of coffee, I brought the subject up again. "Lee, I know you want to protect me and you're telling me not to get involved for that reason, but don't you see? I already am involved! He was my brother. Please answer my questions and tell me what's been going on here."

"Honey—" he said, the tone in his voice telling me he still wanted to put it off.

"I'm not a child!" I blurted it out before he could say anything more. "Don't treat me like one. I'm a trained reporter and I know how to get information. If you don't tell me, I'll go to everyone in this whole damn valley to find out."

His eyes widened and looked at me, seeing me for the first time as a woman rather than the girl he'd known. I felt uncomfortable under his appraisal. He nodded, took another sip of coffee, then spoke. "Maybe you're right. Maybe I have been seeing you as 'little Marti' instead of the woman you've become. Either way, I love you and I'll still do what I can for you. Yes, you do have a right to know, but honestly, I can't tell you that much. I can only tell you what I know.

"Let's go back to the morning of the twelfth. Your brother had a fight with Elaine that day. I'd come over to ask Phil if I could borrow the small tractor for a couple of hours and I heard them arguing. Their voices carried and I could hear it was about a man named Manuel. Phil had fired him a couple of weeks before and I gathered that Elaine was pretty upset about it."

"Upset enough to kill?"

"Elaine? I don't think so. Anyway, they were arguing, but they stopped when they saw me. Elaine told him they'd talk about it later, then left."

"What was her interest in this Manuel? What did he do?"

"I don't know exactly what the story was, but I'm pretty sure Elaine liked him. That he was more than just another worker..."

"Did she love him?"

"I couldn't say. I saw her with him once. They touched, held hands, that kind of thing. But that's hardly enough to speculate about her feelings for him."

I smiled at the delicate way Lee put it, then asked, "What did he look like?"

"About my height, a little heavier, black hair, dark skin... a Mexican worker. I didn't pay much attention to him."

The man Elaine met! I was sure of it.

"Phil was evidently dissatisfied enough with his work to let him go. He was pretty angry. When I asked to borrow the tractor, he suggested we go to town for a drink. You know, I'm still not much of a drinker, Marti—at least not in the middle of the morning without a good reason, so I said no. My mistake—"

"Wait a minute!" I interrupted again. "He asked you to go for a drink with him? I thought you guys weren't getting along."

He looked perplexed. "Where did you get that idea?"

"My father said—"

"Your father!" His voice exploded with annoyment. "Look, honey, I don't know exactly what your old man has told you, but don't believe all of it. Yes, Phil and I had a few go-around's and matters got tense between us quite often, but we were still the best of friends. Hell, we were like brothers!" He paused, frowned and let his head drop toward the ground as if something weighed him down.

When he raised his head, he seemed weary. It was the look of a man who'd fought a difficult battle. "Your father, my darling Martinique, caused more trouble for us–Phil, my dad, this whole valley–than anyone or anything else could. He stirred up a hornet's nest while you were in your San Francisco tower. You don't know anything of what happened here, do you?"

Totally bewildered, I shook my head. What in heaven's name was he talking about?

"This valley—this whole area, the wine industry–is a political issue. The use of Mexican labor at low wages is the main issue. Have you heard of Cesar Chavez? Do you know what he's into?"

"Of course," I answered with sharp annoyance. "I am a reporter. I know that he's pressing for fair wages and better working conditions for migrant workers. I'm aware of that, but I thought the trouble was down south, around the San Jose area where the food crops are grown."

"Right. Except for a wildcat strike here. A man organized the laborers in this valley, trying to do the same thing. But your father fought their requests tooth and nail. Are you aware of that? He used every means he had to try to keep this valley from agreeing to give them fair wages. Marti, we were desperate to get the grapes picked. He threatened everyone— even my family."

I felt my face heat up with anger. "What do you mean 'threatened'? How could my father threaten them?"

"Don't you realize your father's power? He controls half this damn valley!"

My mouth dropped open. "I don't believe you!"

"Don't then. But it wouldn't be hard to find out, Miss Reporter. It's a matter of public record." He breathed deeply, then stood up. "I've got to move."

As he began walking, I jerked myself to my feet and went after him. I shouted his name and he turned. I swallowed hard. "Whether that's true or not, I can't say, but that wasn't what we were talking about. Please continue about my brother."

He didn't say anything, just stared hard at me, his face still reflecting the heat of the argument.

"I'm sorry. There were a lot of things said that I find... difficult to believe. You must know that. I am a Claremont, after all, and it's my father you're talking about."

"How can you know so little about your family?" He tilted his head and looked up at the sky, then back to me. As his eyes met mine, he bit his lower lip and reached out his hand. I grasped it, feeling it was a chasm rather than a few feet of ground that separated us. When I was beside him, he pulled me against him, and nudged me as we started to walk.

A narrow path wound its way to a mid-point up the bluff. From here the view covered a large section of the flat, even ground of the valley. We climbed up in silence. Above us, a black and white bird made a long sweeping flight toward one of the oak trees. I recognized the familiar patch of red on its head, an acorn woodpecker. It looked like he had a nut to deposit in his storehouse.

While a few thoughts pecked at my brain, they were fleeting and there was an intense awareness of the man beside me. The scent of his cologne was woodsy, masculine and mingled with his own body scents. Where his skin touched mine, I could feel the steady pulse of blood throbbing through his veins almost well as I could feel my own racing within me.

"There are a few points you need to understand about what's been happening here," he said quietly. We had seated ourselves on the ledge, backs to the bluff. His arm went around me and I dropped my head on his shoulder.

"I can't understand how you can be so totally involved in news and be so unaware of the problems in the wine industry in this area. Most of the people are just grape growers. They don't have the presses and vats your father does. Problems that affect the produce industry also affect grape growers. We've been having labor disputes you wouldn't believe. Heads of lettuce don't have all the headaches."

"Lame joke," I said with a small chuckle, appreciating his attempt to lighten the conversation.

"Yeah. Well, Phil and I got into it more than once about the situation. With your father opposed to increasing wages and holding out, Phil naturally had to take his side publicly although I know he felt a lot differently about it privately. I guess this was our main battleground. Not so much that he was for or against the wage increase, but more that he wouldn't assert himself over your father's dominance."

"Lee, I have to tell you something," I said as he paused and he tilted his head to look at me. I almost faltered on that attentive, handsome face as I imagined pulling it closer and caressing it. How had I not been aware of how sexy he was? Pulling myself together, I continued. "I've been terribly ignorant of what's been happening here. Maybe it's because I wanted to forget my past, but I've really shut anything to do with it or wine production out of my mind. I can read the news and skim right over it without it making an impression at all."

His eyes narrowed as I spoke. I could tell he was puzzled by this.

"It's true. Think of how it was for me. There were a lot of things about here that I wanted to forget. Mostly that I had no claims to it. It wasn't mine, none of it. When I left this valley, I left the vineyards, the presses, the cellars, everything. They belonged to a Martinique Claremont who once lived here, but not the woman who moved to San Francisco. I didn't even know that girl still existed until three days ago when I drove my car up the lane in front of the house."

I could feel tears welling in the corners of my eyes. Tears for the teenaged-girl I'd forgotten so long ago. Ashamed, I pressed my face against his shoulder.

Very lightly, his fingers touched my cheek, slid down it to my chin, then lifted my face up to meet his. "I hadn't thought the winery meant that much to you," he said in his soft, seductive voice just before he kissed me.

I yielded to the kiss, indulging in it until I pulled my wits back together, caught my breath, and whispered, "Not just the winery. I hadn't realized how much I missed you." With a burst of passion, I kissed him back as I ran my hands over his face and clenched them in his hair.

Investigation forgotten for now, I gave in to his fervor and met it with my unleashed need. His lips burned over my throat and along my collarbone, filling me with so much desire to be with him, to merge with him. Lee's touch, the gentle rub of his fingers over my blouse, touching my breasts through the fabric, made me squirm in his arms. He could have had me right then, but he was the one who backed off.

"Not here, honey. Not on an open hillside. Not now." He released me and climbed to his feet, then took several deliberate steps away from me.

Stunned by the sudden switch, I sat up and straightened my clothes, wiped at my lips, still tasting him on them, then looked the other direction to gather my thoughts. He was right, of course. Now was not the time or the place. *For gosh sakes, my brother had died a short distance from here. What was I thinking?*

We made our way back down to the oak where our picnic cloth, thermos, and plates were spread out. His hands flew over them clearing the items back to the basket he'd brought and we sat on the grass next to each other, holding hands for a little longer.

Lee rubbed the back of my hand, focusing on it, then said, "Marti, I want you to understand. I want our first time to be special, not a sudden burst of passion under circumstances that have twisted our emotions. I need to be sure that you want me, that it's not just a lust-filled moment."

Moisture filled my eyes as I realized what he was saying. He wouldn't take advantage of the moment because he loved me and unless I reciprocated, he wouldn't go any further. Just like that, I was sure, very sure, that I loved him. Whatever doubts I'd held vanished in that perfect afternoon and I felt secure in his embrace.

One other thing emerged from that excursion. The doubts I'd had about becoming heir to my vineyard had also dissipated. I admitted I wanted it as much as I once had when I was a little girl before I understood it would all go to my brother. But the questions about his death were still with me and would need to be answered.

As we laid back on the grass and watched the clouds drifting across, one reminded me of the sickle of death. Whether it was actually shaped that way or it was just the imagining of my troubled mind, I couldn't say. I only knew that the burden of discovering the truth had been dumped in my hands.

Chapter Eight

e didn't speak of Philip again until we were on our way back to the house. Lee couldn't tell me much more about what happened. My brother had gone to the bar alone and Lee had gone back to his fields. When Philip returned, he was in a happier, albeit whiskey-induced, frame of mind. Evidently, he'd gotten into a row with Papa and left again, or so Jacques had told Lee. As far as anyone knew, he went into town, finished getting drunk and, on the way home, drove over a cliff.

"Why did he go to the bluff?" I asked.

"What?" Lee was taken by surprise at the question.

"It wasn't on the route home. In fact, it was the opposite direction unless he went all the way over to Sonoma. I can't really see him doing that just to get drunk. So why did he go to the bluff?"

Lee's face went blank. He hadn't thought of it before. I could tell. "I don't know. Funny, no one asked that."

"It seems to me a lot of questions should have been asked that weren't."

"I think you could be right."

He stopped the Rover about twenty yards from the house and just in front of a curve where it was hidden from the view of anyone at the front of the house. Lee felt the need for secrecy from my family as much as I did. For a few more minutes we just sat there, his hand resting in mine, neither of us saying or doing anything, then he leaned over and kissed me with deep passion, drawing it out for what felt like a minute or more.

"Be careful. Could be there's something going on; maybe there isn't, but I'm not certain that you're safe in that house. If you need me, call me. Okay?"

I nodded, clung to him a moment more, then hurried up the road to the house. Lee backed out as I walked, but even as I went around the curve, I couldn't see where he'd been.

Near the house, Elaine waited for me. For a moment I thought I saw a face at the window above the tasting rooms—my father's office. I pursed my lips and wondered if he'd seen Lee's bright-colored Land Rover. Somehow I didn't think he would approve.

"Where have you been? I've been looking all over for you," Elaine asked as I came up the walk.

"What did you want?" I ignored her question.

"Your boss called from San Francisco. He wants you to call him back. Also, your father has been looking for you. Impatiently, I might add." Although she looked me over pretty closely, she said no more.

I went ahead of her into the house. "What does Papa want? Can it wait?"

She shrugged. "Who knows? I certainly don't have an inside track into his mind. All I know is that he wants you to come to his room as soon as you can."

I sighed. "I guess that means it won't wait. Too bad; I'm going to call Paul first anyway."

My gaze lingered on Elaine for a few heartbeats as I tried to imagine her with the tall, dark man I'd seen her with last night. I wondered if she loved him and he felt the same for her. I suppose she had some good qualities, but I sure didn't know what they were. If that man was Manual, why was he still here, holed up in the shack? To be with Elaine? No, I dismissed that idea immediately. There had to be another reason. It puzzled me. But I had to admit that I knew very little about my half-sister. I'd given up trying to understand her years ago when I realized that she resented me. For that matter, how much did I really know about my brother or my father?

Turning away, I picked up the hallway telephone and dialed the magazine office. Paul answered on the fifth ring.

"Where's the receptionist?" I asked.

"On a coffee break. When are you coming back?"

"Well, that was brief and to the point. I'm not sure yet."

There was silence on the other end.

"There are a few things here I'd like to clear up before I return. I may need a few weeks—"

"A few weeks! Marti, I need you here. You know the magazine isn't overstaffed. Things are hectic enough right now. I even have to answer my own phone."

"I know that, but—"

"But what? Your old man, from what you've told me, is hardly the type to need his hand held."

"Paul, you're getting upset. Why don't you hire a temp?"

"Oh, sure. I'll run right out and do that," he replied, the sarcasm oozing in his voice. "You know better than that. I'm not going to find a decent journalist on the street. I'll give you another week and a half... till the end of the month, then you'd bloody well better get your ass back here."

"I'll try. Goodbye." I hung up without waiting for any further comment. That was one of the worst moods I'd ever caught Paul in. I wasn't that indispensable at the magazine, so what the heck was going on with him?

Granted, Paul hadn't been happy with my taking the time off, but I hadn't been happy that he'd been gone all weekend on a jaunt to Sacramento to meet with a friend who happened to be a state senator. He had expected to interview her about some new legislation, but he hadn't returned until after lunchtime on Monday. By that point I was impatient to get on the road home. I'd had to come into the office to take care of the Monday business that he wasn't there to handle and I needed his approval of my leave.

But this? Paul was perfectly capable of running the magazine without my help. I'd brought along my articles that I would work on, so I couldn't fathom what was bothering him.

While my father was next on the agenda, I needed a little preparation before facing him again. Madame Boucher was not in the kitchen, but I didn't need permission to take a bottle from the wine rack. I selected the Cabernet Sauvignon, poured a large glass, then took it up to my room. I brushed my hair, straightened my shirt and decided I looked as presentable as I was going to get. I sipped the last of the wine in my glass and went to face my father.

He was fidgety. He played with a pencil, a paper clip, and a rubber band. He rearranged his papers for the third time and he talked a lot but said nothing. I avoided meeting his eyes. I studied the furniture, the floor, the ceiling, anything to keep from looking directly at him. He was rambling about the vineyard, how Jacques was an excellent foreman, but now he would have to find someone to replace Philip. He would need a wine expert with a background in chemistry and agriculture.

I stared at the rug while my mind replayed images of the bright green grass and blue sky of the early afternoon. With no effort, I could picture Lee's face, the gentle brown eyes overflowing with passion and love for me. How had I put him out of my mind these past few years?

"Martinique!" My father's sharp voice jolted me out of my daydream.

"I'm sorry, Papa," I said at once, without thought, a conditioned reflex from the past.

"I want you to pay attention. You are still the same child with your head off in the clouds when I am talking to you."

"Yes." What could I do but agree? Tell him he was the same demanding father who never cared much about what I wanted?

He paused, watched me shift to a more alert position in the chair, then got to the point. "My daughter, I signed my new will today. It is as I told you it would be. The vineyards will be yours at my death. Now, will you tell me where you went today with Leland Kellog?"

I glanced toward the window. I should have known he would know. But I gave him a straight forward, simple answer. "To the bluff. I wanted to go out there to see and he was kind enough to take me."

"*C'est bien.* Now there is no more business with the Kellogs. I do not wish for you to see him again." He said it flatly, without emotion. He was issuing a command for a servant to follow.

At first I wanted to give in to my urge to tell him off, to tell him that what I did with Lee Kellog or anybody else was none of his business. I was not one of his workers to have to follow his orders or risk being fired. I was his daughter, yes, but that was all. I had my own mind, my own will, and the right to my own decisions.

Instead, I rose and strolled with evenly paced, deliberate steps to the window. Biting my lower lip to keep my mouth shut, I leaned against the wall and made a slow mental count to ten. Below me, I could see the road from the highway to the house, every twist and curve in easy view. All he had to do was stand and watch. Did he see Lee kiss me also? What if he did? The thought angered me and I breathed deeply to calm myself again.

When I turned back to my father, he was watching me, a half-smile curving his lips and his pale eyes narrowing with ill intent. He was thoroughly enjoying this.

"Papa, Lee is a long-time friend." I kept my voice as calm as I could. "Just because you disagree with the Kellog family is no reason for me to shun them and I have no intention of doing so."

To my surprise, he laughed instead of being angry or annoyed. "I expected that you would feel that way. However, you will reach your own conclusions in due time and you will do as I wish anyway." His voice resonated with the confidence he'd always had that he could still dominate those around him.

It was the kind of bravado and self-assurance that cut through my nerves, making me uneasy in his presence. All I wanted was to get out—out of this room and out of this house! With as much control as I could muster, I replied, "In that case, there's nothing more to say now, so you will excuse me, Father. I have some errands to do while it's still daylight."

Although I was aware of my too hasty exit from the room and my near breakneck flight down the stairs, I could do nothing to slow myself. It seemed my father had laughed as I left the room, but I couldn't be sure. Nor could I be sure of what it was that had made me so uncomfortable.

I grabbed my purse and a notebook and I headed out the door to my car. I was not at the beck and call of my father or Paul, dammit! I had other things on my mind and I needed to find some answers.

Driving down the highway to Sonoma, I reflected that the whole interview had been odd. My father was playing a game with me, a game I didn't understand. But then, what did I understand of my father? He was an oddity himself, this American-born winemaker who clung to the traditions of his French grandparents and even spoke English as stiffly as a foreigner.

Very curious. I still felt like I was in Wonderland with a smiling, sinister Cheshire cat directing me two ways at once.

* * * * *

Sonoma is a picturesque little town in the heart of the wine country of Northern California. It is also a historic town with many of the original buildings still in use. For instance, the Blue Wing Inn, which was one of the oldest hotels north of San Francisco Bay, was still being used although it now housed shops rather than travelers. Sebastiani Winery was relatively new, founded in 1904. However, Samuel Sebastiani planted the first vineyard in the valley in 1825, just a few years before my great-great-grandfather planted his.

Our family went shopping for most of our supplies in Napa, but I always preferred coming to Sonoma. And, because Sonoma was a smaller town and more attuned to the wine industry, I figured I would find more information here than in Napa.

As I pulled into town, I turned toward the Sonoma Plaza, a beautiful park-like town square where the Bear Flag Monument stood proudly. There were few people in the park this time of day, but I knew that at lunch time it had been crowded. I had many fond memories of summer picnics, holiday celebrations and service club sponsored dinners in this centrally-located space. A twinge of longing for those happy days shot through me as I wondered if the town still gathered for festivities in the square.

Skirting the park, I turned onto a street a little past the Solano Mission, properly called the Mission San Francisco Solano, the last of the Mexican missions established in California. Although the main building was constructed around 1823, the two other structures that resided in the historical park were actually rebuilt around 1913 when the historical society acquired the original broken down mission. I had been through the place a few times when I was growing up and its history was interesting but short-lived.

Going past charming old houses with neatly groomed front yards, I steered the car down another street and stopped in front of a building whose single front window bore the logo of the Valley of the Moon Gazette, a small local newspaper.

I pushed against the door, and the distinctive odor of printer's ink greeted me. A small, skinny girl with enormous wire-framed glasses and straight, long dark blond hair glanced up from her typewriter.

"May I help you?" she asked. Her voice was flat and dull, as if the question was a constant routine.

With a quick flick of my fingers into the side pocket of my purse, I extracted my press card and presented it to her as I explained that I was researching an article and wanted to use the Gazette's Library. She peered at my card for a minute, bobbed her head up and down a couple of times, looked at me again as if to verify the photo on it, then handed it back and instructed me to follow her. I'd endured less scrutiny going into the state prison.

She led me through a door into a small newsroom where two of the paper's four reporters, both male, typed out their stories. As I followed her around a row of cabinets, I observed a single Associated Press teletype machine and portable television set in the corner. I was also aware of the interested gaze the young, dark-haired reporter cast my way as I passed his desk.

On the other side of the cabinets, a desk and a film viewer on a small table were ready for use. Like most newspapers, the Gazette had started filming their issues, each roll of film recording a month or more.

"The films are filed in here," the girl said, indicating a metal cabinet by the table. "Each roll is marked by month and year. Do you know how to work the viewer?"

"Yes. Thank you, I'm familiar with it."

"All right, then. If you have any questions or problems, I'll be out front. Is there anything specific I can locate for you?"

"I can find what I need. Thank you." It only took a few moments to locate the roll of film from a year earlier and I loaded it into the viewer. Settling myself in the wooden chair, I began skimming through the old issues.

For the next three hours, I read every account I could locate of the labor situation in the upper valley. I was dismayed to read my father's words in print. He did, indeed, take a strong stand against wage increases, pointing out that it would result in increases in the cost of wine and other produce to the consumer. He also emphasized that some producers, such as Claremont Vineyards, provided free housing to the workers and that should be taken into consideration.

Other articles echoed much the same viewpoint and, in fact, nearly the same words mimicked by my brother. From across the road, the Kellogs agreed that an increase in wages would mean a higher market price for fruit and vegetables as well as wine, but considering the wages being paid, they didn't feel the increase was an unreasonable request. Following the lead of the two major landowners in the valley, the rest of the growers either sided for or against and the majority went with my father.

Through it all was printed the strong voice of the workers, one Hector Escobar. It seemed Escobar was Cesar Chavez's strong right arm in our valley–or at least, Escobar thought so. There were several photographs of him in the pages. One was a close-up of him talking to Lee. Although the image on the screen was small, I realized that he could fit the shadowed man I'd seen leaving Elaine and going to Philip's shack. Except Escobar had a beard and moustache and I was sure the man with Elaine did not.

One thing was certain. This labor problem had been restricted to the area around Claremont Vineyards. The rest of the Napa and Sonoma valleys didn't seem to be affected by it. Evidently Escobar had somehow managed to unite the migrant workers in that area to follow the lead of the striking workers led by Chavez. A minor problem in the eyes of the rest of the valley, but a major headache for vineyard owners, who had to get the grapes picked and to the crushers before they rotted on the vines.

About Escobar's background there was very little. He seemed to come from nowhere and to disappear after it was settled. Against great pressure from the workers and other growers, my father had yielded, but it was almost a disaster. That had concluded about eight months ago and, as I skimmed through the papers since October, I found nothing more about it. I paused for a few minutes and read the account of my brother's death. For the most part, it was lacking any specific information about the accident although it covered a great deal about Philip.

At last I stretched my arms to get the weariness out of my shoulders and glanced at my watch. Nearly six o'clock–time to quit. I cleared the film from the viewer and replaced it in the cabinet. Although there were possibly more reports I hadn't yet read, I had ample information now to get a firm understanding of what Lee had said. I was sure he was equally correct about my father's influence and probable financial involvement with the surrounding vineyards.

And being a reporter, my nose told me there was a good story here from an angle the newspaper hadn't printed. I already knew a great deal of the background from my years of growing up on the vineyard. I felt the trembling eagerness in my fingers as I pulled on my sweater while I went out the door. Even though it did involve my own father, I was excited at the prospect of doing this story.

I found a parking place near the town center and in a short time, my footsteps had carried me to the Sonoma Plaza. A quick perusal revealed a pair of phone booths near the theater. One of the booths was occupied by a long-haired teenage boy whose look of rapture indicated he would be quite a while talking to his girl. An elderly man was just exiting from the other one, which I claimed as soon as he stepped out.

Instructing the operator to charge the call to the magazine's credit card, I gave her Paul's home number. When I didn't get an answer there, I asked her to try the office number and was about to give up when he picked up on the eighth ring. His voice sounded much more delighted to hear from me than he had been earlier.

"If you're not calling to tell me you're coming back right away, I don't want to talk to you."

Maybe not the delight I had thought. "Paul, will you listen to me? I think I have the makings of a really good article."

"About what?"

I tried to keep my voice calm as I began filling him in on the turmoil that had taken place here in the past year. I could feel my excitement growing again as I talked about it. "So, if I just have a little more time, I'm sure I can turn out a top notch article from this."

There was a long pause. "I don't know, Marti," he finally said. "It seems a bit stale. The issue has settled down, more or less."

"But it hasn't," I interrupted. "Don't you see? It's still going on here. It's calm on the surface, but the battle still rages. Just because it's not a headline doesn't mean it's gone away. This is a viewpoint that hasn't been exposed before–a viewpoint only I can write. Let me do it, Paul. Please."

"Possibly," he replied, his voice sounded like he was considering it. I could almost see him stroking his beard and nodding his head in thought. "You could be right. Go ahead. But if it doesn't seem to be coming together well, drop it." He didn't sound as enthusiastic as I had hoped he would, but it was still a go.

"Okay, boss," I agreed. I knew what he meant. If I started the research and it didn't shape up with just a few hours of work, I was to leave it. Most of the time, Paul trusted my judgment on these things and I was grateful that he was doing it again. I had good instincts and I was sure of this story, and somehow, this just might be a tie-in with Philip's death.

As I stepped out of the phone booth, I sighed with relief. Convincing Paul could have been the hardest part and that went easily enough. I crossed the street into the park and marched through it in triumph as the last of the daylight outlined the palm trees against the darkening sky. Pausing before the Bear Flag Monument, I studied it for a few moments. I didn't need to read the plaque; I knew it was to commemorate the Bear Flag Republic of California. Often, as a child, I'd stood proudly in front of the memorial and gazed at the powerful statue holding the sculptured, wind-filled flag.

As I turned from the statue, I spotted the lights of a coffee shop a couple of blocks away. A cup of coffee and a sandwich seemed like a good idea before heading back to the vineyard.

Although the shop was somewhat crowded, I was able to get a small booth at the back. After a quick scan of the menu, I settled on the all-American hamburger, then turned my attention to my notebook. I'd made quite a few entries at the Gazette and I reviewed them now, making additional notes of people and particular items I wanted to pursue. As a nudge of unease hit me, I became aware of someone standing near me and a vaguely familiar voice startled me.

"It is Marti Claremont, isn't it?"

I looked up and my eyes met the chocolate brown eyes of the waitress. Her light brown skin, high cheekbones, and thick reddish-brown hair defined her Mexican-Indian heritage. As I gazed at her, fragments of memories flashed into my mind. A girl in the hallway at school, small and dark-haired, talking to a football player. The same quiet, dark girl at the track meet waiting to talk to Philip after a race, a pad and pencil clutched in her hands. All at once, the images began clicking into place. She was a reporter for the school newspaper. I'd seen her often, but I didn't know her that well. As I struggled to dredge up a name, she spoke again.

"You probably don't remember me. I'm Consuelo Vargas. I was a grade behind you in school. We didn't really go in the same circles, but I knew who you were—the most popular girl in school." She smiled, a big, even grin showing straight, very white teeth.

"I couldn't remember your name," I admitted. "But I definitely remember your face. Did you give up reporting?"

She laughed, delighted that I remembered her. "Yes. And you took it up!" Abruptly, her expression grew serious. "I am so sorry about your brother. I always liked Philip. He was very kind."

I studied her for a moment. "Kind" was an odd word to describe him. Even I, his adoring sister, would never call him kind. Exciting, vibrant, even lordly—yes, he was all of these, as well as arrogant, charming when he chose to be and irascible many times. Why did she say kind? She mistook my silence.

"I'm sorry. I didn't mean to upset you."

"It's not that. Of course, it was a shock. But I was surprised at your comment. I didn't know you knew Philip."

She blushed. "Not very well. I'd talked to him a few times." She paused and glanced down as if she was uncomfortable. There was a sadness in her face that I'd missed before and I recalled the crying woman from the funeral. It could have been her. She changed the subject. "Are you ready to order?"

I nodded and gave her my order. Although I wanted to talk to her more, she scooped up the menu and left before I could say anything else. But she was back a few minutes later with the coffee and three individual containers of cream.

"Had you talked with or seen Philip before his death?" I asked before she could dart away again.

She appeared wary as she replied, "No. Why do you ask?"

I smiled at her, hoping to put her at ease. "I was just wondering. I wanted to know what state of mind he was in before his accident. A few people I've talked to seem to think he might have committed suicide." Of course, this wasn't true, but it elicited the desired reaction.

"No! He wouldn't have done that!" Her voice rose a little, not enough to draw attention, but still more emphatic and her eyes blazing. It was clear that she'd known Philip better than she would have me believe. As she realized that she'd revealed this to me, Consuelo lowered her eyes. "He was not that kind of person."

"Tell me what kind of person he was," I said seriously. Now I was a reporter and I wanted to know this girl's point of view. I wanted to know why she called my brother kind and why she was vehement about his death not being a suicide.

She stared at me, a puzzled expression on her face. "But you are his sister."

"That's true, Consuelo. However, I'm a sister who hasn't seen her brother in several years."

She hesitated. "I can't talk now–or here. I get off at ten. Will you meet me back here then?"

"Ten, it is." I added a cream to my coffee and sipped it as I watched her move on to another customer.

She chatted easily with him, probably a regular, then she continued to the next table. Her small, muscular body bent over to clean it. She was a little shorter than I, but heavier. Her legs were shapely although powerful-looking, the legs of an athlete, a surfer. I'd seen the firm, heavier thighs on many California beach girls who spent a good deal of their time riding the crests of the waves. I tried to remember if she'd been on the girls' track team in school, but it evaded me. Her breasts were full, round and firm and I doubted if she wore a bra. In that respect, I could envy her. My own bust line lacked that kind of fullness, even if it was passable.

In some way, Consuelo seemed out of place in this coffee shop. She didn't seem to be the kind of girl who would settle for a career as a waitress. For one thing, her eyes revealed a keen intelligence and a determination that would soon grow impatient with a mundane job. She was not a soft, gentle creature; of that, I was sure. As she went about her work, I noticed that she didn't smile much and she was very efficient. She came back once more to fill my coffee cup and leave the bill. She smiled and thanked me, the courteous waitress.

I glanced at my watch. It was eight forty and I had almost an hour and a half until she was off. As I left the coffee shop, I noticed her nervous glance toward me. Perhaps, I thought, she was trying to size me up, to judge what I really wanted. As for me, I had a little over an hour to pass before I could get any of my questions answered.

I made my way back across the dimly lit plaza to where I'd left the car and considered the possibilities of my article again as I walked. While the upper level of my brain worked at that, the lower level kept pondering over the liaison I was sure existed between my brother and Consuelo. I was almost certain that it was she who was mourning my brother.

If my mind hadn't been so absorbed in those thoughts, I'm sure I would have heard or felt someone moving closer behind me much sooner than I did. I became aware of a presence and felt the hairs on the back of my neck prickle just in time to half turn to observe the raised hand briefly before something struck my head and a red-black wave obscured my vision.

Chapter Nine

A repetitive throbbing, synchronized to my heartbeat, pulsed at my temple as I woke up. I attempted to open my eyes, but the lids were heavy, feeling almost as if they were glued together. Slowly, the throbbing became an echo. From somewhere near me, I heard a soft voice moan, then I realized it was coming from me. I moved my hand to the source of the pain at my temple. The not-too-well-coordinated touch of my fingers caused an instant sharp twinge to flood through me.

As it cleared, I recalled seeing a man just before he struck me. Although it was only a brief glimpse, his face was permanently imprinted on my mind. He was a young, slim youth of Mexican heritage with a dominant long, narrow nose in his angular face and almond-shaped eyes. Next to his right eye there was a small, not more than half-an-inch, but noticeable scar. I remembered that he looked very young and frightened.

Along with the memory came the awareness of my surroundings. I could feel I was lying on a bed or a cot. It was hard and uncomfortable. The odor of frijoles beans cooking dominated the room and added to the nausea I already felt. Gathering my strength, I tried again to force my eyes open. Abruptly, they popped free and immediately shut against the light. A little more cautiously, I forced the lids up again and adjusted to the brightness.

It was a small room, sparsely and poorly furnished. The light came from the single naked light bulb in the center of the ceiling. Moving with caution, I turned my head toward the opposite wall. A faded, flowered curtain hung across the doorway rather than a door. The dull green plaster walls were cracked and patched. In the corner, an old wash basin stood on uneven legs. A scratched up uneven dresser filled half the small wall adjacent to the doorway.

My captor obviously didn't consider me much of a threat, I thought without amusement. He didn't even bother to tie me up or watch me. Pushing up on my elbows, I raised to a sitting position on the hard bed. For a moment, my head and the room appeared to be moving in opposite directions. I squeezed my eyes shut and when I opened them again, the room had settled.

As I considered what my next move should be, I heard a door open and the curtain across the doorway fluttered with the breeze.

"Where is she?" An annoyed voice that sounded very much like Consuelo asked.

There was a pause, but no response I could hear.

"Is she all right?" Consuelo's voice again.

"I don't know. I think so." A young man's voice sounding scared and defensive. "I hadn't meant to hit her on the temple, but she turned just as I struck her."

"What did you hit her for at all, you idiot? She's Philip's sister–possibly a friend. Have you no brains?"

"I didn't know that! How could I? I saw you talking to her and you looked alarmed. I thought she meant trouble." His voice was a low growl.

"That's the trouble with you, Ernesto. You don't think enough and you act too swiftly." Consuelo's voice was moving toward the room where I lay propped up on one elbow. So much for my next move.

Sweeping the curtains to one side, she stepped through the doorway, then froze in place when she saw me. I forced a sickly and uncertain smile at her and tried to speak only to have a slight croak emerge from my throat. I hadn't realized it was so dry.

Consuelo's eyes filled with pain. "*Ay yi yi!* Ernesto, bring water and a wet towel." Then she rattled something else in Spanish that my tired mind couldn't follow. At best my Spanish was poor, but now it was limited to very elementary phrases.

Letting the curtain shut behind her, Consuelo walked quickly to me. *"Ay, amiga,* I am so sorry this happened."

I wet my lips a little with my dry tongue and tried again to speak. I finally croaked out a few words. "You wanted to be sure I kept our appointment?"

That produced a hard head shake and a brief smile at the poor joke before she peered at me more closely. "Oh, you're going to have a nasty bruise there. My stupid cousin..." Her voice trailed off as she looked toward the other room.

I raised my hand to lightly touch my bruised temple again as if probing it would make the pain go away. All it did was cause another sharp pain and I winced, a quick gasping sound accompanying it.

"That idiot!" Consuelo repeated.

It wasn't hard to deduce that the attack and abduction had been an error on Cousin Ernesto's part. But why was he afraid for Consuelo? Certainly, he must have considered me a real threat to attack without knowing any details. Had Consuelo indicated it in any way? I tried to think back to our conversation. Perhaps she'd shown enough alarm when I questioned her about Philip for Ernesto to misinterpret what had happened.

Consuelo held her hands out, palms up, toward me, imploring me to believe her. "I'm sorry, Marti. This was an accident. My cousin is very impulsive and he thought you meant to cause me harm. Are you all right?"

Still having difficulty talking, I shook my head, which caused it to ache again. At this point, Ernesto hurried into the room carrying a large glass of water and a limp, white kitchen towel. I took the water he offered and gulped it, relieved to get the dryness from my mouth and throat. Consuelo reached for the wet towel. I could see it was worn but clean. Folding it as small as possible, she pressed it against my bruised temple with light pressure. The cool dampness relieved the aching a little and I raised my hand to hold it in place.

Again Consuelo rattled at Ernesto in Spanish. As nearly as I could translate, she'd said something to the effect that he'd almost killed me. Her eyes flashed as she spoke and I suspected she had a rather hot Latin temperament. As she turned her head, her thick dark hair, no longer tied back, fell from a neat central part to her shoulders.

The young man accepted his scolding without complaint. He'd ceased to look frightened although concern still etched lines in his face. His eyes met mine, then flicked down to the floor. He looked to be about seventeen and extremely thin. The dark planes of his face revealed nothing and I wondered what he was thinking. If he was worried, it wasn't for me.

"Why don't you tell me what this is all about?" I felt much better now and was sure the only damage done was the bruise at my temple. As I sat up straight, Consuelo visibly relaxed a little. But she still seemed reluctant to tell me anything.

"It's very complicated, Marti. I don't know how much I can tell you. How much I would feel safe telling you."

Alarmed, Ernesto's eyes darted to her. He, for one, did not trust me. Certainly if distrust should exist, that should be my privilege and at this moment, I was ready to claim that option. Ernesto made me nervous, to say the least. I was beginning to wonder just exactly what this pair was hiding and if I did find out, would I be able to leave here with that knowledge?

Consuelo's eyes met her cousin's before she turned and walked slowly to the curtained doorway. Drawing the curtains back part-way, she stared into the room beyond and sighed heavily. I could see the room was dark, lit by a red light bulb. Ernesto watched her, his face expressionless. Tension made my shoulders ache and I felt like screaming to relieve my nerves. Instead, I said, "Might I have a cigarette? There's a pack in my purse."

Turning from the doorway, Consuelo gave an affirmative nod to her cousin who produced a pack from his shirt pocket and thrust it toward me. My hand shook as I lit one, but after a couple of puffs, I felt calmer. "So, what is this about? Illegal marijuana or something worse?"

She gaped at me a moment, then motioned Ernesto to her. She spoke to him, her voice very low so I couldn't hear what was being said. He glanced at me, scowled, then left the room. The slam of the front door shook the house as he went out. It was clear he didn't agree with Consuelo.

"Do you think you can make it into the other room?" she asked. "The furnishings are more comfortable."

I stood up, felt dizzy a moment, then it evened out. "I think so." She offered me her arm for support, but after a few steps I was all right.

The other room was the living room and was in better condition, although not richly furnished. An overstuffed sofa, old but serviceable, was against the far wall. Near the curtained doorway was a large wooden rocking chair. Opting for the sofa, I made my way across the room and sat. A bookshelf divider separated this room from the small kitchen.

As I looked around Consuelo disappeared behind the divider. I heard the clink of glasses and the hum as the refrigerator door was opened. When she returned, she had two glasses and a bottle of white wine. I noted the gold and blue Claremont label on the bottle.

"This is not the meeting I had intended," she said as she handed me a glass. "I would have rather gone to my apartment than my cousin's *casucha*." She paused for a sip of wine and folded one leg under her on the couch. "My cousin is suspicious of everybody and, as I said, he is very impulsive. He really thought you meant trouble for me. Do you?"

I swirled the wine in my glass, then looked directly at her, making eye contact. "How could I? I know nothing about you. I suspected you knew my brother. How well, I couldn't say, but that's not a crime. I was curious to know more. That's why I wanted to talk to you. There's no harm in that... Or is there?"

For a moment, she studied my face as she gnawed at her lower lip. "Did you know that your father and your brother did not get along?"

I laughed. "My father and brother never got along. Philip was always too volatile, like a bomb waiting to go off. And my father was the detonator, but he loved Philip dearly and there was a deep mutual respect."

My hostess sipped her wine and seemed to struggle to make a decision. "You asked me to tell you about Philip. He came into the coffee shop about a year ago, bombed out of his mind. He sat through at least half of my shift just drinking coffee. When I got off work, he followed me, then offered to take me home. I'd had a crush on Philip since high school, so it was easy to tell him yes. You didn't know that, did you?"

She smiled at my surprised look as I shook my head.

"We went to my place and talked. He'd argued with your father that day about the vineyard and he needed to talk. One thing led to another and, well, he spent the night. After that, I saw him pretty regularly. Of course, he didn't want anyone to know. Especially not your father. It wouldn't do for Philip Claremont to be connected with a poor Mexican girl, you see." She cast an almost bitter look at me as if defying me to challenge it.

Then, in a gentler tone, she went on. 'But Philip was good to me. He saw to it that I had money to go to college so I wouldn't have to spend all I made on my apartment and school." She held up the wine bottle. "He even brought me wine. And sometimes food." Her eyes dropped to her wine glass and she fell silent.

Stunned by this information, I tried to think. Even though I'd been certain she knew Philip, I hadn't expected this. Why shouldn't my brother have a lover? After all, he was a handsome, vital young man and it could be expected of most men to seek an affair where they could. Or was it that I didn't expect my brother to go with a Mexican girl? I felt a pang of guilt. I'd never considered myself prejudice before, and yet I had unconsciously marked Consuelo as beneath me. For my father, there would be no question of it.

Consuelo looked at me, a slow smile spreading across her face. "You find that hard to believe, don't you?"

I forced myself to meet her eyes. "I guess I do. I told you I really didn't know much about my brother, especially since I've been gone several years."

"But you don't believe he killed himself, do you?"

"No, I don't. Nor do I think his death was an accident."

Without hesitation, she said, "Neither do I. But, of course, there's no way to prove it."

"How can you be sure?"

She didn't answer. Instead, she rose from the sofa and walked to the window. Pulling back the curtain, she stared into the darkness. For Ernesto? I doubted it. She didn't seem to be looking for anyone or anything in particular. She was so absorbed in her own thoughts that I doubted she was truly aware of anything else.

I was growing weary. I hadn't had a full night's sleep since I arrived and now the dull headache was working at making me feel more worn. A glance at my watch showed it was nearly midnight. The drive back to Claremont Vineyards was long and lonely and I knew I should be starting back, but something held me. As if I knew there was more to come, I remained still on the sofa, waiting. If Consuelo had more to tell me, I had to wait for her.

I speculated what she might be feeling, what she was thinking or deciding, as she gazed out the window. Trying to insert myself into her place, I considered how she must regard me. I was her lover's sister, but also my father's daughter. Which was I more like? My father would not have favored any part of this affair and I'm sure Philip had made that clear. She knew very little about me other than who I was and what I did for a living. Most of what she might have thought she knew was based on high school and its attendant cliques. With growing apprehension, I wondered what secrets she held back, afraid to tell me.

"You don't trust me, do you?" My voice startled her. Small wonder. It seemed so loud in that quiet room that it jolted me also. Her shoulders had jerked at the sound and she let the curtain drop. She spun around to face me. It was almost as if she'd forgotten I was there.

"Why should I? Just because you're his sister?" She paused. "No, I don't really trust you... and yet, I do." Returning, she sank onto the sofa once more. She sighed, a deep heavy sigh as if her heart was breaking.

"Your father dominated Philip. He never let him really be himself, make his own decisions, choose his own ideals. When I met Philip, he was confused. He had his ideas about the vineyard and how it should be run, but they didn't match your father's."

"That's not unusual. Parents and children don't always agree... especially when a parent is old enough to be a grandparent. I don't agree with my father either. And I doubt that you agree with yours."

A half smile. "No. I don't, but he doesn't dominate my life. I do what I please. You probably do as you wish. Philip didn't. It was like he couldn't. He had no will of his own."

Finding that hard to believe, I interrupted again. "That hardly sounds like my brother. As I recall, he had quite a will and temper to go with it. Granted, my father is domineering, but that never bothered Philip. He was often at odds with him."

She studied my face for a moment. "How long has it been since you spoke with him?"

Ashamed, I told her. My lack of communication with the family was painful for me now. Logic told me that I probably couldn't have prevented what happened, but I could have maintained a better relationship with them.

Defensively, I said, "At any rate, I can't see that my brother and my father would disagree intensely on anything of major importance."

"But they did!" Consuelo's response was quick and defensive.

"They disagreed about the whole vineyard. Philip knew better ways to run it, ways to produce more and better grapes and to process the wines better, but your father wouldn't listen. He sent Philip to Europe and to college to study, to learn, and to come back with better ideas, but he wouldn't let him try them. He wouldn't listen to Philip about a lot of things. They even disagreed over the labor issue–the attempts to get—"

"Not publicly!" I blurted it out. "I've read the news accounts and Philip's words parroted my father's."

"I know! I know! I read the papers, too. It bothered me as much as it bothered him. Don't you see? It wasn't his opinion. I told you he didn't have power over himself. He did what your father wanted, no matter what he believed. We argued over it because I'd counted on his support. His siding with your father was a blow to me. Marti, he couldn't tell me why he defended his father's position, only that he must. Why?"

She stared hard at me. Her eyes tried to drag words from me, an answer of some kind. An answer I didn't have.

"Why?" she repeated. "What kind of hold did that man have over him?"

Put on the defensive again, I could only shake my head. "How do you know Philip told you the truth? Maybe he truly agreed with Father." Even as I said it, I knew I didn't believe it. What was it Lee had said? He was upset more with Philip because of his lack of conviction? His exact phrasing escaped me.

Consuelo shook her head in denial. "No! I knew Philip! He wouldn't lie to me. Not about that!"

"What did you mean, you were 'counting on his support'? Why? What's your concern with the workers?" I leaned toward her and fixed my eyes on her, the reporter closing in on a story.

She licked her lips nervously, then turned her face away. "I...I can't tell you."

"Are you so afraid of me?" I asked. "Lord! Your cousin attacked me and brought me here. You've told me all kinds of tales about my brother, but you can't trust me. Do you think I'm going to go running to my father? Is that it? Don't you think he'd be pretty concerned about someone hitting his daughter over the head?"

She stared at the floor, silent.

"Consuelo, I am my own person," I said more gently. "I owe my father nothing. I'm here in town because I'm certain that Philip was killed. I came looking for evidence. I intend to find out who and why. That's the only reason I wanted to talk to you. You seemed to know my brother and I thought you might give me a clue. Now I wonder what else I've gotten involved with?"

Her head came up in slow motion. In the dim lighting of the room, I could see tears glistening in her eyes and the shiny streaks down her cheeks. Her voice cracked as she spoke.

"I loved your brother, Marti. I really loved him." Her lips trembled. "I had to find out he was dead by reading the morning papers. No one knew about us except Ernesto. I've had to go through my daily routine pretending nothing had changed, smiling at my customers, joking with friends and meeting with people who hated Philip because he was a Claremont."

Moved by what she had suffered, I opened my arms to her and embraced her as a sister. For a few minutes, we sat close together, holding each other, then she pulled away, reached for a tissue and wiped her eyes. She poured more wine and found her voice again. "It's hard to listen to them talking and you find yourself wondering if one of those people you're associated with or called friends might have killed him. They never knew he was in sympathy with them."

Tilting her head against the back of the sofa, she closed her eyes and swallowed hard. "You see, Marti, I belong to an organization called Los Latinos Amigos. We're a Mexican-American equal rights group. When we can, we try to change things and support Mexican laborers, native born or not.

"Ernesto's a field worker. You can see how he lives. This is his place. Me, I'm working to get through college so I won't end up like him. Philip tried to help me. He really did care about me and others like me. He didn't think your father was fair to us, but he couldn't do anything about it. He didn't own the vineyards; your father did and he controlled them. Philip could never openly oppose him. What about you?"

"There but for fortune," I mumbled, then took a deep breath. "If you've read anything I've written, you know where I stand. I've always been for equal rights—no matter whose. Don't misunderstand me. I love my father and I respect him, but I don't agree with him. I was born his daughter, nothing more."

After a long pause, I asked, "Is this organization of yours illegal?"

She shook her head. "No, not exactly, but I couldn't say we are always within the law. We try to do things, accomplish our goals, without any legal actions, but sometimes..." She let it drop.

"So you believe that someone in your organization might have killed Philip?"

"Not really. I've thought about it ever since the accident and I've considered a few members who might be capable, but when it comes down to it... no. Nothing was to be gained by Philip's death. If they were to kill someone, it would be your father."

"Maybe they wanted to frighten him?" I suggested.

"By making his death look like an accident? That would hardly do the job. Perhaps we're both wrong. Maybe it really was an accident."

"You don't believe that and neither do I." If anything my conviction that it was murder was stronger.

With most of the pressure off now, Consuelo talked more freely, but not about the organization. She told me more about Philip and her relationship with him. She spoke a little about her college studies and I learned that she was a second-year law student. It was clear by the change of subject that she'd told me all about Los Latinos Amigos she was willing to relate.

By the time Consuelo escorted me to my car, which Ernesto had kidnapped along with me, I felt I knew, or at least understood, this woman of my brother's. Likewise, she knew enough about me to trust that everything she'd said would stay between us and to know she could count on me if she needed me. The link my brother's death had provided connected us and our mutual need to know what had really happened to him.

Chapter Ten

*A*lthough my head still ached a little, I felt clear-headed as the car zipped along the highway. I was at ease and taking my time driving back to the vineyard. With the almost complete absence of traffic, I was making good time. Once a truck went rumbling past me, but other than that no headlights crossed mine in the dark. Ernesto lived closer to Sonoma than Napa and I'd found it easier to take the Sonoma route home.

The new moon was barely visible high in the sky and the stars glittered and pulsed through the clear night air. I picked out the Big and Little Dippers easily–something I hadn't done in my years in San Francisco. Seeing them now, I realized I had never been able to pick out any constellations other than the Dippers unless you counted the North Star.

I came upon the bluff before I realized it. The ease of the drive had lulled my senses so that I didn't recognize any landmarks until then. In spite of that, I'd begun to slow even before I'd entered the curve, my automatic memory sense aware of the road even if my conscious mind wasn't. In fact, I slowed far more than was necessary. I was halfway through the turn before I knew it. It was an easy curve, even at high speed. One more thing to convince me that Philip did not miss that turn. Not unless he was unconscious or dead.

The view of the valley from here at this hour was one of just a few tree-like sticks rising from the blackness beneath them and the buildings in the distance weren't even visible. On a night with a full moon, the whole area would be illuminated and almost as visible as in daylight.

Across the valley, tiny pinpricks of light sparkled in the area near Claremont Vineyards. They weren't moving so they were likely house lights. As I swung around the curve, I could see the road below and over it, a pair of lights raced. Obviously, these were automobile lights and judging from the flickering of yellow, it was traveling rapidly. My curiosity was aroused. Who was hurrying down this road at nearly two-thirty in the morning and whose house was lit at this hour? Curious, yes, but I was too tired to concern myself with it.

It had been a long day and it felt like several. The idea of a warm, cozy bed was more than a little pleasant. I rolled the window down part way to let cool air revive me. The fresh, sweet scent of damp grape fields flooded my nose and I inhaled deeply.

As I neared our vineyard the pinpoints of light began to grow rapidly. They could only come from my house or the Kellogs. Once I was closer, I realized that several lights were burning, then I was certain it was my home. Alarmed, I stepped on the gas and the little sports car shot forward. My concern increased as I swung around the corner onto the long curved driveway a little too fast. The back tires slid and I fought to control the MG. Snapping back, the low automobile gripped the road and zipped on as if nothing had happened.

Just before the house, I rounded the curve and was appalled to find the whole house blazing with lights and a sheriff's vehicle parked out front. I whipped my MG in behind the black and white sedan and ran into the house.

Madame Boucher stood at the front of the stairs, her slight form covered with a thick blue robe. Her fuzzy blue slippers stuck out at the bottom and at any other time I might have laughed at the picture she presented. Next to her stood Elaine, also in a robe and looking as if she'd just straggled from her bed. They both turned as I burst into the house and ran toward them.

"What's happened? Why is the sheriff here?"

Elaine stepped toward me, annoyance in her eyes and accusation on her lips. "It's about time you got home. We've been worried. Papa claims a burglar was in his room."

I couldn't miss the sarcasm in her voice. "Did anybody see him?"

"Only Papa and he raised enough ruckus to scare him away as well as wake up the whole house. He kept screaming about being attacked." Her tone suggested that she thought my father might have dreamed it.

Alarmed, I asked, "Is he all right?"

"I think so," she replied. "We've called Dr. Turner. He should be here soon." She peered at me with a puzzled expression.

Madame Boucher had said nothing, but she had stared at me the whole time. Now, she sounded concerned as she asked in French, *"Ma Cherie, ce que vous a fait du mal ?*

I realized then that I must look a mess with my clothes smudged and wrinkled and a blue-black bruise at my temple. Although I hadn't seen a mirror, I knew I probably looked as strung out as I felt.

In French, I replied, "It's nothing. I tripped and bumped my head." Then, in English, I said, "Is the sheriff with Papa? I want to see him."

Madame Boucher nodded, still staring at me.

"You look a sight," Elaine commented. "I hope you don't frighten him."

I ignored her and went up the stairs two at a time. With some effort, I tried to think through what had happened. Someone had been in Philip's room the night before. Now it was my father's room and where else in the house?

Sheriff Eberman was a big man. Big in all ways. He was nearly six-foot three-inches tall and he was broad. The width of his shoulders was comparable to the back of an overstuffed easy chair and he filled a doorway completely. His hair was a reddish brown, now streaked with gray, and he had been sheriff for as long as I could remember.

Standing before my father, the sheriff seemed massive in his gray-green uniform with the revolver hanging low on his hip. On his bed, my father sat propped up by several pillows and Jacques perched in a straight-backed chair next to him. I entered this room much more quietly than I had the living room.

"... it was too dark," my father was saying, his voice as strong as ever. "When I heard him in the room, I wasn't sure at first that it wasn't my imagination, but I could see his movement and I called out to him. I started to turn on the light and he rushed me then, knocking over the lamp and hitting me with his fists, Then he ran out. By the time I was able to get out to the stairs, he'd disappeared."

"Don't you think it was a little dumb to call out to a prowler?" the sheriff asked bluntly.

My father raised his hand in a familiar dismissive gesture. "I suppose so, but who thinks clearly in that type of situation I did what came into my mind first—asked the bastard what he was doing in my house. Stupid, perhaps, but—" He spotted me as I stepped around the sheriff. "Ah, Martinique. It's about time! Where have you been? Sheriff, you remember my daughter, Martinique?"

I came to his bedside. "Are you hurt, Papa?"

He shook his head. "No, no! I am all right. He only struck me a few times. It takes more than that to hurt me, *ma petite*."

But I could see his color was high. Obviously, the excitement was not good for him. His eyes glittered in the subtly lit room. Beside the left side of the bed lay the broken fragments of the bedside lamp. Across the room, desk drawers were standing open and the papers on the top were scattered. Other than that, the room did not look disturbed. Whoever came was not after money or jewelry—not in the desk. The intruder was after something else.

Jacques made a slow negative motion with his head. I could see that he was very concerned about my father.

"Did you see anything, Jacques?" Eberman asked. He pronounced it "Jock", the Scottish way.

"No, nothing. I was asleep and I heard Monsieur Claremont yelling, but by the time I reached the stairway, there was only monsieur on them."

"You weren't here, Miss Claremont?" The sheriff addressed me. It was definitely a question, not a statement.

"No. I'd gone into Sonoma earlier and I ran into some friends from school. We began talking and the next thing we knew, it was one-thirty. I just now got home."

Eberman acknowledged with a nod as he thoughtfully chewed on his lip. "Who else was in the house? Mrs. Boucher?" He pronounced it "Bootcher", causing Jacques to cringe a bit.

Jacques wet his lips with his tongue nervously. "My wife did not get up until after me. We were both awakened at the same time."

"Elaine was here," I said softly. "My half-sister," I added as the sheriff shot me a questioning look.

"She's downstairs?"

I nodded.

"What happened to you?" He pointed to my head.

The question was so unrelated in my mind that it took a moment for me to answer. "Oh, the bruise! It was silly. I stumbled and fell." I hoped I sounded convincing. "At my friend's house. I was on my way to the kitchen for a drink when I caught my heel on the rug. Stupid, really." That sounded so weak that I didn't think anybody would believe it.

Whether he believed it or not, the sheriff dropped it. He addressed my father again. "Okay, Mr. Claremont, let's see if I got this straight. You were awakened by noises a little before one a.m. Across the room, you could see the outline of someone at your desk going through each of your drawers. You called out to him, reached for the light and were hit by this person, who then ran out of the room. Is that correct?"

"Yes, that is correct."

"And you couldn't recognize him at all? Nothing about him seemed familiar? The way he walked? His build? Did he say anything?"

Wearily, my father shook his head. "No. I couldn't see anything distinguishing about him. Nothing that stood out or was familiar. He didn't speak at all."

The questioning went on. Bit by bit, the sheriff managed to piece together a rough silhouette of the man, but it was surely not enough to go on. He was around five foot nine inches tall, about one hundred fifty pounds, and moved very quickly–a description that would fit hundreds of men in the area.

From the grayness now slipping into his face, I could tell my father was tiring, but his voice still held the excitement. I'm sure he expected the sheriff to locate the prowler immediately. That was my father's way. Jacques sat very quietly, saying little and then only when asked.

I heard the faint ring of the front doorbell then, a short time later, the footsteps plodding upstairs as Dr. Turner made his way to the master bedroom. The doctor was nearly as old as my father and was one of the few doctors left who would make a house call. A rotund little man, the doctor reminded me of a cartoon dwarf with his smooth, pink bald head and the tufts of white hair sticking out just above his ears. He still looked sleepy as he came into the room, but he soon shooed everyone out to leave him alone with his patient.

In the hallway, we met Eberman's deputy, who had just come looking for his boss. He'd been out checking the grounds but hadn't found anything. "Not even a footprint. Nothing near the house but the fields are loaded with them," he said. "Don't imagine he went that way anyhow. Fields are too open... too easy to be spotted."

As the deputy and Eberman went down the stairs with Jacques to question Elaine and Madame Boucher, I slipped down the hallway to my room. I stopped at the bathroom for a moment. Glancing in the mirror, I was amazed at the disheveled girl reflected in the glass.

My golden hair was tangled and the bruise on my temple was a vivid purple and red. My clothes were not only wrinkled but also spotted with smudges from the parking lot. I looked as if I'd been in a drunken brawl. I was sure now that Eberman didn't believe my story and probably figured this was not connected with the events here unless something else turned up. I hardly fit the description of the burglar.

As I washed my face, I hoped I wouldn't be expected to explain to anybody about it and that I could make the "tripped-over-a-rug" story stick. Of course, that offered no justification at all for the state of my clothes. With a clean face and my hair brushed, I looked much better, but there was nothing to be done about the bruise.

The moment I stepped into my room, I felt something was amiss. I wasn't sure what it was, only that something wasn't right–out of place. Uneasily, I looked around. I wondered if the sheriff had checked the entire house. Reaching for the closet door, I jerked it open and was relieved to find only my clothes in it.

I sighed, feeling a little foolish, and gazed around the room again. Nothing seemed disturbed. I sat down on my bed and began undressing. As I pulled my robe about my shoulders, it dawned on me. Slowly at first, a merely curious thing, then I investigated. The window was open. Totally open! No screen covered the frame. A man could have easily come in or gone out the window. Cautiously, I leaned against the sill and looked out. A narrow ledge ran along the house, just below the window.

Narrow, yes, but still wide enough for an agile man to make his way out on it and to the tree to my left... or to Philip's room! Looking the other way, I saw the screen lying at an angle against the house. I started to reach for it, then remembered the sheriff. Best to let him see it.

I pulled my head back and gazed around the room. Had it, too, been searched? My first thought was my jewelry box. I pulled the box out of its spot in my dresser drawer.

Whether the box had been touched or not, the drawer had. I'd put some papers and a couple of notebooks in it and these were messed up as if someone had gone through them hurriedly. I couldn't tell if any of them were missing, but I doubted anybody would take those. They were only notes for articles that I'd brought with me. When I checked the jewelry box, it appeared untouched. The little golden St. Christopher's medal was still there as well as my emerald ring and black pearl choker. Nothing seemed to have been moved at all. Whatever the prowler was looking for, it wouldn't fit into a jewelry box or under a stack of papers. Or maybe it was the paper itself?

I pulled out the other drawers, checking each of them. A couple had been shifted a bit, but nothing was missing. I went back to my closet. There were books and belongings that had been in there for ages. I'd left them when I moved to San Francisco. They were part of the young Marti who'd grown up here. From the dust covering them, it was obvious they hadn't been disturbed.

The growing sounds of voices outside my door told me the sheriff and his deputy were returning. Tying my robe about me, I stepped out into the hallway to greet them.

"You take that side," the sheriff told his deputy, pointing to the room opposite mine. They were making a room by room check.

"I believe he was in my room, " I said. "Come, look."

Eberman followed me. In that delicate setting, he appeared tremendous and out of place.

"A few of my drawers have been disturbed and it doesn't look as if he took anything. But the window—" I pointed even as I walked toward it. "The screen is on the ledge outside. He either came or went this way. Possibly both."

He grunted, then leaned out the window. "Quite a drop," he mumbled. His eyes took in the narrow ledge, the nearby trees, and the rooms down from me. He pulled his head back in. "Don't touch anything, Miss Claremont. I want to check these rooms."

As I followed him into the hall, I almost collided with Elaine. She spoke irritably. "Lee's downstairs. He wants to see you."

My eyes flashed to the sheriff as his broad back disappeared into the next room, then back to Elaine. "Would you tell him I'll be down in a few minutes?"

For a moment, she glared at me as if to say, "I'm not your servant," but only nodded, turned and stomped back down the stairs.

As I turned, the sheriff emerged from the room and went into the next one. The one I was interested in was the end room–Philip's. The other ones were empty except for furnishings. These were the guest rooms. I debated whether I should say anything about the light in Philip's room the previous night or not.

Good Lord! I thought suddenly. Had it only been one day?

As I expected, the room was locked and the deputy went downstairs to find Madame Boucher for the key. While we waited, I answered a few questions for Eberman. He wanted to know if I always kept my window open. I replied that I did not and, in fact, didn't recall leaving it open when I'd left that morning.

Philip's room was neat and orderly. Surprisingly, it was as I had remembered it. The window was open slightly and the screen was in place. I had no doubt in my mind how the intruder had gotten into a locked room the night before. And it was probably the same person who'd come tonight. The question was, what was he after?

The same question occurred to the sheriff as he asked me, "Do you have any idea, Miss Claremont, what this prowler was searching for? Doesn't seem to be jewelry or money."

I had no answer to that and only gave my head a negative shake. He stared at me a moment, expression unreadable, then said that he would like to dust my room for fingerprints. He told rather than asked.

"Mine are everywhere," I volunteered.

He smiled for the first time. "I'm sure they are, but maybe his are on the windowsill or screen. I doubt it though. Most every burglar these days knows to wear gloves. But maybe he's not a professional."

I left him to his task then went downstairs to meet Lee.

He was pacing the floor, a quick pace taking him across the room away from me. I paused at the doorway to watch him as he swung toward the fire again. His hair was tossed and he wore a blue windbreaker. No doubt he'd dressed in a hurry. What had awakened him? I called his name as I entered the room. Turning, he came to me, his arms open. I went into them instinctively and he held me in his secure embrace.

"Elaine told me what happened," he said. "I heard your car squeal around the corner, saw all the lights, and came as quickly as I could. Is your father okay?"

I mumbled something in the affirmative. My head rested against his shoulder and my arms and body clung to him. There was no denying it; I was glad to see him.

Still holding me, he guided me to the sofa near the fireplace. Then he saw the bruise and a worried expression appeared. "What happened to you? Marti, you didn't run into the burglar?"

"No, nothing like that," I replied and told him my story about tripping over the rug. I noticed I layered it with more dressings each time I told it. I'd have to be careful about that. But Lee accepted it with no questions.

"What was he after?" His tone was strange, a little sharper than he usually spoke.

"I don't know. It doesn't look like he took anything, but he seemed to be searching for something." It didn't dawn on me then that he'd asked what the prowler was after rather than what he took, which would have been the normal assumption.

For several minutes, we sat without speaking, his left arm still wrapped around my shoulders. His eyes focused on the fire and something seemed to burn in them as the log flamed and sparked on the hearth. "What are you thinking about?" I asked.

He tilted his face toward mine and answered in a low voice, afraid someone might overhear us. "Meet me for lunch tomorrow–about eleven at Scotty's. I have to talk to you."

"Does it have to be tomorrow?" I was exhausted already and I still had half a dozen things to do.

"Please, Marti. It's important... Very important." His eyes pleaded with me, an expression I'd only seen once or twice in his face.

"All right. But I've got to get to bed now. I'm really beat."

I walked him to the door. His fingers were light touches on my cheek as he leaned down to kiss me. "Until tomorrow then."

When I climbed upstairs, I saw the sheriff exiting from my room and he gave me the okay to go in. I was relieved to see he'd replaced the screen and the room wasn't any more out of order than it had been earlier. Without another thought, I dropped onto the bed and turned off the light.

Chapter Eleven

C lad in a pale green pantsuit, the color of new leaves that hadn't basked in the sun's rays, I walked across the now dry fields to the tool shed. It was not yet ten, the day was warm and cloudless, and I had plenty of time to investigate before I needed to leave to meet Lee. As I walked across, I noted that there were many old-looking footprints in the ground, including mine from the night before last, but nothing that looked recent. Whoever broke in last night didn't come this way.

I'd slept poorly, over-exhaustion and uneasiness taking its toll. I'd tossed and turned and woken up several times. Finally, about dawn, I'd fallen asleep and slept soundly until nine when something, an unidentified noise of some sort, had awakened me and I couldn't fall back to sleep.

With last night's events still in my mind, I'd decided to go through the tool shed again. Armed with a flashlight, I opened the door and stepped into the dark building. It was an old structure, built by my grandfather, and when the large door was thrown open to allow the tractor to go in or out, there was ample light inside. The smaller door through which I entered allowed enough sunshine to make objects discernible.

Hanging on racks along the east wall were the hand tools— pruners, saws, wrenches, hammers; that kind of thing. Along the west wall, bags of chemicals, fertilizers, and other plant nutrients were lined up in uneven stacks. The tractor itself was a smaller model than you might expect. The grapes were never dug up unless they'd died or had ceased to produce ample or quality grapes, so the tractor wheels had to fit into the furrows between the rows. It was used primarily to spread fertilizers and such on plants before the growing season started.

Switching on the flashlight, I ran it along the floor. There was not much to see. Grease and oil spattered across the floor. Kneeling carefully to avoid dirtying my pants, I ran the light under the tractor. Here again I found grease, oil, and dirt, but there was nothing to indicate a struggle of any kind had taken place.

As I swept the flashlight across again, I saw something shine in the light. A button. A plain, brown, plastic button. Not much of a clue, I reflected, as I turned it over in my hand. It could have popped off anyone's shirt at any time. Or it could have been torn off during the struggle with Philip.

It didn't even occur to me to doubt that there'd been a struggle. Even though I'd only pieced this together in my mind with little to substantiate it, I knew what I knew. It was odd that I was so positive of this. I'm not gifted with clairvoyance, but my intuition has always proven to be amazingly accurate. And that my brother had met with some trouble here, I was certain.

I made one more round of the shed. Not even the oily, dirty floor gave any clues. There were footprints, yes. Hundreds of them, it seemed, but none that could be labeled to any particular person or event. Discouraged, I leaned against the wall. Somewhere was the clue I needed. Something to link someone to Philip.

I stepped outside, closing the door behind me and back into the cheery sunlight. A slight breeze ruffled my hair and brought with it the sweet smell of flowers in bloom, a potpourri of fragrance. Inhaling deeply, I reflected on the sweetness of the earth, then thought blackly of my brother's body buried in it. Another thought followed this; that another girl mourned his death as much, or possibly more, as I and that she shared my conviction that his death was no accident.

Standing crookedly against the bright blue sky was Philip's ramshackle shack. Lee was right; it was a wonder it was still standing. It looked even worse in daylight than it had at night.

With sudden decision, I began walking to it. Perhaps I could at least find out who was staying there and why. I ignored the possibility that the occupant might be there now and might not appreciate my intrusion. But then, this was not his property. Of course, by law, neither was it mine, but mine more than his.

As luck would have it, the shack was empty. That is to say, no one was in it, but it was far from empty. I closed the door. Enough light came from the skylight to illuminate the room completely. A cot sat against one wall with an opened sleeping bag spread on it. Two wooden crates held clothes that seemed to be sorted to clean and soiled. Neither crate held very many. On one wall were dozens of newspaper clippings, some yellowed with age, others more recent. Looking them over, I discovered I might have saved myself a trip to the Gazette's "morgue" had I come here first. If I had though, I wouldn't have met Consuelo, or, I remembered painfully, been hit by her cousin.

Lying on the floor beside the crates were several books, among them a book on union organization. Picking up one, I flipped the cover open hoping that, like me, the owner would have inscribed his name. The owner had; the name on the inside cover was the Napa County Library. As I turned the book, I noticed the thin white band with the catalog numbers on it at the bottom of the jacket. A glance at the rest of the books confirmed they were also from the public library.

The clothes in the crates were men's work clothes and blue jeans. Obviously, their owner didn't dress up much and from the looks of them, he had very little or no money to buy anything dressier. I picked up a pair of clean jeans. They were well-worn and patched several times. Likewise, a blue chambray shirt bore patches of different shades of blue.

Above the cot, tacked on the wall, was a color illustration of Christ on the Cross. It was probably the only crucifix he had. The edges of the picture were bent and torn. He'd had it quite a while, I surmised.

Near to the door was possibly the only valuable thing he owned, a Coleman camp stove with a small pot and skillet on it. By it, almost in the corner, sat a bag of groceries and fuel for the stove.

I gazed around the shack again. Just the bed, the books, the clothes, the picture and the stove. Not much to live with. He was educated; his selection of reading material revealed that. It was probable that he could do more than hide out in this lean-to. Now, more than ever, I asked myself, who is he? Why is he here? And what's his connection with Elaine?

Footsteps outside the door interrupted my thoughts. One of the problems with Philip's shack was that it only had one entrance and one exit and they were both the same. I braced myself to meet whoever came through the door. Within seconds, the door opened and Elaine stepped through. She carried a bottle of wine and a loaf of bread with something wrapped in aluminum foil beside it in a cardboard box top. As she saw me, she stopped, stunned to find me there.

"Hello, Elaine," I said. I sounded calmer than I felt.

Her answer wasn't friendly. "What the hell are you doing here?"

I glanced at the wine in her hand. "I might ask you the same question. As it happens, I was out walking around this morning when I passed this old shack Philip had built and decided to take a look inside." I turned my head toward the cot. "It appears someone has moved in. Do you know who?"

Her face flushed to crimson. "I don't believe that's any concern of yours. You have no right to be here!"

"Don't I?" My voice was as sharp as hers and I took a step closer to her. "This is my father's property, isn't it? Don't tell me you've rented out this shack."

Her hand clenched the bottle and I thought she was going to throw it at me. Hatred burned in her eyes. Until this moment, I hadn't realized how very much she disliked me. Then her hand on the bottle relaxed and the tension preparatory to dodging left my shoulders.

"One of the workers stays here. Philip said he could."

"And you bring him food and drink? Come now, Elaine. Why would one of the workers want to stay here when we have much better facilities for them?"

"He—he likes privacy. Anyway, Philip gave him permission so that doesn't concern you. And what I do is none of your business."

I paused, gathering my thoughts. For once, I decided to think before speaking. My head tilted toward the skylight. The glass was streaked with dirt, but through it the sun's rays filtered down and motes of dust shimmered in the light. Incredible that we were arguing over this worthless shack. But that wasn't the point.

I took a deep breath and met Elaine's glaring look again. She'd set the wine and bread down and waited for me to get out. She still scowled, but she was more composed, ready to challenge me. My next words threw her off balance again.

"Who's staying here, Elaine? Manuel?"

Her face drained of color. "Manuel? I don't know who you're talking about."

"The one Philip fired. You were there at the time, I believe." I elaborated slightly and with second-hand knowledge.

There was a long pause before she spoke. "What do you know about Manuel?"

"Only that Philip fired him and you were upset by it. From what I heard, you were upset enough to argue with him about it. Were you upset enough to kill?" I'd asked the question almost casually, but Elaine gawked at me strangely.

"What the hell are you talking about?"

"You and Manuel. Was he upset also? Did you figure out between you that if Philip was dead you'd have control here?" I was accusing now, not really thinking about how I was saying it.

"You must be kidding!" She was incredulous.

"Is it so hard to believe? You can't expect me to accept it was really an accident. Come now. Be serious. Manuel seems to have a motive... Not a great one, but men have killed for less. And you wanted Manuel around. Is he your lover?"

I knew I was taking a chance in approaching her like this, but I was fairly certain she wouldn't harm me. At least not until she knew if there was anyone else I might have told.

Still with a look of disbelief, she collapsed on the cot. "You have got to be kidding. Marti, you don't know what you're saying. I never wanted Philip dead. I had nothing to gain from it. I never really believed for even a moment that your father would leave this vineyard to me. You would get it before I did; you know that. Why do you think anyone killed Philip? The coroner and the sheriff both ruled it accidental. Is there anything to indicate otherwise?"

The plain round face had lost its look of hatred now and she watched me in genuine amazement as if I were turning into a strange creature before her eyes. Suddenly, I was sure she was telling the truth that she didn't want my brother dead and had nothing to do with it.

"Is Manuel staying here?" I asked again. I still wanted that answer.

"No. He left after Philip fired him. He was not my lover, only a friend. The man who stays here now is a laborer. A little more intelligent than some, better educated than most, but a field worker nonetheless. And," she paused, her face registering dislike again. "If you really do believe someone killed Philip, it wasn't him. It's none of your business, but I was with him the whole night and there are others who can verify it. We went to a bar."

Her voice was bitter and I could see she hated telling me anything. In control of her emotions again, she continued. "Now, Marti, I think you'd better leave. I repeat, you have no business here."

I glanced pointedly at the bread and wine again. The wine was from our cellars and I had no doubt the bread was fresh from Madame Boucher's kitchen. "Do you always supply your 'friend' with bread and wine from our house? Surely he's more than just another worker?" Still I pushed her, reluctant to let her have the upper hand.

"My relationships are none of your concern." Anger colored her face red. It was apparent that I was treading on dangerous ground.

With a knowing smirk, I retreated toward the door.

"Marti!"

I paused with my hand on the door knob.

"Where were you last night? With Lee?"

I almost laughed. She was trying to reverse my own game. I turned and smiled sweetly. "That, Elaine, truly is none of your business."

Stepping through the door, I slammed it behind me and almost hoped the damn shack would collapse.

Chapter Twelve

I thought about my discussion with Elaine all the way to the bar where I was to meet Lee. I was running late again, but I hadn't expected to investigate Philip's shack or run into Elaine.

Now I was positive Elaine and Manuel, as a team, had not killed my brother, but perhaps Manuel alone? Elaine's shock at what I had suggested had been real enough; however, I couldn't be positive about Manuel. The more I thought about it, the less likely it seemed he would do it.

In my somewhat limited experience, when angered, the Hispanic people tended to be hot-tempered, but in a situation of this sort, he would not wait and plot. If he'd been furious enough to kill my brother, he would have done it when Philip fired him and, most likely, hand-to-hand. Unless someone like Elaine prodded him, it would be forgotten, not formulated into pre-meditated murder.

But if it wasn't Elaine or Manuel, who else would have done it? Who else had a motive? What would Lee have gained by my brother's death? Nothing. He would still have to deal with my father if he wanted our property. More would be gained by my father's death than Philip's. Even Consuelo had said that. The murderer would either stand to gain something or wanted Philip out of the way. I had to find a fresh angle on this. There was a solution somewhere and I was determined to find it.

I pulled in next to Lee's Land Rover, which was parked across from the entrance to the small bar. Above it a yellow and red sign proclaimed it as "Scotty's Bar and Grill". It was a popular place in the valley and the man who owned it really was named Scotty. The food was excellent and it was inexpensive. I pushed the heavy, wooden door open and stepped into the low-lighting of the bar-room. A divider separated about one-third of the space into a separate dining area.

Lee was seated at the bar where he could watch the door. As soon as he saw me, he slid off the stool and came to meet me. With barely a word of greeting, he caught my arm and guided me to a booth at the back of the restaurant side.

"I didn't think you were coming," he said as he sat opposite me. "One more beer and I'd be ready to float away."

"I got delayed."

"I guessed."

A waitress ambled over, a pencil and pad in hand, and greeted us with a smile. We both ordered sandwiches and I added a beer.

After she left, Lee caught my hand across the table and asked, "Is anything wrong?"

"Is anything right? Everything under the sun seems to be happening, but if you mean anything else, then, no. Nothing new has happened. What did you want to see me about?"

"Not here," he said quietly. "I'll talk to you about it after lunch. We'll go for a drive—"

"I really don't have time, Lee."

"Please, honey. It's important or I wouldn't hesitate to talk about it here. I don't want anyone to overhear. Trust me... please." His voice was even lower and I had to strain to hear him.

I signaled my agreement with a nod. There was no point in trying to pursue it any further. Experience with Lee had taught me that much. Experience had also taught me that Lee wasn't the type to make a big issue out of nothing, so if he had something important and secret to tell me, it would very likely be exactly that and I would have to be content to wait to find out.

Over our sandwiches and beer, our talk was casual and, for the most part, brief. I didn't tell him anything about meeting Consuelo or the encounter with Elaine this morning.   He asked about the magazine and what kind of articles I'd written.

Afterward, Lee suggested we take my car since it would be better if anyone passing by saw his Land Rover parked in front rather than my MG. I didn't think about better for what at the time. I simply handed him the keys and slid into the passenger side.

He stopped once for gasoline, then drove toward the coast. At first I thought he was going toward San Francisco, but he turned off on Highway 121 leading toward the ocean.

"Where are we going?" I asked, certain of the answer.

He glanced over at me and smiled. "To the Point."

I knew he meant Point Reyes, a secluded beach about fifty miles from the valley and half that distance above San Francisco. It was a spot I knew well. Ever since I could remember, I'd loved it there. Before me, my mother had made it her place. Leaning back, I watched the fields pass beside me and allowed myself to think of happier times when a small, blond girl followed her mother's running and laughing figure across the unmarked sand of a cold Northern California beach.

I must have dozed for a while, but I awakened as I became conscious of the change in the car's speed. Opening my eyes, I saw we'd left the main road and were driving across back roads through wooded canyons toward the point. "I see you decided to take the long way around."

Lee glanced over at me and smiled. "I love driving over in here and you were catnapping, so I thought I'd give you a couple of extra winks."

Now and then we passed a farmhouse or two set back from the road and a few horses and dairy cows grazed on the tall grasses. We passed through the peaceful town of Inverness Ridge with Tomales Bay, looking placid in the early afternoon, on the right. The town itself was a resort village more than anything else. The main road ran through it and shops, cafes, bayside hotels and marinas lined the edges of the road. As I recalled, it was a popular place for artists and writers, as well as romantic lovers.

On a marsh lake, a flock of snowy white egrets waded in their search for food. As I watched the birds, moisture came to my eyes. The birds were among many endangered species. Would they survive even here? I'd done an article once on the plight of these and other wild birds, but my question was still unanswered. For now, I admired their beauty and hoped they would endure.

Coming up over a hill, we were faced with a breath-taking view of Drake's Estero. The verdant hills resembled a thick shag carpet so lush were the grasses on them. The deep blue shades of the fingers of water were enriched by the vivid colors that surrounded them.

As I watched a herd of Holstein cows grazing on the hillsides, I remarked on it to Lee. "Sometimes I think I'd love to have a farm out here–away from the city and not a grapevine in sight. Just the blue and gray of the ocean and the emerald green grasses with the yellow and white flowers. It's so tranquil."

"And the salt smell of the sea along with the mists and the fog. Not to mention the frequently overcast skies," he added. "But it really is peaceful. Of course, some people think the same thing about our little wine-producing countryside."

"If only they knew," I muttered. "Still, there's something about the ocean. Don't you feel it, too?"

He grinned. "Why do you think I brought you out here?"

I laughed. "There better be a real reason behind this trip to the coast, mister."

"There is," he assured me with a wink.

Near here was a place where a crack in the earth sat on the San Andreas Fault. Lee had once told me that you could actually see it move. He said the promontory was drifting northward at something like two inches a year and eventually it would be around Alaska. I'd laughed then and told him it didn't matter because I wouldn't be around to see it. But I wondered about it now, just as I wondered about the fate of the snowy egrets.

Lee turned left toward Drake's Beach. Ahead the sky was beginning to cloud and was already turning a light gray. How odd that just a few miles away to the east, the sky was bright and clear with the sun beaming down on the earth.

As the car rounded another curve, there was the bay stretched before us just as I'd remembered it. Lee stopped the car as near as he could and got out. Coming round the front, he held out his hand to me and I felt reassured as mine slipped into his. At this time, I needed the link to the past that Lee provided.

Once we passed the rocky boundary, we slipped off our shoes and strolled barefoot in the wet sand. His arm went around my shoulder and I slid mine around his waist. I felt joy and satisfaction to be so at ease with him, as if this was the way it had always been with us. Behind us, our footprints were the only ones on the beach.

"It's beautiful, isn't it?" I said. I gazed out toward the vast expanse of the Pacific Ocean. "You know, I can almost see the Golden Hind anchored out there in the bay. Historians say Sir Francis Drake brought it here for repairs. I wonder how they knew?"

"Charts, I suppose." Lee spoke softly as he nuzzled his cheek against the top of my head. "Drake must have made some kind of maps of the coastline. Besides, there's the brass plaque he left behind claiming it for England."

"I forgot about that," I admitted as I sat on a rock and looked up at Lee, the enchantment growing in my soul. "It's funny, the United States seems so settled, but all over there are little places like this... little islands in time. Places untouched over the centuries. It's just as wild and beautiful right here as it was when Drake sailed around the Point and into this quiet harbor. It's easy to imagine a sailing ship coming through and anchoring here. Think what San Francisco Bay must have looked like! Just as wild and unsettled, but much larger with no buildings rising from the hills and no Golden Gate Bridge spanning the entrance."

Leaning back, I inhaled and tasted the fresh salt air. It was different from the City, cleaner with no taste or feel of smog in it, and somehow more moist. A light breeze brought coolness and blew my hair back. Half-lying next to me, Lee's sweater brushed my cheek, then his lips met mine and I turned into his warming embrace.

It is an incredible experience to feel that you and the man you love are alone in the whole universe, but that was how I felt. Time stood still at Point Reyes. The crowds of vacationers hadn't found it yet and developers wouldn't build on it. For this moment, it was ours to share with each other even though I knew it would not remain this way forever. Already, the area was becoming a tourist spot, but on a cool day in the middle of the week, the area was pretty much our private beach. For the first time since Sunday morning, I wasn't thinking about Philip or how to find his murderer.

Lee held me closely, his hands caressing my hair and face. His kisses were gentle, not hard passionate kisses, but affectionate, loving ones. I was the one who kissed him in hunger and pulled him closer to me. Within me, the desire for him rose, but he was fighting it. At length, he shoved me away from him and I thought something was wrong. Then I saw the spark of passion in his eyes and I knew he wanted me as much as I wanted him.

He moistened his lips and his voice was a little raw when he spoke. "Not now, honey. This isn't the time or the place." He sat up, his fingers traced a circle over the back of my hand that reached for him, and gazed at the horizon.

"Lee..." My voice was barely audible as I was so tentative in what I was about to say. Above us, a pair of seagulls cried out to each other as he turned his head toward me. "I love you, Lee."

A smile played at his lips but failed to break across his face. "I've waited ten years to hear you say that. Ten long years... and it has to be now." He stared down at the sand.

After a few moments, a period when I was afraid to speak after that remark, he studied my face as if he might never see me again.

His warm eyes reflected the serious tone of his voice. "I have to tell you something. You know I love you, honey, and it's time I level with you. I realized last night that you're as involved in this as anybody here."

As I started to respond, he raised his right hand to indicate silence. I could see that whatever he wanted to tell me wasn't easy. He seemed to drift off into his own thoughts again.

"Tell me exactly what happened last night," he said at last. "I want to know every detail."

I was confused. I thought he was going to tell me something, but now he was asking me to give him more information. "I thought you had something to say to me."

"I do. But please, indulge me before I tell you."

In the ensuing silence as I considered this, I thought about everything that had happened. I'd gone over it so many times it had lost its reality. Surrounded by the pristine beauty of this quiet cove, I didn't want to bring any of the real world into it. Not into this special place, this dream-like paradise where time seemed to have ceased its steady advance and left it exactly as it had been for centuries.

So it was with great reluctance that I began to tell him about the events of the previous night. About my visit with Consuelo and her cousin, I still said nothing. For some reason, I didn't want to tell him about that. When he asked where I'd been, I answered with a half-truth... that I'd argued with my father, gone into Sonoma, did a little research for an article at the local newspaper, then I'd run into a couple of high-school buddies and visited with them the rest of the time. I was relieved he didn't ask me who the friends were.

I fell silent, waiting for him to speak. Above us, the sun slipped out from behind a gray cloud and filtered rays of sunlight cascaded onto the bay causing white sparkles over the surface. Where the sun touched them, the edges of the clouds blazed with a silvery white light. Lee's hair shone with a warm, reddish brown. I fought the urge to reach across to touch it, but I wrapped my arms around my knees and clasped my hands together. With real effort, I forced my mind back to our discussion.

"Do you have any idea what the prowler was searching for, Marti?"

"No, but I think it must be important. He's not after money or jewelry. From the looks of the desks and the drawers, I'd say he was after papers... documents of some kind."

Lee nodded in agreement. "A document of sorts. For a little over a year, Phil had been keeping a journal. A very secret journal. I don't know exactly what was in it, but I suspect it was everything he knew or guessed."

"About what?"

"About everything and everyone. He kept it locked in his room somewhere and nobody's seen it except Phil. I don't know anything for certain that's in it, but I can speculate about what I think it is. Phil didn't miss much. A lot of people didn't really pay attention to him when he was around, but he noticed far more than anyone would credit to him. People usually had their defenses down around him.

"Well, shortly after the problem with the grape pickers began, he started putting everything down in this journal—names, dates, places, incidents—a complete record of the turmoil and discord. He told me about it. Not the detail of what was in it, but that he was keeping it. He wasn't sure why he'd started it, but he thought it might be useful someday. I would guess that there's been quite a bit written in the book that a few people around here wouldn't want to become public knowledge. The thing is, who knew about the journal?"

I stared at him blankly. He couldn't be expecting me to answer that question. Then I noticed that he was gazing at the sand at his feet, not really seeing it. He was deep in his own thoughts.

I cleared my throat. "Who besides you knew, Lee?"

"I don't know." He shrugged his shoulders and his head came up to face me. "I just don't know. I knew. Your dad. Possibly Elaine—I'm sure she must have walked in on him at some point when he was writing in it. She has a habit of turning up when you least want to see her. Maybe Jacques, but I couldn't say for sure. Who knows how many people Phil might have told about it? At least three people knew it existed. Four, maybe. If Elaine knew about it, odds are her boyfriend did also."

"Who is her boyfriend?"

A quirky smile touched his face. "You tell me. Probably you can make a better guess than I can."

"Hardly. I haven't been here for several years, remember? And she doesn't confide in me. I thought it was Manuel, but she denied it."

"You asked her?"

"In a manner of speaking..."

Lee laughed at that, his eyes crinkling with amusement. "No, I don't think it was him. I'm pretty sure he's gone and I don't think Elaine would have gotten involved with him."

"Then I haven't got a clue," I admitted. Allowing for the shadowed figure of the man that Elaine said was staying in Philip's shack, all I had was a vague description.

For a while, we sat silently, each with our own thoughts. I debated telling Lee everything I knew or had seen. I loved the man, I reasoned, and I should be able to trust him. I did trust him. Ever since I was a child, I had trusted him. As I thought back, I remembered that Lee had always been there for me. He may have been Philip's best friend, but he was my protector. I felt a deeper flow of love as I turned to Lee again.

"I was thinking how crazy this all is. That I'm doubting people I've known for years, even my own family. I could be wrong. Perhaps Philip's death was an accident."

"And maybe it wasn't. Is it only coincidence that your brother's journal is being sought with such intensity? That someone is breaking into your house to hunt for it? Someone is very worried about what's in that book."

"If that's what the burglar is looking for. If so, he may already have it, but if he does, then more than one person is worried about it."

His eyebrows shot upward although the question went unasked.

"Someone was in my brother's room before last night," I continued. "It was Tuesday night and I was outside. There was a light in the window." I told him about what had happened the night I followed Elaine and about finding the door locked when I went to check it.

To my surprise, he laughed. A deep, dry chuckle. "Poor Marti! I'll bet you've really been worried all this time. That was me. Before you say anything, let me finish." He was serious again. "I knew where the spare key was and went in. I thought you'd gone to bed. What were you doing up anyway?"

"I couldn't sleep." It was the truth. As curious as I'd been, my mind had been racing far too much.

Accepting that, he continued. "I was after the journal also, but not because it would incriminate me or anything. I thought there might be a clue to Phil's killer in it. You see, after I talked to you, I realized you'd confirmed what I'd believed already. Knowing Phil, I wouldn't have been surprised at anything I found in his journal, but I didn't find it. I checked every place I could in his bedroom. If there's a secret hiding place there, I couldn't locate it and I'd bet last night's prowler couldn't either."

"Do you think he'll try again?"

"I doubt it. At least, not now. It would be too risky." He seemed worried, doubting his own words. If as much was at stake as Lee said, then whoever it was would not be content to wait for the journal to be found by someone else.

"I think he'll be back," I stated with conviction. "He's not going to want someone else to find it."

He drew in a deep breath and exhaled heavily. "You may be right. Or he may wait and watch for someone else to find it and try to get it then."

"He may have a long wait. It might never be found. As I recall, Philip was pretty good at hiding things he wanted to keep secret. He always had something that he considered private."

I looked around me. The cove seemed silent, not even a bird overhead and the waves hitting the beach were quieter as the sea calmed. It was odd. I shivered.

Without hesitation, Lee wrapped an arm around me and asked, "Are you cold?"

"No. Just frightened." I huddled closer to him, leaning my head against his chest. "I don't understand any of this. It seems incredible that it could be happening. Why? What are you not telling me? What was my brother involved in? There has to be something to make some sense of this."

I could see the reluctance in his eyes. He still didn't want to tell me everything, yet I had the right– No, the need to know. If I got any deeper into it, I'd be swallowed up by it. "Please. Tell me. You know I'm up to my neck in this already. You're endangering me more by not telling me."

With an easy movement, he raised his right hand and plucked a strand of my hair between his fingers. He rubbed it like he was feeling the texture or the silkiness of it. With a deep sigh of decision, he began talking. His rich, baritone narrated the story without emotion, lulling me into a sense of security.

Chapter Thirteen

"J tried to make it easy for Phil to talk to me. We'd always been open with each other, but the strain of events concerning the workers was taking its toll on our friendship," Lee told me. He said my brother had first come to him six months before, stopping by his house late one afternoon. At first casual, his conversation became more strained as they talked and Lee realized that something was bothering him.

"Eventually, Phil got around to it. He related his involvement with a Mexican girl and a Mexican activist group. The group supported the labor strike. Basically, Phil agreed with them, but that put him on a rather obvious collision course with your father. At the time, he was worried your dad would find out he'd been to their meetings. From the way he talked, I gathered a couple of the members were pretty hot that he wouldn't support their viewpoints publicly, but then, they didn't have to live with your old man."

"Did they resent him enough to want to harm him?" I asked, letting the remark about Philip's involvement with Consuelo pass for the moment.

"I don't think so. They aren't a violent group. They just couldn't understand why Phil wouldn't stand up against your dad.

"Anyway, he was trying to raise money without your father knowing, He'd given them a considerable amount already from his own savings and he wanted me to help also. Of course, I did what I could, but we were really very limited. Since we couldn't openly approach people for help, we had to contact those we knew were sympathetic. All in all, we raised a pretty good sum, close to ten thousand dollars. Not nearly enough, but respectable. The majority of the contributions came from sympathizers in town. Since Phil had to keep it quiet around your father, I was more involved on the surface. That didn't help the rift with your dad any."

"Is that what you meant when you said you were upset with Philip for not standing up for his convictions?"

He nodded. "Yeah. He really opposed your dad on the labor issue, but he never would face him on it or publicly state his own views. I guess that's not for me to judge though. I wasn't in his shoes."

Picking up a stick, he began drawing circles in the sand, one inside the other, then another, as if he was deep in thought. After a minute, he continued. "A couple of weeks later, Phil stopped by again. He was sure your dad knew he was going to the meetings with this group. They'd argued and the old man told him to stop opposing him or else. Phil was afraid he'd change his will, leave him out of it. Your dad called him irresponsible and swore he would 'ruin the vineyard' if he continued.

"After that, Phil quit going to the meetings. But his relationship with your dad was still strained and they continued to argue. One day, Phil came to me and asked if Dad and I were interested in buying Claremont Vineyards. He said he had reason to believe your dad was going to sell. Even though I was doubtful, he urged me to talk to him about it, so Dad and I approached him. All we did was ask, but you'd have thought we had stabbed him! Such carrying on and accusations. It was unreal! That was when your father ordered us out of his house and told us never to return."

I shook my head slowly, mulling this over. "My father would never sell, Lee. You know that. The vineyard has belonged to the family too long. Why would Philip think he would sell?"

Lee stood up, reached out his hand to me. "Let's walk. I'm tired of sitting." He slipped an arm around my shoulder and we strolled like lovers with slow, unhurried steps, around the horseshoe-shaped bay.

"Phil didn't really know why," he continued after we'd walked a few yards. "But your dad talked about selling. I guess he must have made several remarks about it. Pretty strong remarks at that for Phil to seriously consider them. Anyway, after that things seemed to calm down a bit and I didn't see much of Phil. In fact, our friendship cooled considerably. I figured your father must have laid down the law again, so I stayed out of his way whenever possible. It was about this time that he began drinking heavily."

Lee came to a standstill, slowing me to a halt by his side. For a few moments, his eyes just gazed into mine as if he could see into me and seek an answer or reassurance, then he made up his mind. "Marti, I don't know if I should go into this, but here goes. That involvement Phil had with a Mexican girl was an affair. He really seemed to love her and he went to her as often as he could, even after his father told him to quit meeting with the group. I believe he would have defied your father for her if it had come to that."

It was my turn to shock him. "I know about Philip and Consuelo."

His mouth dropped open. "What?"

"I was talking to her last night." I laughed a little. "I ran into her in the coffee shop where she worked. We remembered each other from high school and decided to get together after she got off work. Naturally our conversation got around to Philip and she told me about her affair with him. Believe it or not, she loved him, too."

He chewed his lower lip nervously, then said, "A chance meeting, huh? What else did she tell you?"

Now, what the hell was he worried about? I thought. "Only what you've just confirmed about Philip's association with Los Latinos Amigos and that he seemed afraid of my father."

He relaxed a little. "That's all?"

I frowned. He was over-reacting. Did he have a connection with Consuelo also? "What else is there?"

Shaking his head, he replied, "I don't know. I just thought she might have added something." He began walking again. I didn't start after him immediately.

"Lee," I called. "Do you know Consuelo?"

As I spoke, he stopped, but he didn't turn around as he answered.

"No, I only know what Phil told me about her."

Catching up with him, I grabbed his hand. "What are you afraid of, darling? Don't you trust me?"

He looked down. "There's nothing more to say. I don't know Consuelo and that's that! Now, please drop it!"

At the look on my face, he threw both arms around me and pulled me close. "I'm sorry, honey. I'm just a little edgy. So much has been happening and I've been worried about you. When I saw that bruise last night, I thought someone had attacked you. It really scared me."

As I clung to him, I thought that now was definitely not the time to tell him the truth about that.

"Every time I tell you something, I wonder if it's a mistake. Why didn't you tell me before that you'd talked to Consuelo?"

I shrugged, "There wasn't an opportunity last night and I really didn't think it was all that important." I didn't add that I wouldn't have told him at all if he hadn't brought it up.

"Well, maybe it's not that important, but she is one more person who could have known about the journal."

"I don't really think she would have been concerned about what the book said about her." On the defensive, I spoke a bit too sharply, but Lee didn't seem to notice.

"Not about her, but maybe about the organization. We have to consider every possibility, even if you two are friends. I'm not saying that she wanted to harm Phil, but she probably did know a great deal about his business." He squeezed me, then resumed walking, pulling me along with him.

"Anyway, to continue my story, the next time I saw Phil to really talk to him was a couple of months ago. I was at Scotty's place and Phil saw my Rover there, so he stopped and came in."

His face clouded over and his eyes closed as he brought the memory into clear focus. He groped for words, then started again. "He looked... upset, very ill at ease. I remember he grabbed my arm and half-dragged me to the back of the grill. He said he'd been going crazy trying to find me. He kept repeating that he didn't understand his old man over and over. It didn't take much to figure out that something had really come as a blow to him.

"Eventually, he calmed down and told me what was bothering him. It seems your father had the combination on his safe changed and refused to give Phil the new numbers. Among the things in the safe were the company's books, all the records, invoices and other related papers that Phil felt he had a right to see. After all, he thought he was running the vineyard, but your father told him that he would take care of all the business again. Whenever he needed something, Phil was to let him know and he would arrange it."

I must have been staring in disbelief because Lee stopped his story.

"I know it sounds wild, but I don't think Phil imagined it."

"Wild isn't the word. Philip's had that safe combination since he was sixteen. He's been in charge of ordering supplies since he was seventeen. How could my father do that to him? It's not conceivable."

Phil said your father seemed strange and he couldn't understand what was happening or why your father was doing this. Let's put it this way; it was one of the few times I've seen Phil really shook up. You know how confident he was, but this whole thing was strange. He was like another person. Of course, I tried to talk to him, calm him. I reasoned there had to be a good explanation somewhere. I even wondered if he'd found out about Consuelo and was getting back at Phil, but he didn't think so. He said that if that were the case, there would have been more of an explosion."

"He was probably right about that," I agreed. I was getting a very unpleasant picture of my brother; that of a man persecuted by either real or imaginary fears of his own father. "I don't think Papa would have taken kindly to an affair with anybody, let alone to someone he would consider unworthy. Was there anything else that would have caused him to distrust my brother?"

"Nope." Lee shook his head, then stopped suddenly. "Wait a

minute. It might not mean anything but Phil did say that Mr. Klein from the bank had been out to see your dad. When Phil asked him about it, he told him it was nothing important and wouldn't tell him anything more. We both thought it was strange since it was the middle of the day and busy bankers don't tend to leave the business for a friendly chat."

"Certainly not Mr. Klein," I agreed. My father had dealt with Edmund Klein many times over the years and rarely had the man ever come to the house except on business.

We reached the end of the cove where beach, rock, and ocean met. Before us stretched the vast, empty ocean and above it, dark, heavy clouds rolled toward us.

"Looks like a storm coming in. I wonder if it'll come across to the valley?" Sometimes the clouds moved on in and sometimes they drifted further south before moving inland.

"Probably. Storms usually bring us some rain at this time of year." Lee squeezed my shoulder affectionately. "Bet you miss your San Francisco rain."

I laughed. "It's not so unique, you know. Just a little more frequent. Honestly, I don't know what to make of all that you've told me. Did Philip try to talk to Mr. Klein?"

"I don't think so. At least, he didn't tell me if he did." He reached down and picked up a shell that had washed ashore, then leaned against the rock face to study it as he talked. Why didn't he want to meet my eyes?

"Then there was that incident with Elaine over Manuel that I already told you about. I still haven't figured out why Elaine was so upset over it, but I know he wasn't her boyfriend."

"Well, that shoots that theory," I interjected. Then who was she seeing? I had been certain it was Manuel staying at the shack even though Elaine denied it. I didn't expect her to admit it, but I didn't expect it to be anyone else either.

"There's something more I should tell you," he said as he dropped the shell and jammed his hands into his jeans pockets. "I told you Phil asked me to go have a drink with him and I turned him down. What I didn't tell you is that he came over about two hours later and insisted I meet him. He said he'd found out something he needed to talk to me about, something very important. But he couldn't go into it just then. Whatever it was, I think it was in his journal. Now do you see why I thought it was important to try to find that book?"

Folding my arms across my chest, I stared out toward the ocean and counted to three. Wow, I thought, when this man neglects to tell you a detail, it really is a big detail. "Did you go meet him?"

"I went to the bar, but he'd already gone. I waited a couple of hours, then gave up. About four hours later, Jacques came to the house asking for my help to find him."

A strong breeze rose from the ocean blowing my hair back and spraying salt water in my face. I turned to face Lee. "Didn't that seem a little strange? Why was Jacques looking for Philip? I'm sure he'd been out all night before. What made this night different?"

"I've thought about that... and I don't have an answer." He reached out for me. "I'm sorry, honey. I wish I didn't have to tell you any of this. I would have told you before, but I wanted to keep you out of it."

"I know that. The only trouble is you haven't answered any of my questions, just added new ones... and there are too many questions. We can see it so clearly. Why can't anyone else? Why did the sheriff call it an accidental death? It seems he would have investigated more."

Lee gnawed at his lower lip but didn't say anything. As he brushed my hair away from my face with his hand, I rested my head against his shoulder. "I'm glad I have you."

He kissed me then—the hard passionate kiss I'd desired such a short time before. Like a warm candle, I melted into his arms and we slipped to the cool, moist sand, our arms wrapped around each other.

* * * * *

"*W*e should be starting back," Lee said, his voice a low murmur in my ear. I made some incoherent sound of agreement even as I shook my head. He laughed, then with a languid move, he pushed to his feet and offered a hand to help me up.

"Oh darn," I muttered, feeling the wet around the bottom of my skirt. "I'm soaked." As I glanced around, I noticed the tide was rapidly making its way up the beach. "It's really getting late."

As we began back to the car, Lee pulled me close. "Are you cold?"

"A little." To emphasize it, I shivered on purpose. "Let's run!" I didn't wait for an answer but burst into a sprint. Behind me, I could hear Lee's feet slapping the wet sand and knew he wasn't far away. We arrived at the car within seconds of each other, breathless and laughing. It felt good to lose myself in that spurt of energy.

He caught my hand as I started to put my shoes on. "Honey, I know this is the wrong time, but probably the right place... Will you marry me?"

Surprised by the suddenness, if not by the proposal itself, I stared up at him, then finally found my voice. "You asked me that once before and I said no." I paused, thinking about the commitment I was about to make and if it was what I really wanted. I knew I wanted to be with him and if that wasn't love, what was? "But the answer is different this time. Yes! Yes, I will!"

With a laugh, I threw both arms around his neck and kissed him.

Right then, there was a crash of thunder and the sky opened with rain. Giggling, I climbed into the car with Lee following immediately. As he started the engine, I smiled at him, bursting with happiness, then leaned my head back and floated back to the valley on a cloud of euphoria.

Chapter Fourteen

*S*till elated, I drove back toward the vineyard as the sun began its descent. A few clouds had worked their way into the valley and I expected the next day would be rainy. A quick glance at my watch told me I should arrive just in time for dinner.

As I pulled up in front of the house, I spotted the familiar steel-gray Mercedes and the all too familiar figure leaning against it, legs crossed at the ankles and arms folded across his chest. Paul. Now, what was he doing here?

"It's about time," he said as he opened the door for me. "I've been waiting hours for you. What've you been up to?"

With a quick hug and a sisterly kiss, I told him I'd been out for a drive with a friend. "And what's brought you out into wine country?"

"The overwhelming desire to see you again, of course. I miss your beautiful little face around the office, pet. Besides I wanted to see more of this vineyard that seems to provide such endless fascination to you suddenly." He flung an arm around my waist and began pulling me toward the door. "Incidentally, I did bring a few notes with me and perhaps we can go over them at some point just to see what articles they might turn out to be."

"I might have known!" I hoped I sounded properly indignant although I was pleased he missed me professionally. "I suppose Gene couldn't handle it?" Gene was one of the other four staff writers for the magazine.

His free hand stroked his beard thoughtfully before he answered. "Well, to tell you the truth, he just doesn't have your touch, your flair with words."

"I thought my touch was too flamboyant. At least that's what you've been telling me for the past two years."

"Oh, maybe a trifle bit, but still they're unique. By the by, pet, you really should tell people when you're leaving. Nobody in this entire household had even an inkling of where you'd gotten to."

I grinned in triumph. "That's the way I planned it, Paul. I like to keep my business private. Why didn't you come in and wait?" I shoved the front door open.

He smiled, a disarming one that had gotten him out of more than one scrape. "Oh, I did the tour of the grounds, inspected the little grape vines and all that. That's a lovely garden out front, but why is it so far from the house?"

"Privacy, Paul. It was a lady's garden and she wanted solitude."

As Madame Boucher met us, I switched to French and introduced Paul, who, likewise, addressed her in French. As he showered her with flowery phrases, Madame Boucher blushed like a school girl.

"You cad." I said, muttering it under my breath.

He heard me and shrugged. "Part of my business, pet."

I frowned at him. "Well, turn off your business around here. Make yourself comfortable while I run upstairs to see my father for a minute."

With perfect ease, he followed my instructions, going first to the bar to pour a scotch, then settling down in a comfortable chair to wait. I shook my head in wonder, decided Paul would fit in any place you put him and hurried on up the stairs.

My father was not in a good mood. Although he was at his desk, he still did not look well and he snapped at me. "It's about time you made an appearance, Martinique. I might ask where you have been all day, but I doubt that you would tell me."

"*Au contraire*, Papa. I've been with Lee," I admitted freely. Sooner or later, he would have to know and accept the fact that I intended to marry Lee, but I wouldn't tell him that now. "He was worried about me."

I bent and kissed him dutifully. I stepped behind the chair and began to knead his shoulders. "You do him an injustice. He's not your enemy. Neither Lee nor his father." I felt his shoulder tense and hurried to jump past the annoyance that was building in him. "But enough of that. We have a guest. My boss is here."

That delighted Papa. "How wonderful! I have wanted to meet this man. It is a good sign that he came here to see you. Tell Madame Boucher that I will be down for dinner."

Surprised, I stopped the shoulder massage. "Are you sure you should?"

"Of course. It will do me good. Now run along, my daughter, and entertain your young man."

Once again, I kissed his cheek and left him. "Now run along–" Just as if I was still a small girl, I reflected with irritation. And Paul was not my "young man," I wanted to shout, Lee is.

Paul had an easy way that seemed to blend into any situation or setting. You could put him in an igloo with several Eskimos and he'd soon be a part of the scene. I found him stretched comfortably in front of the fireplace perusing a book of art reproductions. All that was missing from the scene was a lazy, flop-eared dog to drowse devotedly next to his master.

Comparing him with Lee was inevitable. Paul had a light, carefree manner that masked the strong drive within him. Usually, his blue eyes twinkled with amusement, but I had seen times when they more of a raging sea with anger. Fortunately, that anger had been directed at me only once. Physically, he was smaller than Lee, at least three inches shorter, and very slim. He was good-looking with fine, sharp features and I sometimes wondered if, without the beard, he might look effeminate. Bigger and broad-shouldered, Lee was definitely a more rugged-looking man. Of greater value, Lee conveyed a feeling of security, which Paul did not.

"You are very fortunate," I said as I sat beside him. "Papa has decided to honor us with his presence at dinner. He wants to meet you."

"Is that good or bad?"

"Depends on your viewpoint. It's not bad that he wants to meet you, but for what purpose is the real question. My father is a domineering man. This is his vineyard and he is lord of all that you see. Everything he does relates to this property and to him. People are only of value as to how they can fit into his plans." As I said this, a small voice in mind asked again why Philip would ever have thought Papa would sell the vineyard? While he was alive, Claremont Vineyards was his domain, a kingdom he wouldn't part with for any amount of money.

Paul probably understood this view better than anyone. He wasn't so different when it came to his magazine. They would likely get along very well and that wasn't necessarily good news for me.

"Yes, I see. Well, pet, I am also looking forward to meeting your father. In the meantime, can we go over a couple of these article proposals?"

"Just let me tell Madame Boucher about dinner," I replied as I sprang to my feet and started toward the kitchen.

＊ ＊ ＊ ＊ ＊

"Come on, Marti. You can do better than that," Paul cajoled.

Frustrated, I threw my pencil on the desk, leaned back in my chair and stared at the crisp double-spaced lines of print in my typewriter. They may have looked neat, but they didn't read well. The sentences were awkward and not as succinct as I would like.

"Maybe I could if you would stop hovering over my shoulder!" I bit my lip for snapping at him. Never before had it bothered me to have him read as I typed.

It startled him also and he stepped back, a slightly pained expression on his face. "All right. I'm sorry. I didn't know it bothered you."

He turned and strode over to the window where he stood staring out. We'd come to the library because it was the only place I could think of that was quiet enough to do any work. But it wasn't my favorite room in the house. There was something terribly depressing about it and I felt it especially now. The walls were paneled with a heavy, dark wood as were the shelves that held hundreds of books.

"Your own research room," Paul had said appreciatively when he'd first come into the room. As well stocked with reference and literary volumes as it was, I seldom used the books in here even when growing up. A trip to the library in Napa was preferable.

I swiveled the chair to face Paul. "I'm sorry. I guess I've just had too much on my mind. It's made me very jumpy."

As he turned back, I saw that he still frowned. "I suppose so." His voice was quiet, then his natural resilience took over and a huge grin burst out. "I didn't know you had that much snap in you."

I laughed. I'd seldom known anything to really upset or depress Paul. I suppose it was his survival instinct, otherwise the magazine would probably drive him to ulcers or worse.

Coming over, he began massaging my shoulders. "Relax, pet. All this tension is bad for you. I really think you ought to come back to San Francisco with me."

"You don't give up, do you?" I asked with a shake of my head. "I told you I have this story to write and I'm going to do it. Besides, I'm still on leave."

Just as he started to respond, Madame Boucher poked her head in to announce dinner. Glad to have our conversation cut short, I rose, grabbed Paul's arm, and urged him toward the dining room.

At this point, I didn't want to have to justify my reasons for staying here. In truth, I felt Paul would laugh if I told him the situation, tell me that the whole idea was preposterous, and try to hustle me back to my desk in the city. It did sound absurd, I admitted unless you were involved in it and I wasn't sure I could convince him that it would be a great article.

The dinner table looked magnificent with a fine Belgian lace tablecloth and two bowls of freshly cut roses, one at each end. For this occasion, Madame had brought out the silver candlesticks, chafing dishes, wine decanters, and platters. "In honor of our distinguished guest," I said low enough that only Paul heard me.

He grinned. "I should have worn my tux."

"I wasn't aware you owned a tux," I replied with mock severity.

To that, he only shrugged and helped me to my chair. With tactful planning, Madame indicated the chair next to me for Paul as if she could have kept him out of it if she'd wanted. I noticed there were only five places set. "Who's not joining us?"

"Elaine has a dinner engagement in town," my father said. He'd just come in as I asked my question. Before I could introduce him, he did it himself. "How do you do, young man? I am Martin Claremont. It is an honor to meet you. My daughter has told me much about you." He extended his hand.

A little awed by this formal introduction, but nonetheless polite, Paul took my father's hand in a firm handshake and replied, "No, sir. It is my honor to meet you. You are, I understand, an exceptional man."

Papa had dressed for dinner, not a tuxedo, but a dark blue velvet jacket. Even Jacques was dressier than usual. Curiously, I wondered what Papa was planning now. I noticed the slight nod of approval as Paul waited for him to be seated before seating himself. I had the unsettling hunch he was looking at Paul as a potential son-in-law.

"I didn't know dinner was going to be formal. I would have put on an evening gown," I said with a touch of sarcasm.

Papa raised an eyebrow. "Not formal, Martinique. We are merely honoring our guest."

Glancing over at Paul, I tried to convey my apologies. He, in turn, forced an embarrassed smile. No doubt he'd had the same thoughts. At least, I didn't have to face Elaine. But I wondered with whom she was having dinner.

For a few moments, there was an awkward silence, then Madame

Boucher began passing food around the table. She'd prepared a delicious farmhouse dinner that included a garden salad, *coc-au-vin*, freshly-baked French bread, and broccoli with Hollandaise sauce. The wine was one of our own from Papa's private cellar, a perfectly aged Sauvignon. Papa maintained that chicken cooked in red wine should be served with red wine and he stated this again to Paul as he poured the wine.

As Papa spoke with pride about the wine and the aging, I was amazed again at how little I knew about this business that I'd grown up with, yet not absorbed much knowledge. Paul was attentive and obviously appreciative of the wine although I never recalled him being a wine aficionado. He was more inclined to scotch.

Paul's attention seemed to spark Papa's hospitality and he spoke freely about the wines and the vineyard. "You must tour the whole winery before you leave. Perhaps Martinique will show you around. In spite of her ignorance of fine wines, she is familiar with most of the machinery and the process. Now that my son is gone, she will inherit these vineyards at my death. I trust that she will gain a great deal more knowledge about wine before then."

I caught my breath in a truncated gasp. To my knowledge, this was the first time he'd stated to the household that I would be inheriting and I was not pleased that he'd told Paul before I had a chance to say anything. Why was that? Was he trying to entice Paul with the promised wealth his daughter would have?

Papa paused, cast a reproachful glance at me and took a breath to continue.

Wanting to get a sting in myself, I said, "Well, perhaps I could return to the University to study agriculture and winemaking techniques. Or you can send me to France for a few months. Or I could always marry Lee and solve that problem. He knows plenty about this business." Out of the corner of my eye, I saw Paul's eyebrows arch upward, but my main view was focused on my father's face, which could barely conceal the rage he felt.

Through narrowed eyes and a tightly-controlled voice, he growled, "That is not humorous, Martinique. I was being quite serious."

I almost said so was I, but I bit my tongue and kept tactfully silent.

He forced a laugh. "My daughter likes her little jokes, Paul. However, she will be a very wealthy young lady when all this is hers."

Oh, there it was. Spelled out for my boss. I was too angry to be embarrassed by this snobbish bartering.

"Or a very wealthy old lady if you live another ten or fifteen years, as I expect you will, Papa." I tried to make my voice sound light. I didn't want Paul to see how upset I was by this whole conversation.

However, Paul picked up on Papa's cue. "Well, money isn't everything, Mr. Claremont. I really think quite a bit of Marti as she is—an overpaid, but talented, reporter for my magazine. Of course, I wouldn't stand in the way of her success and when she's ready to return here permanently, I'll just have to reluctantly let her go."

Very diplomatic, I thought. With bosses like that who needs enemies?

Papa nodded his approval.

An awkward lag in the conversation followed that exchange. I noticed Jacques, who sat across the table from me, looked quite uncomfortable as if he had stumbled into a conversation he had no right to hear. His wife had sat next to him after serving the food and now looked as if she would prefer to escape back to her kitchen. In sympathy with Jacques and anxious to divert the conversation from the path Papa had chosen, I said, "We are being a bit rude. Madame Boucher does not speak any English, Paul. Generally, we converse in French. Since you speak it fluently, I suggest we do so now."

Paul not only agreed but promptly apologized to Madame for our discourteous oversight. The conversation moved to more pleasant topics as I had hoped it would. Papa covered the history of our vineyard and explained a little about the wine-making process, a subject on which Jacques was only too happy to comment. Even his usually quiet wife had a few remarks to contribute. As I watched my father's face, I was sure he was growing fonder of Paul. I had to admit, my boss was quite charming, but then I knew how smooth he could be. He'd charmed his way through more than one interview.

"You really should explore the winery cellars," I said. "They are most interesting. Some of the bottles of wine down there—"

The ringing telephone interrupted me and automatically, I started to rise to answer, but Jacques was already on his feet.

I picked up the sentence again. "Some of the bottles are from the first years this winery was started. I suppose they're worth quite a fortune now."

"Yes," Papa agreed. "We do have some very fine old wines. Aging is the key to superb flavor, particularly to the red wines. A white wine can be over-aged." As Papa started on a dissertation on what constitutes a quality wine, Jacques tapped my shoulder and indicated the phone was for me. Excusing myself, I took it in the living room, thinking it must be Lee.

"Marti! I need to talk to you desperately. When can I see you?" The voice was Consuelo's. She sounded upset or frightened. I couldn't tell which. She kept her voice low.

"I can't get into town until tomorrow. What's wrong?"

"I can't tell you over the phone." Her voice was frightened, I decided. What had happened? "What time tomorrow?"

"First thing. About ten by the time I get there."

A pause. "Meet me in front of the Sebastiani Theatre. You remember where it is?"

I said I did.

"I'll be waiting in front. Just pick me up. Okay?"

I agreed and she broke the connection, no goodbyes or anything.

I replaced the phone in its cradle, then stood there a few moments longer to collect my thoughts. The tone of her voice had shouted fear, yet she couldn't talk about it over the phone. I should have gone tonight, I thought, but there was nothing for it. I couldn't get away, not with Paul here. Maybe I could... But no! She didn't want me to meet her at her place, so I'd have to wait. Had she found out something? I stilled my thoughts and shifted them back to the dining room conversation as I returned.

Papa was still discussing wine and Madame Boucher was just bringing dessert, a marvelous display of her specialty, Crepes Suzette. The light, thin pancakes were nestled together in the center waiting to be ignited. I arrived in time for the lighting. As the honored guest, Paul was given the task of flaming the liqueur and he proceeded with nervous caution.

"I feel like an arsonist," he commented, but Madame Boucher had things well in hand. As the liqueur flamed, she spooned the burning sauce over the crepes and served them before the flames vanished.

"Quite impressive, pet," Paul said as he nudged me.

I wasn't paying much attention. My mind drifted back to the phone call and I found it difficult to bring it back to this little dinner party.

The after-dinner brandy in the living room was another ritual to suffer through. Paul was relaxed, enjoying himself as he conversed with my father. Even Papa seemed better than I'd seen him since I'd arrived.

"My daughter has offered you the hospitality of our home while you're here, hasn't she?" Papa asked when Paul mentioned he was staying the weekend.

"She did mention there were a couple of spare rooms and that I was welcome to use one."

"Excellent," Papa said with approval. "I'm glad to see she does have some manners even though she seems to have expressed them poorly." The tone of his voice was biting, evidence that he was still irritated with me.

I set my glass down with a sharp rap on the end of the table. I'd had more than enough of the little digs tonight. "You must excuse me. I'm very tired. It's been a long day and I'm exhausted, so I'll go up to bed now."

Paul looked up as I rose to leave. "Do you have to go now, Marti? I really wanted to talk with you more."

I forced a weary smile. "I'm sorry, Paul. I just can't make it any longer. But go ahead and visit with my father and I'll talk to you tomorrow."

Accepting that, he rose to kiss me good night, a peck on the cheek, then, in turn, I kissed my father's cheek in the same manner, and made my exit to the stairs without any further words.

It was another hour before I managed to get to bed. I'd reviewed the whole phone conversation again in my mind, searching for any clues as to what it was about and had drawn another blank. I resolved to also pay a visit to Papa's banker while I was in Sonoma. That was another lead I wanted to investigate further.

So, on a night when my head should have been filled with delightful thoughts of my engagement to Lee, I fell into a restless sleep with a mystery on my mind.

Chapter Fifteen

*T*he early morning air was cool and fragrant as I hastened toward my car. So far, the rest of the household was still sleeping. With a plan to stop at a coffee shop, I had awakened early and slipped out unnoticed–or so I had thought.

As I started to get into my car, Jacques caught up with me. "Martinique, you are going off again with a guest in the house?"

I nodded.

"But what will he do?"

"Paul? Don't worry about him. He'll find plenty to keep him busy. I have to go into town. I don't know how long I'll be, but I'll be back as soon as I can. Please do me a favor. Don't tell anyone that you saw me this morning. I was gone when you got up, okay?"

"Of course." He hesitated as if he had something more to say.

"Yes?"

He took a deep breath, preparing himself to tell me something that might not be pleasant. I was completely alert now. "Elaine has not been home all night. Be careful, Martinique."

"Of Elaine?"

"Of everyone. Trust no one. *Écouter...pas une.*" He hurried away from me.

A shiver of uncertainty and fear rose up my spine. My hand still rested on the door handle and it was several seconds before I recovered enough to push the button and open it. As I slid in and laid my hands on the steering wheel, I discovered they were shaking. Something about the way Jacques spoke his warning unnerved me.

Not one.

"Oh, Jesus," I whispered. What did he mean? No. Who was he warning me about? I turned the key and the engine roared to life, sounding as loud as a jet engine in that quiet morning. I glanced toward the house, but it still seemed asleep. I eased the car out of the drive and onto the highway where I sped toward Sonoma.

I was fifteen minutes early, but Consuelo was already there, waiting. Her long black hair swung freely as she paced back and forth, a nervous young woman in a pale blue dress. She kept looking up the street, then down again at the sidewalk. She may not have expected me for fifteen more minutes, but like me, she was anxious and keyed-up. When she spotted my car, she stopped pacing and stood on the curb. As soon as I pulled over, she got in without a word.

"Where to?"

"Some place where we can talk privately. How about the river?" Her voice was tight and she looked exhausted with black rings circling her tired eyes. I didn't think she'd slept since I talked to her. Whatever was bothering her was taking its toll.

She didn't seem willing to talk at the moment, so I didn't try to start a conversation, but drove in silence to the Sonoma Creek where I found a quiet place to pull off the road and park the car. Consuelo got out and walked to stand beside the bank, then looked around carefully. Satisfied that we were alone, she let out a deep breath and appeared to relax.

"Now, do you want to tell me what this is about?" As I joined her, I sipped the last of my coffee and sat on the grass by the water.

She paced back and forth a couple of times while she gathered her thoughts or worked up her nerves. When she spoke, her voice was low enough that only I could hear. "Marti, I'm not exactly sure what it means, but someone broke into my apartment early yesterday morning. Ernesto was there. He was asleep on the couch and the lights were out. I think whoever it was must have thought no one was home. When he surprised Ernesto, they struggled and the man pulled a knife and cut him."

"Oh, my God! How bad is it?"

"Not serious. He just cut his arm, then knocked him out. He'll be okay. Evidently, the man just wanted to get away, He wasn't a killer, just a burglar. Ernesto didn't see him clearly enough to give the police much to identify him."

"Did the man find anything?"

She looked up sharply. "How do you know he was looking for something?" The question had surprised her.

"Because someone broke into our house also, looking for something. Not after jewelry or money. I'm sure it's the same person or someone in league with him. So, I repeat, did he find anything?"

Dumbfounded, she stared at me a moment before answering. "No. Nothing. What was he looking for?"

I leveled my eyes with hers, studying her, then I made up my mind. If she was to be my friend, I would have to trust her. "Philip kept a journal that someone seems to want badly. No one appears to know where it is. Do you?"

She collapsed into a heap next to me. "Philip's journal?" She ran her dominant hand through her hair, twisting the end. "I'd forgotten all about it."

My heart jumped. Could it be she had it? I was almost afraid to ask. "Do you know where it is? Have you seen it?"

"No. I'd seen it once and I knew he had it. But he never told me where he kept it. I always figured it was in his room somewhere. For some reason, he thought it was valuable, but he never told me much about it."

I was disappointed, yet, at the same time, relieved. Philip did not even trust her with it or the knowledge of its hiding place. For the first time since I'd found out about it, I felt that it really might be safe.

Her voice cut through my thoughts. "Is it so important?"

"To someone it is. I wish I knew exactly what he'd written in it.

How much did he tell you about it? Did he give you any clues at all?"

"He just told me he was keeping a journal of everything that happened and that it might prove valuable some day. At the time, he seemed very pleased with himself, but he only mentioned it a couple of times."

"I figured as much. Did Ernesto know about it?"

"Philip didn't confide in him and I didn't tell him. There was no reason to talk about it." She pulled her knees up to her chest, folded her arms around them and dropped her head on her arms, her face reflecting her worries. "Why would anyone think I had it? Who would know about us except you?"

I'd already thought about that and I didn't like the answers. Consuelo put the sound to my thoughts. "Wait... Lee Kellog knew about us. Philip told me he'd told him. But he would have no reason!"

"Who else, Consuelo? Think of someone else. There has to be another answer." I wouldn't believe that, couldn't believe it. I loved Lee and I believed him. *Don't trust anyone*, Jacques had said. Did that include Lee? "Did Elaine know?" I asked.

She thought about it carefully. "I don't know. She might have, but I don't think so. Philip was very careful. He was afraid of what your father would do if he found out. I can't recall if anyone ever saw us together who could have told someone. People saw us at meetings, but not as a couple. Just two people with a common goal." She dropped her head again and moaned. "I can't think, Marti. There might have been someone..."

Another thought chilled me. "Someone might have followed me to you. Maybe he thought I knew and I could lead him to it." I looked around me nervously, half-expecting to see someone watching me.

Oh, you are getting spooked, I thought. If I hadn't been so frightened at the prospect of being followed, it would have been laughable.

Consuelo watched me, her eyes wide. I'd scared her also. She swore in Spanish, then pulled herself together. "I think we'd better find out who it is. Tell me about the burglar at your place."

I nodded in agreement, then went over the details of the break-in again. When I gave her Papa's description of the burglar, her eyebrows dropped and she frowned. "What's wrong?"

"That doesn't match Ernesto's description. He said the man was shorter than that, maybe five-nine, slender build, and he was very quick."

It didn't fit Lee either, I realized, and felt relieved. "Is Ernesto sure? The man woke him. Maybe he wasn't aware of his true size? He didn't have time to really look."

"He's sure," she said matter-of-factly, "When you are struggling with someone, you know how large he is."

"Then we're looking for two different people. The next question would be, 'are they each independent or are they working together?'" Would two people be any easier to find than one? I leaned back against the tree. Something had bothered me ever since my talk with Lee on the beach yesterday, and I decided to ask it now. "Consuelo, why did you tell me that the members of your organization didn't know that Philip was in sympathy with them? He was involved with them, wasn't he?"

Her head came up quickly and the shock in her eyes told me she'd lied about that. She drew in a deep breath. "How did you find that out?"

"Lee Kellog told me." I think the regret that she hadn't trusted me with that must have showed. "Why don't you tell me about it now? Tell me everything."

Dropping her eyes from mine, she shook her head. "Sometimes you do what you think is best, but then you end up getting caught. I didn't think it was necessary to tell you that Philip had been to a few of the meetings. Yes, he was in sympathy with the Amigos, but they didn't all believe that. A few of them felt he was just trying to find out what their plans were. If he had not quit himself, he would have been asked to resign. But those who felt that way would not have hurt him;

they just didn't trust him."

She smiled, a sad expression in her eyes. "He never gave them a reason to believe... not when he publicly supported his father. You couldn't blame them. He didn't. But he still wanted to help. He tried to get money for the organization. Believe me, they wouldn't have killed him. I know these people and they are not murderers."

"Neither is Ernesto. Yet, he attacked me," I said, a sharp retort that caused a pained look on her face.

"Ernesto is not like the rest. Besides, he didn't mean to hurt you. He was just worried about me."

"That's another thing. Suppose I hadn't been your friend? What would he have done then? I might have gone to the police. As it was, I had a hard time explaining this bruise. I'm lucky anyone believed me. My excuse sounded so incredible they must have thought it was true."

Her face morphed to an am imploring expression. "I know it looked bad, but he wouldn't have really hurt you. He acted impulsively and made the wrong moves. He's young and doesn't think. I thought you understood."

I closed my eyes, annoyed that I'd brought it into the conversation. "I'm sorry. I didn't mean to get into that again. I was just trying to illustrate my point—that like Ernesto, the members of the Amigos may not intentionally want to harm anyone, but there might have been one who, under a given set of circumstances, could have been motivated to kill."

"Sure," she agreed. "Many people could be persuaded by a 'certain set of circumstances' to commit homicide. That's nothing new. I'm afraid that's a mighty thin straw you're grasping, *amiga*. What we're talking about is not spontaneous murder. It was planned to look like an accident."

Restless, I began plucking long grass blades, twisting them together. "You're right. I'm trying to fit pieces together that don't match." I turned to her. "Lee said he thought Philip found out something that last day. Something really important, maybe something that got him killed. Did you see him that night?"

"No, I didn't," she answered, climbing to her feet. "Let's go. This place gives me the chills." As we started back to the car, she added, "That was one of the things that bothered me. I expected him that night, but he never came."

She opened the car door and leaned against it, her chin resting on a hand across the top. I paused as she continued. "When he went off the road, he was returning from Sonoma, not coming here. If he'd come to town, I know he'd have come by to see me."

Consuelo gasped suddenly and grabbed for me. The blood had drained from my face and I leaned against the car. My train of thought had connected with something else I didn't want to believe.

"Are you all right?" she asked anxiously as she still offered support.

I nodded, pulled myself upright and lurched around the car to pull open the door and collapsed behind the steering wheel. Finally, I managed to say, "If someone wanted it to look like an accident, all he had to do was make it look as if the car went over the edge. The direction didn't matter, but he intentionally made sure the car looked like it was returning from Sonoma."

The blank expression on her face told me that she didn't understand.

"Don't you see? He knew Philip was going to Sonoma that night. Now that means it was somebody who knew he would be coming to see you. I think whoever did it was trying to tell you that he knew about you and—"

"But Ernesto was the only one who really knew about us," she interrupted as she realized at last what I meant. "Who would know he was coming here that night?"

"Lee knew also," I said flatly. "He told me."

"What else did Lee tell you?" she asked, a touch of bitterness in her voice. "Did he tell you he belonged to Los Latinos Amigos?"

My heart jumped and I gaped at her. "What?"

"He's a member. He's been in for over six months."

"Son of a bitch," I swore with emphasis. *Don't trust anyone.* Angrily, I thought that he hadn't lied to me, only told me a half-truth. How many other half-truths did he tell? Was he the one who planned Philip's death? But I was back to the same old question of why.

As if she read my thoughts, Consuelo said, "No. Lee didn't do it. He and Philip were too close. I think there's more than one person involved. The burglars are two different people and neither description fits Lee. Granted, Lee knew about Philip and me, but so could someone else if they followed him. We're jumping to too many conclusions."

Calming down, I acknowledged. "Okay. You're right. We've got to find that journal. Should we tell the Sheriff?"

"Do you think he'd believe you?"

With another shake of my head, I started the car. "Probably not. This whole thing is unbelievable." I was sure the journal was somewhere around the house and it was up to me to find it now. We both realized we would have to be cautious in case someone was watching us.

As I dropped her off near the coffee shop where she worked, she turned to me before she opened the door. "Be careful. I think you're in more danger than I am... especially if you find that journal."

* * * * *

My next stop turned out to be the sheriff's office after all. I'd decided to do a little fishing, see if the man knew a little more than he was letting on. Sheriff Eberman was in and studying reports.

"I was just wondering if you'd found out anything about our burglar," I said without a greeting.

"No, Miss Claremont," he said, barely glancing up from his papers. "As a matter of fact, I've run into an interesting side development. We've had another 'break and enter' incident with all the same characteristics as the one at your place, except the description of the burglar doesn't seem to be the same. What do you make of that?"

I feigned surprise. "You mean there could be two people? Perhaps they aren't related. Where was the other break-in? Another vineyard."

"Nope," he drawled. "The apartment of a waitress. Nothing in the way of similarity there, but the method of entering was the same and there are no fingerprints or footprints. It's not much to go on, but I have a hunch they're related. What puzzles me is what it is that someone is looking for at the home of Martin Claremont and the home of a Mexican waitress. What common denominator could both have? I don't suppose you have any idea?"

I glanced around, pulled up a chair and, since I hadn't been invited to sit, made myself at home anyway. "Sheriff, I've been in San Francisco for seven years and I only came home to attend my brother's funeral. I really don't know what kind of connections there might have been. I've read the newspapers and I know there were labor problems and maybe this connects somehow, but I can't give you any kind of answer."

He watched me closely, then said very quietly, "Maybe you'd like to tell me how you really got that bruise?"

He was no fool, our sheriff. Although I had deep respect for this man who'd kept the law in this valley for so many years, I couldn't tell him everything. For one thing, I still heard Jacques' warning and I wasn't sure of even the sheriff.

I smiled. "As crazy as it sounds, I did fall and bump my head against the door jamb. Almost knocked myself out, too. I'm not too well-coordinated when I've had a few drinks." I wet my lips as he continued to stare at me. He didn't believe that. Quickly, I went on, getting away from that subject. "Actually, I wanted to ask you something else. You investigated my brother's accident, didn't you?"

He nodded.

"I was wondering how you arrived at the conclusion it was an accidental death?"

Typically, he answered with a question. "Do you have reason to think otherwise, Miss Claremont?"

Since I was sure he would ask that, I'd thought the answer out carefully. "Not really, I guess. But I remember my brother as being both a drinker that could hold his liquor well and an excellent driver. I find it very hard to believe he could have lost control on that curve."

He nodded thoughtfully. "Yes, that was an easy curve. However, I based my final evaluation on the coroner's report, which did not indicate any foul play. If you have any evidence to suggest otherwise, I would, of course, open the investigation again. Do you?"

"No, I don't. I'm just a little unsettled about it, that's all. Call it a sister's intuition. Well, thank you for your time, Sheriff." I rose to leave.

"Miss Claremont..." He started in a slow drawl and I paused. "If someone, like yourself, had anything unusual happen, it might be a good idea to report it. You can't always be sure who your friends are and your father hasn't made too many lately."

I hoped I looked calmer than I felt. "Thank you for the warning. I'll keep it in mind." My second warning today.

His head bobbed again, then he returned to his reports. I let myself out, feeling as if I'd made a mistake by coming here at all. As I walked toward the bank, I noticed that the clouds were heavy and dark today. I guessed it would rain before nightfall. With determination, I shut Lee and the previous day at Point Reyes out of my mind. I still felt betrayed on that count.

Aaron Klein was friendly, courteous and not very helpful. He was a small, thin man who had a way of answering, but not answering questions. Without hesitation, he made his position clear. "Well, Miss Claremont, I naturally want to help you all I can. However, our bank records are confidential and any dealings our bank has with

Claremont Vineyards fall into that category."

"I understand that, Mr. Klein," I said patiently, putting on my best professional look. "But since I am heir to the business, I had hoped that you might give me some insight into the financial background. I would like to know what I'm going to inherit. It's only since my brother's death that I've given it any thought and I haven't any idea what the vineyard is worth."

He smiled, revealing slightly crooked teeth. "All I can tell you is that your father's business is worth a great deal of money. For more than that, I would suggest you ask your father. That would be the logical course, I would think." The tone of his voice suggested that the subject was closed. So much for my charm.

Picking up my purse, I started to get up, then hesitated to make one more try. "By the way, I heard that you called on my father at the vineyard a few months ago. Did that have anything to do with the business?"

He laughed drily. "I'm sure you'll be a good business woman, Miss Claremont. All I will tell you is that my visit to your father was strictly personal. Now, if that's all, I'll wish you a good day." Polite dismissal.

With a sharp nod of acknowledgment, I turned and left. I hadn't expected to find out anything and for some reason, I had the feeling he revealed more to me than he intended. By telling me that his visit to my father was personal, he didn't deny that it was related to the business, only that it was not related to the bank.

Like the caterpillar with the pipe who spoke to Alice in riddles, I thought wryly. Was the Red Queen waiting somewhere to call "off with her head"? Or in this case, was it the Knave of Hearts?

Chapter Sixteen

*P*aul was waiting for me by the tasting room. For the first time since Philip's death, the room was open and a pair of cars were parked in front. Of course, Papa wouldn't want to miss any weekend business, I thought bitterly, then reprimanded myself. I was being unfair. After all, he was a businessman and no one in any business could afford to be closed more than a day or two.

Putting on a smile, I waved at Paul and called out. "Hi! Have you been waiting out here long?"

"No, I saw you driving up and came out. Where've you been, pet?" He met me and folded an arm around my shoulder.

"I had to go into town. Come on into the house while I fix a sandwich. I'm starving." I started toward the door.

He pulled back on my shoulder lightly. "Only if you promise to take me on a tour of this place after you eat."

As I turned to look at Paul, I noticed the sparkle in his eyes and the slight flush to his cheeks. With a laugh, I said, "It looks like you already started on the tour."

He grinned. "I just sampled a little, but I really don't know that much about wine. I need an expert guide."

"And you're turning to me?" I asked, disbelief clear in my voice.

He shrugged. "Well, you're bound to know more than I do. Didn't you pick it up by osmosis? I mean, being around it all the time, you must've."

"Very little, but enough to impress you, I guess." I opened the door and went straight to the kitchen. Although Paul had released me, he still stuck close. How was I going to hunt for the journal with him hanging onto me? Trying not to show my annoyance, I began putting a ham and cheese sandwich together while I considered possible amusements to keep Paul busy and away from me.

It was several minutes before I became aware that he was staring at me. He'd turned a chair around and laid his chin on his arms across the back of it, then watched me. He was quiet and his expression more serious than it had been a short time before.

"What's wrong?"

He shook his head. "I'm just watching and thinking you're really quite beautiful. A little short for my tastes, actually, but beautiful, nonetheless."

"Thanks a bunch," I said as I reached into the refrigerator for a soda. "For your information, there are some men who don't care that I'm short."

"Lee, for instance?"

I stared hard at him. Had my father said something? "He's one. Yes."

Paul's eyes didn't waver. "I might ask exactly who he is, but I shan't. I like your father. He's a very interesting person. But you two don't get along, do you?"

"Look who's getting nosy."

"And look who's dodging the subject." His laugh was short and he wore a smug look. He did drop it though. "Oh, I forgot to tell you. I have something for you—your mail. I stopped by your apartment yesterday morning and brought it. Forgot to give it to you last evening."

I waited, then said, "Well, where is it?"

His eyebrows arched. "Oh, no! You don't get it until after the tour. You might decide to answer your mail right away instead of showing me around."

"Black mail."

"No, actually it's mostly white and one pale blue envelope."

I groaned. I should have known better. I finished my sandwich, picked up my soda and started for the door. Grabbing his arm, I yanked him out. "Come on, then. Let's get this going."

Near the edge of the grape fields, I pointed to a large, leafy plant with several small bunches of grapes forming and spoke knowledgeably. "That is a grape vine. In fact, its exact species name is *Vitis vinifera* with some other Eastern strain mixed in to make it hardier. Grapes like sandy soil and lots of sun. It takes a certain temperature to ripen them. I forget what it is, but my brother explained it to me once. It had to do with calculating the temperatures in the growing season that exceeded a certain degree or something like that. Anyway, it's rather complicated and I don't really understand it."

I waved my arm to encompass all the vineyards. "Now, this species of grapes has many varieties from which almost all wines are made except for fruit wines and a few other unusual ones. The diversity of the wines results from the character the grapes get from the climate, the soil and the techniques which the Claremont family have used for centuries, even when they were in France."

"I'm impressed," Paul said as he looked over the fields which seemingly stretched for miles. "How many acres of grapes do you have here?"

"You would ask that. To be honest, I don't know. I have no concept of the amount of land we have, but I expect it's a couple of hundred acres. The vineyards go all the way back to those low hills there." I pointed into the distance. "You'll have to ask Papa if you want to know exactly. He or Jacques could tell you just like that..." I snapped my fingers together for emphasis.

As I set a quick pace toward the buildings that housed the fermenting and cooling machinery, Paul caught my hand and pulled me back beside him so that we took at it his gait rather than mine. "What's your hurry?" he asked. "After all, I did come all the way up here to see you."

"And bring along some articles to write," I reminded him.

He ignored that but pointed toward the storage vats. "What are those?"

"Grapes used to be stored in those until they could be crushed. Usually, it wasn't very long. We don't use them at all anymore. Our equipment now is a lot faster than when my great-great grandfather founded the winery. We can crush the grapes as soon as they arrive; no waiting." Wondering if this was boring Paul, I turned and asked, "Are you really interested in all this?"

"Of course. I think the whole place is fascinating. You may be right about that story you want to do. Only please get your degrees right if you explain about grapes ripening on the vines. I don't want to be bombarded with letters from would-be wine experts."

"I hadn't planned to include that." A big smile crossed my face as it appeared that Paul was warming up to the article idea. We reached the buildings and I guided him to the far side. To my surprise, I was enjoying this and he was right that I did know more than I thought. "Now, this is the crushing section. The first monster machine you see there is the crusher. Actually, it crushes and removes the stems at the same time."

Before us was an eight-foot-long machine, currently disassembled, with revolving paddles and a perforated cylinder. "That's an odd looking creature," Paul commented. "How does it work?"

"It's very simple," I said. "At least, it's one of the machines I understand. As you can see, it's been taken apart for cleaning. When it's together, the paddles fit inside the cylinder and they revolve very fast crushing the grapes, which then fall through the perforations in the cylinder. The stems are discarded at the end." I motioned him to the next machine. "It's not enough that the grapes are crushed, they have to be pressed also. Now, we use a screw press to extract the juice..."

"What? No lovely maidens dancing on the grapes?" he interrupted. "I'm terribly disappointed. There goes another concept shot to hell."

I laughed. "You're batty, Paul. Girls haven't stomped grapes in years. Not since I went away to school. Before that, it was quite a job and my feet used to wrinkle up like prunes."

Paul's abrupt outrageous laugh sounded like a whooping crane and resonated through the building. The next minute we were both laughing hysterically. I guess it was a relief of some sort because nothing was that funny. Paul and I held on to each other and my head dropped against his chest. I had to admit I really liked the man. For the moment, his insane sense of humor had pulled my mind away from my worries. Granted, people seldom saw that side of him, but at least it was there when I needed it.

Pulling my wits together again, I urged him to follow me through the rest of the processing plant. I explained what little I knew about the fermentation process and watched as he made a disgusted face while I described the caps of yeast and crushed fruit that float on top of a warm vat of fermenting grape juice.

"It's really much more impressive when we're actually making wine." I waved my arm to the next door on the other side of the fermenting vats. "The next area is the aging room where we store the wine in fifty-gallon redwood or oak barrels to age. Papa's already told you about that process."

As we stood examining the barrels, something touched my mind. Something about the barrels... from long ago. But I couldn't quite get it, then it was gone.

Paul saw the distant look on my face as my brow wrinkled with the thought. "Marti? Is anything wrong?"

"No. It's nothing. Just something I was trying to remember, but it's escaped me. Let's go on to the wine tasting rooms." I walked ahead of him, my mind still trying to recall what it was about the wine barrels that had stirred in my memory. It was too vague and Paul kept talking to me.

The tasting room was in a charming, chalet-designed building not too far from the house. A small parking lot in front accommodated about twenty-five cars and it was adequate unless it was a holiday. At this time of year we had only a few cars in it at a time. This was the only building open to visitors, unless they were taking a tour, and it was normally all they wanted to see. The building front was covered with flowers–climbing roses, geraniums, hydrangea, and several other varieties in a rainbow of colors, reminding our guests, and potential customers, that almost everything grew in the mild California climate. Built from redwood trees, it featured a roofed porch with redwood furniture and a hanging swing made from a wine barrel. My lips curved into a fond smile as I recalled swinging on it whenever I could sneak away before Jacques or Madame Boucher would shoo me off. The massive front doors were also made from wine barrel slats that were held together with metal straps.

Inside, close to a hundred wine racks lined the walls and made aisles. The variety of wines seemed endless, but not all the wines sold here were our manufacture. Papa stocked an assortment of other wines that we did not produce, including some rather expensive European imports. One label I recognized as being the French branch of the family. Several wine barrels were in here also and the rooms, three of them, had a musty smell.

In the first room, engraved on a bronze plaque, were my great-great-grandfather's words. Not in the original French, but translated to English so that any visitor could read them and understand the considerable pride that went into Claremont wines.

"This, my friends, is the fruit of all our labors, this clear delightful nectar to please the palate of even Bacchus, the god of wines.

Martin Claremont–1908"

The date was the founding date of the winery although the vineyards themselves had been planted many years before. The same words were printed on the labels of all our wines. "It sounds better in French," I said softly as I automatically translated the words back to the almost poetic French phrasing I'd heard my father say many times.

Below the plaque was the visitor's guest book which I insisted Paul sign. "You're one of the most distinguished guests we've had visit," I argued. "Paul Thorpe, well-known magazine editor. Just think what people will do when they see your name on our guest register."

"I'd rather not," he replied with a shake of his head, but he did sign the book.

"This is where I really don't know anything," I told him as I looked around the rooms. "I've never been much of a wine drinker other than cream sherry. Kind of a rebellion against the whole thing, I guess. I do know the difference between aroma and bouquet though, at least in definition." I could tell by his befuddled look that Paul didn't, so I clarified it. "The aroma is from the grape variety and the bouquet is from the aging. But I can't distinguish one from the other when tasting wine."

"You can tell good from bad, can't you?" Paul asked, selecting a bottle of Chardonnay from a rack.

"Of course! But only because bad tastes so terrible. Would you like to taste that?"

He nodded and I handed the bottle to the young man behind the tasting counter, a quiet Mexican boy with wide, dark eyes that reminded me of Ernesto. I knew he had to be at least twenty-one to work behind the bar, but he looked much younger. Without a word, he poured a sample, which I handed to Paul while I explained the process of proper wine tasting—look for the clarity of the wine, smell the aroma and bouquet, then roll it around the tongue to fully taste it. At least my student caught on to the "rolling it around the tongue" part fairly well.

Over the next thirty-five minutes, we repeated the process of selecting a wine and tasting it, cleansing the palate between wines with little crackers. The first wines had been dry varieties as we moved toward the sweeter dessert wines with each selection. After about seven wines, it becomes difficult to distinguish differences, so when Paul selected an eighth bottle, I suggested it be the last one. It was a rich cream sherry with a superb bouquet.

I congratulated myself that I did know more about wines than I'd believed. I had absorbed a great deal while growing up and, of course, wine was always served at the dinner table. Even when we were small, it had been mixed with water so that Philip and I could enjoy it with our food. Papa wanted us to learn early to appreciate the product of the vineyard and I had accepted it as part of my life, but not really taken the effort to learn about it. Yet here I was, able to show someone about it and amazing myself with the knowledge I had tucked away in my memory.

Paul selected three bottles and reached for his wallet. "You don't have to do that," I told him. "Take them with the compliments of my father."

He chuckled. "Oh, no. I want to pay for them. I had enough of your dear father's hospitality this morning. After all, he is in business to make money and I believe in free enterprise. So, if you will step out of my way, I will attend to this matter." He motioned me aside and advanced to the register.

I waited by the side exit as Paul paid for his choices and charmed the cashier. I could tell he'd had more than enough to drink and I suspected my father's hospitality hadn't been restricted to the fruit of the vine. He had a nice selection of stronger spirits as well. As Paul staggered a bit toward the door, I thought that he'd had a tendency to laugh more than usual and at almost anything. It was a state I didn't see him in too often and never this early in the day. Almost always, he was well in control of himself and you had to know him very well to know he'd been drinking at all.

Throwing an arm around my shoulder, he pushed me out into the garden. This was a large area by the tasting room that Papa wanted to make into an outdoor café. "People like to eat when they drive out from San Francisco," he'd told me several times when I was younger.

So far, it was still only a garden with redwood tables and chairs scattered around for visitors to sit, sip wine, and eat the cheese and crackers, which were also sold in the tasting room. The patio area floor was redwood and trellises of the same wood formed the walls where grapevines, Thompson seedless eating grapes, climbed and covered the area. Around the edges and in planters were numerous varieties of shade plants and several dwarf fruit trees in redwood tubs. The side opposite the winery wall was completely open except for the supporting pillars of redwood logs, around which honeysuckle vines, crowned with tiny white and pink flours, wound vigorously. The early afternoon air was heavy with their sweet fragrance.

Paul looked around in appreciation. "This is a little paradise here. Which of the Claremont ancestors did this?"

I smiled and answered with some pride. "This is Papa's contribution. Both the tasting room and the garden are his creations. Before this was built, the wines were sold from the house. Quite a bit of it is still stored in the cellars."

Without warning, Paul spun me in his arms and kissed me in a more than friendly way, his mouth locking on mine, demanding more. I responded automatically to a man I'd been with so many times that it took a few moments to recall I'd accepted Lee's proposal the previous day. As I started to pull away, he held me even tighter, then I quit resisting.

With a pang of guilt, I realized I still enjoyed Paul's kisses, his touch, even his beard brushing against my face. I didn't doubt that I loved Lee, only I wondered if I loved him enough? I also loved Paul. Not enough to marry him, but I did respond to him as the lover he had been. That didn't disappear overnight.

"Sometimes I think I really do love you, Marti," he murmured, shattering any hint that there might be a real connection between us. He gently pushed my hair back from my face and gazed into my eyes like a man who was sure he had captivated his woman.

Disengaging, I moved away from him, then reached out and fingered a cluster of hydrangea blossoms as I avoided looking directly at him. "You only think that. But we've gone through this before, Paul. It's easy enough to take me to your bed, but you won't commit yourself to anything more. It's always like now. You 'think'. You can't even commit to saying 'I love you.'" I turned toward him then, meeting his eyes to sever this aspect of our relationship. "I can't continue this way. I need more than a half-hearted lover. And I've found it. I'm getting married."

For a few moments he gaped at me, shocked and stunned by this announcement. Recovering, he lurched to one of the redwood benches and plopped down like a dropped sack of potatoes. His eyes focused at a point somewhere between his feet. The silence that followed was total—no birds, no nearby voices, not even the wind rustling the trees.

I shook my head and the sound resumed as if it—or I—had been suspended for those few seconds. I hadn't realized until that moment what marriage to Lee might mean to me or its effect on Paul. Over the past few years, my life had been intertwined with Paul's in almost every way. Our mutual interest was the magazine. I was the eager, ambitious writer and he, the untiring boss. We'd developed our personal relationship almost as fast as the professional one and most times, the two overlapped each other. I'd been attracted to him the day I interviewed with him and it had been an easy relationship to slip into, but over the past few months, I'd felt the personal side cooling. I did need more than he offered and I realized now it was this that had made me ready for Lee's proposal.

"Married?" Paul's voice was a harsh croak. "Jesus! Isn't this sudden?"

I took a deep breath. "I've known him for a long time." I felt a little weak myself and sank down on the bench next to him. "I'm sorry, Paul. I didn't mean to tell you this way. I've known him since I was a child. We grew up together."

He considered my words as my heart beat in anxiety. This could shatter so much with him, my whole relationship and my job. "Childhood sweethearts, eh, pet? No wonder you were anxious to stay. Were you planning on coming back at all?"

"Of course! I'm not going to marry him right away. I wouldn't cut out on you like that. I mean, there's... Well, there's all kinds of things to think about before we get married. Like my brother just died and I certainly can't get married right away. It just wouldn't be right. Then there's my father. He doesn't like Lee."

"Lee Kellog?" Paul raised an eyebrow and he frowned. "He's your fiancé? I should say your father doesn't like him. Even I got an earful about that."

"It's all so complicated..."

"What?"

"Oh, everything! I don't really understand why Papa doesn't like him at the moment. We were all close when I was growing up and Lee and his sister Beth were here as much as we were at his house. And there's something else going on here. Things don't quite add up right. Paul, you're my closest friend who is not from this valley. Can I talk to you in confidence?"

His mouth was a serious straight line and I thought he was going to reject me, but he gave me a short nod. In relief, I broke down with tears flooding down my face like a dam in a cloudburst. He pulled me into his arms and I pressed my face against his shoulder as he held me until I could get control again. As usual, he was the proper gentleman with the handy handkerchief, which I accepted with more gratitude than he knew. All through this whole ordeal, I'd not really let my guard down and the loss of my brother, the funeral, the fights with my father and the whole mystery surrounding it all came out in that burst of emotion. When I gained control again, I told him what I believed had happened. He listened without interrupting until I'd told him everything, even about Consuelo, but I did hold back on my suspicions of Lee. I couldn't tell him that I had doubts about my future husband. I wasn't even prepared to admit it to myself.

"So that's it," I said after I'd dumped everything on him. I wiped at my eyes again. "I've been investigating as much as I can. Something inflammatory must be in that journal to make it so important. I didn't realize that all of this had been such a strain until now. I haven't been able to trust anybody here."

"Not even Lee?" His mouth wore a cynical smile I was familiar with that said it all.

I shook my head. "No. He's too close to everything that has been happening here. But I don't distrust him either."

"And you've told no one else all this?"

"No." I had told Consuelo part and Lee part of it, but not everything. Just as Lee held back information for me, I did the same.

"Good. Don't say anything to anyone else. Don't even let them know that you know about the journal. It certainly does seem to be the clue. You have no idea where your brother hid it?"

Again, I shook my head.

"He must have had some special places for storing his treasures. Maybe a secret drawer somewhere or a hidden box?"

"I've been trying to think, but I keep drawing a blank. Remember, I haven't seen him in years and we weren't too close after we grew up. Any place I might remember would be from childhood and that was a long time ago."

"You said he and Lee were good friends. Is it possible Lee would know? Or even have it?"

"I don't think so." My voice was firm although the possibility had crossed my mind.

He took my face in his hands and kissed me on the forehead. "Well, promise me one thing. If you do think of any hiding places, don't go looking there alone. Come to me and I'll go with you. It may be dangerous and I don't want you there alone. Okay?"

I hugged him, my arms going around his neck. "Okay! I am glad you're here, Paul."

"Think twice about marrying Lee, pet," he whispered in my ear. "You don't love him. You love me."

He lifted my arms away. "I have to take care of some business. Why don't you go relax for a while and I'll see you later? You look beat." He stood up, then reached inside his linen jacket pocket and produced a handful of letters. "I almost forgot again. Your mail."

Taking the letters, I slid them in my pocket and watched him walk away. Now, I felt more confused. Who did I love?

Chapter Seventeen

*L*eft to myself, I sat unmoving until a young couple came out onto the patio, then I got to my feet, gave them an acknowledging tip of my head, and started back toward the house. I wanted to be alone to think, so I skirted the house and headed toward my garden, my sanctuary. My thoughts were jumbled together until I was unsure of anything. What had seemed so clear this morning was now muddled and uncertain. I was so sure I loved Lee that it would mean nothing to me to cast Paul from my life, but this encounter had left me wallowing in a pit of uncertainty. I knew there was no future with Paul. He would never commit to the relationship, even his parting statement confirmed that.

Leaning against a walnut tree, I tried to look at every angle. First, if I married Lee that would mean leaving my position with the magazine and coming back to this valley to live. I looked around me at the clear blue sky, the pleasant green vineyards and the numerous trees and flowers. It was a big change from San Francisco and promised calm, relaxing days. On the other hand, if I couldn't reconcile the differences between Lee and my father, it would be continual turmoil. Could I come home again, really? Or had I changed too much since I had been in San Francisco? Had the girl I had been here grown beyond this pleasant valley to the point that it would be dull and lonely until it ate at me like a disease?

If I went back with Paul, what would it be like there? The same old story, a three-way love affair–Paul, me and the magazine, with his magazine winning most of the time. True, I enjoyed working on the staff and I'd become a pretty good journalist over the past few years, but was that enough?

An unexpected rage burst within me. Angry that I had accepted Lee's proposal so readily and angry that I let Paul inflict so much uncertainty into my thoughts. And now, all it once, it seemed I was uncertain about what I wanted from life. I slammed my fist against the tree to vent my anger and almost cried out as I bruised my knuckles. Shaking the damaged hand, I chastised myself more. All that accomplished was to give me an aching hand. With weariness riding my shoulders, I dropped onto the concrete edge of the duck pond. Even the ducks had skittered away to the opposite side.

A poking at my side reminded me that my mail was still in my pocket. Without enthusiasm, I pulled the letters out and went through them. There was the usual assortment; a power bill, a couple of credit card bills, what looked like an invitation of some kind and a letter with no return address and a Napa postmark. The handwriting was familiar and the postmark showed the day before Philip's death.

Tearing the envelope open, I quickly scanned the one-page letter to the signature on the bottom–Philip's! A cold chill raced up my spine. What an eerie feeling to see his handwriting. I read the brief missive with eagerness.

Marti,

Today, I thought of you again. You've been on my mind more and more frequently. Sometimes I recall those things we did as children and all of those marvelous hiding places we found. You do remember, don't you? Something of value may still be there. Who knows? Lee often asks about you although I don't see him as frequently as I used to. Things are not going well between our family and the Kellogs. A few difficulties. But why I am writing is to ask you to please come for a visit. I have much to tell you that can't be put in a letter. Please call me with your answer. I am hopeful that it will be yes and you will come as soon as possible.

With deepest love,
Philip

I stared at the page in my hand, a simple request from a brother to his sister, but in spite of the phrasing, the urgency of it screamed at me. Even if all this had not happened, I would have known that he had something important to tell me, something he had to see me in person to say, and I would have come. But knowing what I knew now, I realized that he was trying to give me clues in case something did happen to him before I came. The references to "childhood hiding places" and "something of value" indicated his journal. He'd hidden it someplace I should remember. My heart sank. By not remembering, I felt I had let him down. In the end, he'd turned to me, his sister, and in the one way I could help him, my memory failed me.

Trying to shake off my feelings of despair, I turned my gaze to the duck pond, hoping to release the helpless feeling. A large white swan eyed me with curiosity, probably hoping for a handout of something tasty. I regretted that I didn't have some stale bread with me. As I watched, the magnificent creature glided with regal grace and an air of arrogance over the water in a demonstration to the ducks that he was, indeed, a superior creature.

With that, a memory from the past broke through and I was a small, blond girl with puppy-dog-eared strands of hair caught by ribbons that hung about my face as I peered into the water. In the reflection, I saw a fair-haired boy with beautiful blue eyes, who was only a little older than I. We were giggling as we tossed bread crumbs to the ducks. A smile tugged at my lips as I recalled the happy moment. We used to keep bread in a hollowed out hole in a tree. Stale bread wasn't always available, so we used to sneak some fresh from the kitchen and hide it in the tree. I'm sure Madame Boucher knew we did it, yet she never said a word.

Would a journal fit in that hollow? I was on my feet as soon as the thought connected. It took a little longer to remember which direction it was from the pond, but at last I recalled the unmarked path we took. It was quite a ways back from this garden area, I remembered as I picked my way through the trees and shrubs, careful to avoid any roots or vines that could trip me. Whether the hole had been made by woodpeckers or disease or both, I wasn't certain, but it had been in the tree for years even then so it was a natural cache for children's special treasures . Or, as I hoped, a spot to hide a book.

But when I finally found the tree, I was disappointed. Not only did it not contain the journal, but the hole was gone entirely. It had been cemented and all that remained was the smooth surface of whitish gray in which someone had carved the initials "DK" and "LM". With a touch of irritation, I noted that once again the lure of wet cement had prompted a visitor to the vineyard to inscribe his mark for posterity. It had happened before, but Papa had those smoothed out. This one, on this tree, no one would notice except me. I felt as if whoever had done it had violated a sacred place. My place.

For that matter, I wasn't happy to see the hole filled in at all. It closed the door on that memory and left me trying to find other hiding places. Was Philip's memory so much better than mine or was it just that he was here and surrounded by our childhood?

Feeling restless, I walked a winding path back to the duck pond. The swan had found something to eat and was busily trying to keep it away from the ducks. This time I sat on the stone bench away from the pond and found myself wishing I had a cigarette with me. The problem with being an ex-smoker was than when situations like this arose, you wanted a cigarette desperately and since you didn't buy them anymore, unless someone was handy with a pack, you had to suffer or break down and buy some.

That was when Jacques came strolling up. He'd been looking for me; I could tell by the way his face lit up when he saw me and a grin spread across his face.

"*Ma cherie. Comment-allez-vous?*"

"*Tres bien, Jacques.* But I'm dying for a cigarette. Do you have one I can steal from you?"

"But of course," he replied immediately, pulling out his pack and tapping one out into his fingers. "But I smoke menthol and I don't think you like that kind."

"It doesn't matter." I took it and allowed him to light it for me. "I hate times like this when I feel that I have to smoke. I gave it up, you know." With a little hesitation, I inhaled. One taste told me I still didn't like menthol, but it was better than nothing. I waited while he lit one for himself, then asked, "Were you looking for me?"

At once, a look of concern altered his face and his kind eyes rested on mine for a moment. He sat beside me, caught my hand and pressed it between his. "Yes, I was, *cherie*. How much longer do you plan to stay here?"

I flashed a smile. "Are you trying to get rid of me?" But he didn't laugh and the smile dropped from my face. "What is it? What's wrong?"

"It's delightful having you here, Martinique. You know that. If only your brother was not gone, it would have been perfect. But..." He shrugged, evading the answer.

"But what?"

He puffed on his cigarette, quick little draws that showed he was fidgety, his head weaving from side to side slowly. I knew his habits, knew when he was reluctant to say something. "How can I tell you without hurting you? It is so difficult and complicated."

"What's difficult? You never had trouble talking to me before." My voice was sharp and I felt my eyes narrow as I looked at him. Still, he said nothing, just continued to puff and gaze straight ahead. Maybe he was trying to gather his thoughts or just build his courage. Exasperated, I said, "Jacques, you were always more like an uncle to me than my father's foreman. Haven't we always been friends?"

Now, he gazed directly at me, the lean face looking tired. "Ah, *ma petite*. Yes, it is so. But your father... Regrettably, he is not really well. He is changing and he says and does things that are sometimes irrational. I do not think that having you around too much is good for him. A visit is all right, but to stay here so long... He begins to get ideas..."

"What kind of ideas?" I interrupted, although I was still feeling an unsettling lump in the pit of my stomach at the suggestion that my father's mind might be slipping.

"Ideas that you are going to stay permanently and learn his business. That you are going to take Philip's place here." He paused as his eyes searched my face for my reaction. "He thinks you are home to stay."

I laughed with relief. "Is that all? He knows I'm going back to San Francisco. Why do you think he would believe I'm staying? Has he said anything directly to you?"

He glanced away, casting a sharp look toward the house, before turning back to me, then he spoke in a low voice. "For your own sake, I think you should leave here at once. Go the first thing in the morning, please."

I was surprised and I could see that he was earnest in this request, but I didn't know what prompted this much concern for my safety. "For my sake? I don't understand, Jacques."

"I can't explain it, but I am afraid for you. My wife and I both feel that you may be in danger. Many things have happened here that are not good. I do not think your brother's death was an accident and I would not like to see you follow that same path. I cannot tell you more than that. Just believe that there is evil here and go as soon as you can."

Goosebumps raised on my flesh as he talked and I shivered. He'd admitted it at last. He, too, did not believe that Philip had an accident. "You mean you think someone may try to kill me?"

"I don't know. I'm just afraid of the possibility." He stood up, pulling himself slowly as if bone weary. "I must get back to the house. Please think about what I've said."

"But, Jacques!"

He paused a moment, shook his head, then walked on. I stood

staring after him, knowing he'd heard me. There was no doubt of that. Obviously, he had no more to tell me other than to leave. This whole thing was feeling like a nightmare. It was too incredible that Jacques could sit here and tell me that someone may want me dead, then just walk away. Who? Who had I harmed? Unless... Unless whoever had killed Philip had decided I was getting too close to the truth. But what did I have? Just a few suspicions and a clue to a journal that may or may not answer some questions. Perhaps it was enough that I knew about the journal. If that were the case, then so did Lee, Consuelo, and now, Paul. Did that put them in danger also, or only me because I would be the one most likely to find it?

Jacques must have known more than he told me. And what was all that about my father changing and getting ideas? Was he trying to warn me about my father? I had to know what happened between my father and Philip. If the journal was the only way to find the answer, then I wasn't leaving here until I found it. Not after my brother had sent me that letter.

Wracking my brain again for possible hiding places, I walked slowly back to the house. I would find a clue somewhere. Somehow, I had to find it.

As I was about to step onto the path back to the house, I heard voices coming around the bend... a man and a woman. Without any real reason, I chose to step back into the shadows of the trees rather them meet them head on.

Chapter Eighteen

"What about your half-sister?" The man's voice carried clearly to where I was hiding. His English was good, but with an accent that indicated he was Mexican or Spanish. "How much does she know?"

"I don't know. She's been snooping around a lot. I told you that I found her in your place yesterday. Heaven knows how many other places she's been! Then her boss turned up here yesterday. That's peculiar, too."

Even though I couldn't see them yet, I knew the couple approaching was Elaine and the boarder in the shack. I pressed myself tightly against the tree. It was well back from the path, but not so far that I couldn't hear even low voices as sound carried well along that tree-lined walkway. And they were talking about me.

"What's odd about the man turning up here?"

"Not so much that he's come, but that he seems familiar to me. Of course, I've never met him before and he says this is the first time he's been in this area, but I'm sure I've seen someone who looks like him before."

The man laughed. They were coming into the range of my limited vision now. "It could have been someone in Napa. After all, there are likely many people who resemble him."

Elaine's head bobbed up and down in agreement. She wore blue jeans and a man's work shirt, the tails un-tucked and dropping bulkily over her hips. It disguised her dumpy figure well. Then it dawned on me... a man's work shirt! Just the kind that would have a button like the one I'd found in the tool shed. Now I made the leap to a conclusion that might or might not be valid. If I could just get into her room and check it out, I might discover if this shirt or another like it was missing a button. Of course, that wouldn't be real proof of anything, but it might be a start.

"Do you really think Philip included you in his journal? Why should he and what could he possibly say? That you were an instigator, the leader of a revolution? Some revolution!" Elaine's voice rose a little in disdain.

"I admit I didn't do much except stir things up a little. If it hadn't been for your stepfather, I might have gotten a lot accomplished. But to answer your first question, yes, I do think he included me in that damned book of his. There are some things he knows about me that could be harmful to me and to the cause." His voice had dropped and I barely heard the last words.

"How did he find out?" Elaine voiced the question that was in my mind.

The man's laugh was bitter. "My own stupidity and loose tongue. You know how sociable Philip was. We went out drinking and the next thing I knew, I was telling him my life story. And there are parts that do not bear repeating."

"What? Have you done something wrong?"

"Let's put it this way. I have been in trouble, but I'm not going into any more detail. That's all behind me now. It's bad enough I told Philip and it may be recorded in that infernal book. Are you sure it exists, Elena?" I noticed the Spanish pronunciation of her name. A touch of endearment perhaps?

"Of course, I'm sure." Her voice sounded exasperated with this line of questioning. "I told you I saw it myself. Even if I didn't know what it was, I saw that Philip was writing in it all the time. Besides, I heard Marti tell her boss about it this afternoon."

My breath caught. She'd overheard me talking to Paul? Just how much had she heard? I could kick myself. Lee had been so careful when he'd told me about the journal and I'd just blurted it out where anyone could hear me. How could I be so stupid!

By now they'd come even with my hiding place and I could see them clearly. The man looked familiar. Not just that I'd seen him before, although I had from a distance, but that I'd seen a photograph of him somewhere and I couldn't quite place where. Carefully, I tried to inch my way a little closer without giving up my cover. As I stepped against a tree root, my foot slipped and I stumbled. Although I quickly regained my balance, the slip made enough of a thumping sound to be heard only a few feet away. And my half-sister caught it.

"Hector! Did you hear that?" Elaine's voice practically hissed. "A noise... from over there." She pointed into the trees toward me.

I held my breath and pressed back against the tree as if I expected it to make me invisible. At least I knew now who the man was and where I'd seen his picture. Hector Escobar. The leader of the local labor strikes, the self-proclaimed right arm of Cesar Chavez in this valley. And he was living on my father's land! I could have laughed except that I didn't think they would appreciate me overhearing their conversation.

Elaine stepped off the path and started into the trees with Hector close behind her. I knew they would find me easily and there was no excuse I could possibly offer for spying on them. I'd almost decided to confront them, claiming to have just come through the trees, when a small, furry animal darted past me and out onto the path just in front of Elaine and Hector.

"It's only Jezebel," Elaine laughed, relief in her voice. "She must have been in a tree."

As they retraced their footsteps to the pathway, I breathed out and thanked my lucky stars. Jezebel to the rescue! The same white cat I'd seen the first night. Where she'd come from, I didn't know, but I silently promised her a bowl of fresh cream the first chance I got.

They walked on in silence for a bit, then just as they were getting out of the range of my hearing, Hector spoke up. "We must find that journal before anyone else does."

The last words I heard Elaine say were, "With her luck, that idiot Marti will probably locate it."

I bit my lip. I may have been an idiot, but I would be the one to find it. I was the one Philip had left the clue and the only one who could possibly know where he'd put it. All I had to do was remember.

Although I wanted to follow them to hear what else they might say, I was afraid any movement might draw their attention and I couldn't count on Jezebel to save me again. Taking small, well-placed steps to try to avoid making any noise, I eased out from behind the tree and made my way toward the road. Instead of returning to the house, I decided to visit the Kellog home. There was still something I wanted to settle with Lee.

* * * * *

As I stood before the expansive ranch-style house, I felt a twinge of bittersweet pain. I'd spent so much time in this place when I was a child that it was like an old friend welcoming me home. The broad brick walkway curved across the freshly sheared green lawn and up to the bricked front porch flower boxes. In constructing the house, the architect had used a combination of white brick and redwood to create an eye-pleasing structure, which the Kellogs maintained in every way. I recalled hearing that this house replaced a smaller version that had existed until Lee was six, but this was the house I knew and loved.

This land had been in the Hayden family for almost as long as ours had been handed through the Claremont clan. Like me, Constance Hayden Kellog was the last of her line and she'd inherited the vineyard shortly after she'd married James Kellog. Unlike me, she'd known how to run it, had prepared all her life for it, had taught her husband and son all she knew. However, this vineyard was just that—no winery to go with it. Along with most of the valley landowners, they either sold their grapes to my father or shipped them to other markets.

I hesitated, then pressed the doorbell. Behind the door, I heard the muffled tones of the Westminster door chimes and finally the rhythmic clicks of high heels against ceramic tiles followed by the scrape of the door opening. I smiled at the dark haired woman who peered at me. At first, she didn't recognize me. Her brows lifted in question as her eyes searched my face until the features matched a picture in her memory, then she grinned.

"Marti! How good to see you. Do come in. Oh my, how you've changed. No longer a young girl in braids." She flung the door wide and caught my arm.

Even in her mid-forties, Lee's mother was still petite and beautiful with her bright brown eyes and naturally curly dark hair, which was now frosted with silver. Once inside, she hugged me, kissed my check and displayed me to her husband as if I were a prize she'd won. A perfect pair of in-laws, I thought, going through the whole scene again with Lee's father. I wondered if Lee had told them about us yet.

At last, unable to ignore the commotion any longer, Lee stepped out of the study. He was surprised to see me, but his smile reflected genuine pleasure. "It's about time you made it over here," he said as he hugged me.

"You are staying to dinner, aren't you?" Constance Kellog asked. Her eyes were so hopeful that I found it hard to say no, but I explained that we had a guest and I needed to get back.

"Actually, I came to see Lee for a few minutes. Perhaps I could get a rain check on that invitation."

Masking her disappointment, she caught my hand in hers and replied, "Of course, dear. You're welcome here anytime and you know it."

"Could I see you alone, Lee?" I spoke softly so that he was the only one who heard.

He nodded and motioned me out to the patio in back. Just outside the door I came to a halt as a sparkling blue sheen temporarily blinded me. I blinked my eyes, then grinned. "You've put in a pool." Quite a pool it was, I noted, as I observed the huge comma-shaped basin of water. I longed to throw myself into it, clothes and all.

"Very observant. Let's go to the other side." He caught my elbow and urged me around the pool. Motioning to the chairs at the circular redwood umbrella table, he pulled out his cigarettes and lit one for each of us, then sat down and stared at me intently. The expected kiss hadn't materialized. Had he sensed something?

"What's on your mind, honey?"

I shifted uncomfortably in the deck chair. I hadn't even thought about what I would say. Avoiding his eyes, I let words trickle out of my mouth, as I tried to phrase them without it sounding like an accusation. "I'm not sure how to say this. Someone told me about..." My voice stalled, then I just blurted it out. "I've been told you were a member of Los Latinos Amigos. Why didn't you tell me? Why did I have to hear it from someone else?"

His face darkened for a moment and I thought he was on the edge of telling me it was none of my business. Then he exhaled a puff of smoke and spoke in a calm, even tone. "You're right, Marti. I should have told you. If you're going to be my wife, you have a right to know all about me. I haven't lied to you; I just haven't told you everything. Wait here. I'm going to get us a couple of drinks. This could take a while. What would you like?"

"Tom Collins," I answered, my usual drink of choice popping out of my mouth without thought. As he left, I wondered how I could tell him everything I had to say. How could I tell him that I couldn't marry him? At least, not now. That I was still unsure of my feelings for Paul? And worse, that I wasn't sure that I trusted him?

Lee returned, not with two glasses, but with an iced pitcher full. He must have expected a long conversation.

"This isn't lemonade, you know," I said while he poured two glasses. I took a sip and winked at him. "But it is delicious. Thanks."

Leaning back in his chair, Lee talked, sounding as if he was giving a lecture. "I joined the organization shortly after Phil did. Naturally, it was easier for me since I didn't have your father to contend with. Phil couldn't let it be known that he was part of the group. In all fairness to your father, it was understandable why he didn't want to increase wages. It would have cost him thousands of dollars."

"But you and your father were willing to pay a fair wage. My father makes more than you or anyone else in the valley," I objected, surprised that Lee was defending my father.

"Observe, my love," he said, pointing toward a carport-like structure near the start of the vineyard. Underneath was a huge machine with a sort of chute to a bin at the side. "That's a harvester. We got it three years ago and that makes it easier for us to go along with the wage increase. We don't have that many workers. Our automatic grape picker does all the work. Phil wanted to get one for your place, but your father opposed it, wanted to continue with the old ways. I'm surprised he didn't want the grapes stomped."

My mouth fell open in surprise. Before I could respond, he continued.

"Maybe I should go into a little more background on the relationship between Phil and your father. When we got out of college and came home, we were both full of ideas. We'd been taught ways to increase production twenty-five percent, to make our lands more profitable and to use machinery to cut costs. My mom and dad were delighted and more or less gave me a free hand. We bought the machinery and raised a variety of produce, not just the grapes.

"Meanwhile, Phil was being frustrated at every turn. He felt his education was wasted because your father didn't want to change anything. They quarreled a lot, but Phil couldn't get around him. At first, he came here and we'd talk and he'd get it out of his system, then shrug it off and say he would change the vineyard when it was his. But it got harder and harder for him and pretty soon, he quit coming over. I guess he couldn't stand to see our machines and how well we were doing."

As Lee paused to take a sip of his drink, I reflected on what he'd said. It wasn't hard to imagine my ambitious brother growing bitter over his wasted education and abilities. He was ready to prove his value and utilize his knowledge but was denied the opportunity. Yes, that must have hurt.

"At that point, I wouldn't have been surprised if he'd killed your father he was getting so frustrated," Lee went on. "They battled more and more frequently and Phil would take off to Napa, Sonoma or even Santa Rosa then come home later, drunker and drunker. Eventually, he gave up trying to change things and began to coast, letting Jacques handle the mechanics of running the vineyard. Your father controlled the books, so Phil didn't even see those to know how the business was doing.

"So, when this whole thing with the farm workers began, he saw his first ray of hope. He reasoned that if your father had to pay higher wages to the grape pickers, he would finally see the light and realize things had to progress. Phil thought it would convince him to begin buying the machinery, then he would be able to get a foothold in the business and sooner or later, the old man would turn it over to him."

I was beginning to see the picture quite clearly. No wonder Philip joined Los Latinos Amigos. As if he'd read my thoughts, Lee confirmed them.

"When your father began fighting Escobar, Phil joined the organization. He channeled all his energy into it, not that he cared that much for equal wages, but because he believed it would force your father to his knees. Phil became convinced that the vineyard was in financial trouble and that was why your father resisted progress. And that's when he came to dad and me about buying the place."

"Did he have any proof?" I had to ask it although I was sure I knew the answer. What proof could there be?

Lee shook his head. "No. Just suspicions. He thought that was why your father wouldn't let him see the books. He wasn't sure what was wrong, but he felt certain it was financial."

"I can't imagine Philip wanting someone else to buy the vineyard. Even if everything had gone sour, it was still his life." I was amazed that he'd asked the Kellogs to purchase it.

"You don't know the deal, honey. We would buy it, but Phil would take over running it. Eventually, he would pay us back for what we put into it and we'd quit claim it to him. He figured he could get control that way and although Dad didn't like the idea too much, he went along with it because of Phil." He paused, sighed deeply and his mouth curved into a rueful smile. "You know the rest of that part. Your father misunderstood us and Phil didn't have the gumption to straighten him out. After that, the banker paid a visit and if there were any financial problems, they must've been solved then. Phil returned to his campaign to force your father to modern methods, but progress was nonexistent. And that's where he was until he died."

Understanding my brother more now than I ever had, I said, "I wish you had told me all this sooner. I can appreciate how he must have felt. The man in his shack—that's Hector Escobar, isn't it?"

He nodded. "I wondered how long it would take you to figure that out. I didn't want to keep any of this from you, but I didn't know how much you could handle."

"What do you mean how much I could handle?" Did he figure I would fall apart over it? I was annoyed and showed it.

His tone was pacifying. "I mean it's a difficult story to believe. How did I know you wouldn't go to your father and tell him everything only to have him tell you it's a pack of lies? Then there was Elaine and Escobar to consider."

"Yes. That's a combination, isn't it? What's with those two?"

"They're engaged. Have been for a month."

In shock, I stared at him. "I think you'd better tell me about that!"

He smiled again. "I thought that would surprise you. Phil let Escobar take the shack. It was easier for him to meet with him that way. Naturally, Elaine found out about it. To keep her quiet, Phil agreed to give her a part of the vineyard. That was all Elaine really wanted, just a piece of land of her own. Escobar dropped out of sight, grew the beard and Elaine and Phil passed him off as a new employee. Your father never goes out of the house, so he's never seen Escobar on his property. In due time, Elaine and Escobar fell in love and they decided about a month ago to get married."

"And she was so hostile toward me because she figured I wouldn't let her have her property," I surmised. "I don't guess I can blame her there. She had no way of knowing how I would be."

"None of us did. It's been quite a while since you were here last. A teenager left here and a woman returned, a woman who'd lived in the big city, done a lot of things, made a name for herself and changed in God knows how many ways. You have changed a lot, honey, but basically the good parts are still there. Of course, Elaine's spent better than half her life hating you. She couldn't change."

"I can see your point there." While I conceded, it bothered me that I was trusted so little even if I had been away a long time. Was I that much of a stranger? "But that doesn't really tell me why you joined Escobar's group. It is Escobar's, isn't it?"

"Essentially, yes." He held up two fingers. "Two reasons. First, I honestly believe that all the itinerant workers, no matter the nationality, should get higher wages than the bare minimum most growers are paying them. Sure it would cost more, but these people have the right to a decent way of life. God knows, I'd hate to try to live on their wages. Second, I wanted to help Phil and I thought I might be able to do it by working through the group."

My lips pressed together into a bitter line. "I see. You and your friends figured if they banded together you might be able to overthrow my father, the dictator. This is incredible! Granted, my father was unfair to Philip, but to resort to this kind of thing! Practically destroy the business! I just can't believe it."

Lee fired back, his voice reflecting his irritation. "I tried to keep Phil under control. I was here, Marti. Here! I watched his whole life deteriorating and it hurt him. He was my best friend and I wanted to make sure he didn't do anything violent. If I hadn't been there, I don't know what might have happened. There were members of that group who wouldn't hesitate to resort to violence and so far, Escobar and I are the only ones who can keep them under control."

"Maybe one of them slipped from under your control," I said, my anger making the words sharper. "My brother is dead and one way or the other, that group is responsible for it."

"You don't know what you're saying. Let's just drop it for now. We're not proving anything by this." When I didn't answer, he stood, stretched, and forced a grin. "Enough of this. Let's go see my folks and tell them we're getting married."

As he rose to his feet, I followed suit, but asked, "You haven't told them yet?" The question was to confirm what he'd indicated. He shook his head.

"Then let's not." I saw the surprise then apprehension in his face as I met his eyes and dropped the bomb. "I think I was a bit hasty in accepting your proposal. I believe we ought to wait longer." I looked away, staring into the clear water of the pool, unable to force myself to meet his eyes again.

For a few moments he was silent, then I heard the chair scrape as he sat back down. The hurricane in his voice was apparent. "What's wrong, Marti? Is it because I didn't tell you everything? Do you feel you can't trust me? Or do you disagree with my viewpoint? Honey, I tried to do what was best. Please believe me."

I couldn't speak. Feeling tightness in my throat, I tried to swallow and I felt tears stinging my eyes. Oh, Lord! I was hurting him again and I didn't want it to be like this. Why did I keep doing it to him? Only this time it was hurting me, too, because I did love him with all my soul. I felt so confused.

"Marti, look at me, please. What's happened?"

As my hand tugged at my hair, I felt very weary. "Nothing. Everything. It's hard to say. I love you, Lee. Honestly, I do. But there's more to it than that."

"I don't understand," he said as he got to his feet again to reach for me.

"Don't touch me!" I jerked back from him. "If you try to hold me, I'll break down and I can't do that. I'm not ready to marry you, Lee. I have to straighten out another emotional entanglement first. Only when that's done will I be free to know if I love you as much as I think I do. Please give me the time."

"Is it your boss?" he asked. I nodded. His fist crashed to the table sending his glass and several swizzle sticks flying. "Damn it! I love you, Marti. Doesn't that mean anything to you?"

I swallowed hard, anxiety making this more difficult. "Of course, it does. It means everything to me. Just give me a little more time— "

"I've given you ten years! How long do you want me to give you?"

"Time enough to straighten my head out! I just realized I love you, but that doesn't automatically stop a three-year relationship. I still care about Paul, too. I have to be sure."

His face reflected his hurt, then he grabbed me, pulled me tightly into his arms and pressed his lips to mine in a rough kiss that burned through me, raging against my resistance. His tongue pressed against my mouth, forcing entry and I didn't have the will to fight it when my body burned with the desire to taste him. I fell into that passionate heat and returned the kiss, my tongue flicking against his as a little moan of desire escaped from deep within me.

"A sample," he said in a whisper, his breath heavy. I saw the flame burning in his eyes as I gazed up into them, then he shoved me back. "Make up your mind soon, Martinique. I won't wait forever." He turned away and retreated into the house.

Weak-kneed and breathless, I gripped the back of a chair for support until I regained my balance, then I fled down the back exit from the patio. Following the path around the house, I fumbled with the gate, got it open, and sprinted toward the tree-lined drive of Claremont Vineyards as if a demon was after me. My racing footsteps carried me straight into Paul's arms. As he held me, I found I didn't have the strength to pull away.

"What's wrong, pet?" He asked with concern and alarm in his voice. I shook my head. "Well, something's wrong. You were running like you were being chased. Is someone after you?"

I tried to catch my breath. "No. Nothing's wrong. I'm okay."

"You came from the Kellog house."

"Don't go jumping to conclusions!" My voice was a brittle shout, but probably told him more than I wanted him to know.

For a moment, his eyes blazed and his anger started to flare, but he clamped a tight control over it. I knew Paul well enough to know the sharpness in my voice would annoy him. I pulled away and stalked toward the house. He came after me, grabbing my arm.

"Wait a minute! I'd like a little more explanation. What happened at the Kellog's house?"

I swung around to face him. "That's none of your business! What were you doing? Watching me?"

"Maybe I was. God knows, you're behaving strangely." He barked it back at me, anger flaring in his face and making his cheeks red.

I think I would've hit him right then if I hadn't known beyond a doubt that he would slap me back. Aware that I was shaking with anger and nerves, I turned and loped down the tree-lined path leaving Paul staring after me.

Chapter Nineteen

lthough I would have preferred to skip dinner, my father would not permit my absence when we had a guest, particularly when the guest was mine. I was polite, but little else. At the moment, I had nothing to say to Paul. I was still irritated and couldn't help wondering why I was so fond of him. He was a domineering brute, I told myself, but then I had to be honest. Most of the time he was understanding and could be very gentle. Perhaps he was jealous or maybe I was different. Who wouldn't have changed some under the same circumstances?

My father carried the conversation over the first course, a tangy French onion soup, but by the time the roast arrived, the table was strangely silent. Even Jacques and his usually buoyant wife were very quiet. Elaine gazed at everyone curiously, noting the tension, then launched into a brief monologue about the vineyard to which no one appeared to pay attention in the slightest. When, at last, my father shoved back his chair and rose, I gratefully followed suit. Now I could excuse myself as they retired to the living room for after-dinner brandy.

Slipping out the back door, I gazed out over the vineyard. The sky was just beginning to glow with the bluish-pink sunset. No one was outside and I had at least an hour of daylight to search for that troublesome book.

Now all I needed was a clue. Philip's letter indicated it was a hiding place we both knew but not one that was obvious. I thought a slow, casual walk might jar my memory. Rejecting the rows of grapes because there was no possible hiding place among them, I turned toward the tasting room. As I made my way through the gardens, I felt his presence, but it wasn't accompanied by a clear memory of any kind. No, there was no hiding place here, only fleeting memories of warm sunny days when we played tag and hide and seek. Without thinking, I drifted toward the winery buildings. A small, faded, yellow bird house in the tree near the winery caught my attention. I recalled that we'd left notes in it occasionally, providing a bird wasn't occupying it, but it wasn't large enough for a book. Besides, Lee knew about it also. Of course, Philip could have left a note, another clue of some kind.

Once I decided it was worth checking out, I hunted for a foothold in the tree. Finding a knob where a branch had been trimmed, I put my right foot on it and bounced on the other one to get started on the climb. A branch provided a handhold I could pull to reach a split between branches where I wedged my left foot. It took a while, but I managed to climb up to where I could reach the birdhouse. How on earth had we managed that as children? Braced against the trunk, I reached out and tilted the wooden box toward me. It was empty except for some grasses and twigs a bird had used for its nest, which I removed, then I spotted a small slip of paper at the bottom back. Scissoring my index and middle fingers together, I was excited as I caught the paper in them and pulled it out.

My excitement faded when I saw the brittle and yellowed paper. It must have been there for years. Curious, I unfolded it, wondering whose message had never gotten to the person for whom it was intended. It was faded and I couldn't make out the words, only the signature, "Lee." I refolded the note, slid it into my pocket and began working my way down.

"What are you? A monkey?" Paul's voice came from below me. As I turned my head, I saw he was reaching up to lift me down.

"I thought you were with my father," I said, ignoring his arms as I slid down the smooth bark a little less than gracefully. I couldn't seem to have any time to search. What was he doing here?

"Now don't get excited, pet. I came to apologize. I didn't mean to seem so nosy, but you know I do care about you. Now tell me I'm forgiven."

I hesitated a few moments, then forced a smile. "All right. I'm sorry I was so snappy with you, Paul. I guess I'm a little short tempered."

"Small wonder with everything that's been happening. I should have realized that. Have you quite made up your mind to marry Lee?"

"No, I haven't. I still have a couple of things to consider."

"Like me?" He asked gently.

"Among other things."

Lifting my chin in his hand, he turned my face up to meet his lips. His mouth pressing against mine conveyed a sense of urgency and evoked memories of a relationship I was once eager to have, a relationship I felt was almost over. Or perhaps it had grown too predictable and needed a change of scenery to revive it? Even though I physically responded to him, it was not with the same intensity I had returned Lee's embraces. The tingle of electricity that vibrated my spine and warmed my nether regions with Lee's touch was not there.

"I'm really very fond of you, Marti," Paul said softly.

I sighed. "But you've never said you love me." Then, as he started to speak, I added, "No. Don't say anything. You wouldn't mean it anyway."

His lips curled into a half smile. "Think you've got me all figured out, don't you? All right. Let's leave it." Indicating the tree, he asked, "What were you doing up there anyway?"

"There's a birdhouse in that branch. I wanted to see if it was occupied." I didn't want to tell him it had been a post office when I was a young girl. That was my own private memory, mine and Lee's now.

He reached out for my hand. "Come back to the house. Your father's gone up to his room and Elaine is not the best company. Or is there something else you'd rather do?"

I didn't want Paul hunting for the journal with me. When I found it, I wanted to be alone to read the words my brother had written. Somehow, I felt it would be very personal. I covered my annoyance with another smile and shook my head. "I just wanted to walk for a bit. Clear my head, you know."

He was agreeable. "Let's walk then."

Although we wandered about the vineyard for almost an hour, no other memories of childhood even touched my mind. We conversed about dozens of subjects, none of which could I recall in detail even twenty-four hours later so overpowering were the events which were to follow in the next twelve hours.

As we came around the corner, we noticed the Sheriff's car parked in the driveway. Alarmed, I glanced at Paul, then sprinted into the house. I heard his footsteps on the gravel and knew he was right behind me.

Eberman sat on the sofa, a cup of coffee perched delicately in his massive hand. Across from him were Jacques, his wife, and Elaine. The big man eyed me easily, then spoke. "Just the person I wanted to see, Ms. Claremont." He looked inquisitively at Paul. I introduced him and sat down.

"You know..." Eberman was a "you know" type man. "...I was just going over the details of these break-ins with the Bouchers here. You didn't tell them about the other one, did you?"

I shook my head. He already knew that.

"I was trying to match up anything that might point to the same motive to connect to the two. Only problem is I don't seem to have a motive. Whoever broke into both places seem to be looking for something specific. I base that on the fact that nothing was taken from either place. The interesting part is that the descriptions of the burglars don't match. Not even close. Now that suggests that either two different people were involved or one of the witnesses was incorrect in his description. But we'll let that go for now. What I want to know now is what is the object of the burglars' search?"

I suppressed a smile. Our sheriff appeared to be on a hunting trip. "I told you this morning that I didn't know and I still don't." I thanked my guardian angel that Paul didn't say anything.

"I know you did," he conceded with a nod, "but I thought maybe something might have come to mind that you didn't think about this morning. Also, I wanted to see if anyone else here might have any idea what it is. You see, I think that's the key to this whole case."

"You're probably right, Sheriff. I wish I could help you, but I honestly don't have any ideas. I'm afraid I haven't been here enough to know."

Very casually, he asked, "By the way, do you happen to know a Consuelo Vargas?"

I nodded. "We went to school together, more or less. I saw her the other day and we talked, but we're not good friends."

He absorbed that, then rose to leave. "Well, I guess that's all, so I'll be on my way. You know, any information you might have sure would be appreciated."

Madame Boucher escorted him to the door. I had the uneasy feeling that the Sheriff would be back and would keep coming back until he got an answer. Perhaps I was being foolish in not telling him. For a moment, I wondered why Paul hadn't said anything, then decided he was merely backing my denial. I knew why Elaine hadn't mentioned it and doubtless, she knew why I kept silent. Had Consuelo revealed anything to him? And I still didn't know if Jacques knew about it.

"Did the sheriff say anything else?" I asked.

"No. He just wanted to know if I have any other ideas why anyone would break in and not take anything, especially when we have so many valuable items in the house." He looked tired and worried. "He also wanted to know where I was last night."

My mouth dropped open. "He can't suspect you! You don't even fit the description."

Jacques looked a little relieved. "He didn't tell me what the burglar looked like. I am glad to know he does not look like me." With that, he rose and left.

"You seem to know a lot about this," Elaine said, accusation clear in her voice. "What were you doing at the Sheriff's office?"

Turning to face her, I glared in response. "Not that it's any of your business, but I had to go into town today and I thought I would see if he'd found out anything. He told me about the other burglary then."

Angered, her nostrils flared and her eyes narrowed, her resentment of me stronger than ever. Her voice tightly controlled, she said, "You came home to bury your brother and you've done that. Now, why don't you leave and let things get back to normal around here?"

"As you said, sister, this is my home. I'll stay as long as I damn well please." Considering the anger I felt, I managed to keep my voice steady and calm.

"Isn't that marvelous? You leave without a second thought and don't bother to see us at all, then come here calling it your home and taking over as if you were the queen bee. Go back to San Francisco, Ms. Martinique Claremont. You're not needed or wanted here." She whirled and stormed from the room, not waiting for anything else I might say.

It was the second time she'd told me to leave but that was all right; I had no reply. In that respect, she was right. I felt my face flame in anger and embarrassment.

With a polite cough, Paul cleared his throat, no doubt sorry to be caught in the middle of our quarrel. I regretted that he had been placed in that position. Excusing himself, he retreated to the den to work on the magazine articles. Although I realized I should have gone with him, I couldn't face working on a piece of writing just now. Instead, I sat by the fire and stared into the embers, focused on the deep red heart of the flame and tried to reconcile my past self with the person I was now.

True, I had left without a backward glance, and I hadn't come home or really showed any interest... until now. Why couldn't I make peace with my half-sister? We'd never been friends, but neither had we been enemies. Was I such a snob now that I could not even speak to her civilly?

My soul-searching was interrupted by the doorbell. Voices in French echoed in the hall and it took a moment to connect the man's voice with Lee. Madame Boucher was telling him not to go up and it didn't take much to figure out he was intent on seeing my father. As he came barreling through, I tried to stop him.

He only paused a moment. "I need to see your father," he informed me crisply, then shoved me aside and charged up the stairs. Before I could follow, Madame Boucher was beside me repeating frantic apologies for letting him get past her as if she could have stopped him. I assured her it wasn't her fault and vaulted up the steps in pursuit.

When I tried to open the office door it was locked, so I pounded on it. From the other side, Papa's voice shouted, "Leave us alone. Go away!"

I hesitated, then backed away from the door with slow steps. At least I could assume they weren't at each other's throat. Worried about what would happen between them, I trudged back downstairs. Madame was waiting, her eyes filled with concern.

"It's all right," I told her. "I believe they're talking. At least, I heard no shouts or furniture being thrown."

She didn't look much relieved, but she acknowledged me and escaped to the sanctuary of her kitchen. I hoped my words were true and the two men weren't trying to kill each other. Sinking back onto the couch, I lowered my head down to my arms that were folded across my lap and waited until the sharp sounds of footsteps on the stairs brought my head up. Lee was coming down fast and hard to make that much noise. I turned to face the door just as he burst into the room, his face red and his eyes angry.

"What happened?"

"Your father is more stubborn than you are!" He threw himself into the chair across from me.

"What did you tell him?"

The dark brown eyes locked on mine. "That I wanted to marry you. I know you wanted to wait, but part of the problem is this ridiculous quarrel with your father, isn't it? Well, I tried to straighten that out."

I felt the blood drain from my face and my eyebrows shot upward in alarm. All I could think was, how much had Lee told him?

He read the look in my face at once. "No. I didn't tell him about Phil. I just tried to smooth things over, but he's so damn stubborn. Does he know what the word forgive means?"

For a moment, I couldn't speak and my hands were trembling. Finally, I forced out the words. "What did he say? About us, I mean?"

He looked away. "I don't want to repeat it. Let's just say he didn't look upon it favorably. He said he'd disown you if you married me."

"He said that?" I knew he wouldn't be happy, but I hadn't expected him to go that far. If I'd told him it might have been different.

"Not in those words."

"Why, Lee? Why did you do it? I asked you to wait."

His answer was simple. "Because I love you."

And that was where Paul walked in. They didn't need an introduction. Paul took one look at me, sized up the situation, incorrectly, and told Lee to get out. The wrong thing to do.

Lee's hands gripped the arms of the chair until his knuckles turned white with the pressure. I could tell—anyone could tell—he was fighting for control. "I suppose you're the other loose end in Marti's life?" His voice was hoarse with anger.

"You're not exactly neatly tied into it," Paul answered in his most British voice. "Do you think you have her future all wrapped up in a neat little bundle?"

"I plan to marry her," Lee said quietly.

"I don't believe the lady's made up her mind yet."

"And what kind of relationship do you plan to have with her? Do you expect her to go on sleeping in your bed without any kind of promise or commitment?"

My face burned as the blood rushed to my cheeks. How did Lee know that much about our relationship or was it a guess?

Unperturbed, Paul spoke only to Lee. ""I believe that is Marti's business, not yours. If we want to have a relationship of trust, then– "

"Then you don't plan to marry her!" Lee interrupted. "Of course, you don't love her. Does she know that? Does she know about the other women?"

Paul took a deep breath and glared at Lee. "I never told her otherwise. I believe we have an open relation—"

"Stop it! Both of you! How dare you discuss me this way?" I was on my feet now, fighting back tears and ready to start tossing things.

Lee turned to me. "Marti, I was just trying to tell you this clown could care less about you. He doesn't love you. He's only using you..."

Tears were pouring down my cheeks. "I know that! Don't tell me any more." As I pressed both hands over my ears, I cried, "Get out!"

Face showing his uncertainty, Paul took a hesitant step towards me and I cried out, "No!"

Then I bolted out of the room, taking the stairs two at a time. I slammed the bedroom door, locking it behind me, and threw myself face down on the bed and let the tears flow unhindered.

When at last the sobs subsided, I sat up slowly, drained of energy and emotion. For a while I remained motionless, eyes unfocused on an object on my dressing table. I'd been hurt and humiliated having them argue over me like that as if I had no say in the matter. Three men I valued in my life and they had all betrayed me.

Without concern for me, Lee had forced Paul into his admission. I knew Paul didn't love me enough to marry me, but I hadn't wanted it confirmed so totally. I wanted to go on believing, letting it die slowly as it would have. Why hadn't Lee let me handle it? Given me the chance to come to his love on my own? And Paul was spouting that open relationship crap to cover his lack of commitment to me. How did Lee know there were other women anyway? Yet, I knew it was true.

But my father was the worst. He would disown me? Is that how he threatened Philip? Did he say he would take away everything my brother had worked and planned for if he stood up against him? And if I wanted a life of my own, a husband of my own choice, he would cut me out as well? This was not the father I knew and loved. He had always been domineering and tough, but not the father that would deny his own children.

Gathering my strength, I stumbled to the bathroom and splashed cold water on my face. My eyes and throat ached from the intensity of my tears. As I swallowed a glass of water, I looked into the red-rimmed eyes and blotchy face reflected in the mirror. Had I ever been truly happy? I thought I had until this week. If I hadn't come, all this wouldn't have happened. I would have gone on in blissful ignorance at the magazine and now I couldn't go back to the magazine at all. It would be impossible to work with Paul, but I couldn't stay here either. Before I could evaluate my feelings for Lee, I had to get away from him and this memory-laden vineyard.

Journal or no journal, I decided to leave. For now, I would go back to San Francisco, clean out my desk and use part of my savings for a couple of weeks in Hawaii, then I would decide my future. With this resolution made, I went back to my room and began to pack.

As I lifted my jewelry box to put it in my suitcase, I hesitated, then flipped up the lid. My fingers hovered over the contents a moment, picked up the gold St. Christopher's medal and closed the lid. I couldn't take this with me. It belonged here with Philip's belongings.

With light, almost soundless steps, I slipped down the hall and tried the door to Philip's room. The knob turned easily and the door swung open. As I had hoped, it hadn't been locked again after the sheriff checked it. My fingers ran across the wall until I found the light switch, then flipped it on. Leaving the medal on the dresser, I glanced around the room uneasily. Something here tugged at my memory. I turned my eyes, item by item, moving from the chair to the bed, to the dresser, to the desk, studying each object, one by one.

The furniture was redwood, made primarily from wine barrels. In fact, the round, polished table next to the bed was a small wine barrel with the front cut out and shelves installed. My great-great grandfather made this furniture with his own hands for his young son. Times were harder then and the vineyard hadn't built up to a wealthy business yet, so the wine barrels were the only wood available. With the highly shellacked redwood and bright brass fittings, the dresser was a masterpiece.

Because it was handmade by our ancestor, Philip had been very proud of this furniture. It was our heritage and stood along with the house and vineyard as a reminder of the determination the first Claremont's had possessed to turn this raw land into what it was now. Touched with awe that all this had existed so much longer than its makers, I felt disconnected, not a part of the heritage. I shook myself and practically ran to the door, leaving the room to its ghosts.

But while I tried to sleep in my own, much newer, bed, I tossed and turned as something struggled to get its message across. I sat up, located a half-smoked, stale cigarette in the ashtray, lit it and pulled on my blue silk bathrobe. I'd known nights like this before when I was working on an article and something, some niggling detail, was just beyond my reach. A glance at the clock told me it was three-forty-eight. I'd been wrestling with my sleeplessness for nearly four hours. I was certain I had dozed off some, but I didn't feel it.

The cigarette wasn't satisfactory. It left a dryness in my throat and I headed downstairs to make a cup of coffee. As I reach for the instant coffee, I changed my mind and decided to make a pot of fresh. While I waited for it to percolate, I tried to isolate each event or item that was troubling me.

Number one was, naturally enough, the mystery of the missing journal. It had never really left my mind since I first learned of its existence. Without any more clues to its whereabouts, I wasn't likely to locate it.

The second was Paul. Or was it Lee? They were intertwined in the events of the day and I could no more sort them out now than I could earlier. And connected to them were the decisions I'd made to leave in the morning, chuck it all in and go to Hawaii. I began to doubt that I could merely get in my car and leave. Not with all the questions I had about Philip still unanswered. Without a doubt, this is what disturbed me so.

Finally was the warning Jacques had given me. He was determined I should leave; however, he hadn't given me a suitable reason why. I poured a cup of coffee and sipped it slowly. There had to be a good reason or he wouldn't have suggested it. I wanted to comply with his wishes except I felt I owed Philip the truth.

I refilled my cup and returned to my bedroom. In this quiet time in the house, I felt uneasy and deeply troubled. After pulling a chair over to the window, I sat with my coffee and stared out. It was overcast; I could tell by the lightness of the pre-dawn sky. Soon now the sun would be rising and I would have to face either another day here or take my things to my car and drive off. Who was I kidding? As I said, I owed Philip, and myself, the whole truth.

I was beginning to relax now. As always, a hot drink such as coffee or tea, would make me drowsy when I was tired or wake me up if that was what I wanted. I believe that the story about caffeine being a stimulant was a myth and that was one of those items I'd made a note to research one day. As I snuggled in my chair and closed my eyes, an image passed through my mind, crystal clear and easily identifiable— the image of the wine cask end table in Philip's room. The wine cask end table...? I puzzled over it. Why would that come to mind? There was nothing really significant about it.

Then, like a bolt of lightning, it hit me. I jerked to my feet, fully alert. I knew where the journal was now; the only place it could possibly be. I tried to stay as quiet as possible, taking care not to hurry too much, as I dressed in jeans and a shirt and snatched up a sweater. While I tied my tennis shoes, I tried to remember in which drawer of his desk my father kept his keys.

Papa was sleeping soundly and I hoped my memory was accurate. Tip-toeing across the room, I used both hands to open and support the top right-hand drawer as I slid it open. The keys for the winery, the visitor center, and the private office were in the inset well at the front of the drawer. There wasn't enough light to search for the one I needed and I probably wouldn't recognize it anyway, so rather than chancing to wake Papa, I took the whole ring. I muffled them in my palm as I slipped them into my jeans pocket.

As I made my way back toward the door, I banged against a chair. Although it only made a slight thud, it sounded loud to me and I halted for a moment to see if it had disturbed my father. I detected no change in the pattern of his breathing, so I continued across the room and out the door. In the hallway, I breathed a sigh of relief, checked my flashlight to be sure it worked, then crept downstairs and let myself out the back door.

Chapter Twenty

A light breeze brought a chill to the early morning air. As I slipped it on, I was glad I'd brought a sweater, although it could be attributed to the habit I'd developed while living in San Francisco of always having one with me. I judged it would be at least another hour until daylight. I peered across the clearing to the winery and the workers' barn to verify that no one else was up and was reassured by the stillness. Stimulated by excitement and my recent knowledge, I almost flew across the clearing in a quick jog. There was no question in my mind about the hiding place.

The memory had come so quickly and so clearly that I wondered why I hadn't remembered it before. When I'd seen the wine barrels this afternoon I reacted to the hint, but it wasn't until I saw the wine cask table, which still so closely resembled a barrel, that it connected. Then I visualized my brother and myself as young children on a wet winter day as we played in the aging cellars. It was dry and warm even if it was a bit musty. Philip had talked me into playing marbles with him, something I didn't usually enjoy because he always won.

On this particular day, one of the marbles, a big cat's-eye, rolled in between several barrels that were resting on their sides. As Philip reached to retrieve the marble, he overbalanced and half-fell against one of the barrels which gave way. At first we thought the bottom had broken through and expected wine to come pouring onto the floor, then we realized that the bottom had merely slipped out revealing a space about four inches deep between the false bottom and the real bottom. Our eyes popped wide with surprise and we wondered who had made this barrel that way and why. Although it was empty, it must've had some valuable purpose at one time. Being imaginative children, we conjured up several possibilities including one that the barrel had once belonged to a pirate who smuggled gold and jewels in the space. That was our favorite story and the barrel soon became identified as the "smuggler's cask".

I could still hear Philip's childish young voice saying, "This is a special hiding place, Marti. We'll only put extra special and very important things in here. You must promise to tell no one about it."

Wide-eyed and solemn, I crossed my heart and swore I would never reveal the secret.

Extra special was right! Now, if I was correct, it contained something very important. In my recollection, it was never used for anything when we were children and over time I'd forgotten all about it. It took seeing that cask with the shelves to remind me of the false-bottomed barrel. The space would be large enough for a notebook.

Within minutes, I stood outside the winery door. Switching on the flashlight, I dug the keys out of my pocket and fumbled through them searching for the one to match the lock. My hands trembled, half with cold and half with nervousness. For a moment, the key didn't seem to fit, then it slid into the lock and turned easily.

The winery was pitch black and as silent as an empty mausoleum. Summoning up my wavering courage, I advanced with only my flashlight to guide me. Although it was a temptation to turn on the lights, I didn't want to alert anyone, who might be awake and looking this direction, to my presence here. This room, in darkness, seemed to be cavernous and menacing so I tried to hurry through it. At the end, I located the door to the aging cellar, but when I tried the handle, I was amazed to find it locked. I hadn't expected it to be and I thanked my lucky stars that I'd brought all the keys with me. After several false starts, the right key finally slipped into the lock and I eased the door open as the hinges made a loud-sounding squeak.

The familiar musty smell of redwood and oak wine barrels in the dry room greeted me. Now all I had to do was locate the exact barrel, assuming it hadn't been moved, of course. Unless a barrel needed to be replaced, most of these fifty-gallon ones stayed in the same location and were filled and emptied as the aging process was completed. As if to confirm it, I ran the flashlight over one of the many rows of wine bottle racks, which were filled with Claremont Vineyard wines. I wasn't too sure how they were arranged, but I knew it would be by year and the time allocated to aging.

Being careful to avoid noise, I made my way to the back where the wine barrels were stacked in long rows, barrel upon barrel creating a formidable wall of redwood and oak. Without actually counting them, I guessed there were around five hundred barrels. Again, I was tempted to turn on the lights, but rejected the idea. Perhaps it was a premonition or just caution, but for whatever reason, I continued my search in the dark.

It was virtually impossible to distinguish any difference in the containers. To my inexperienced eye and with only the flashlight for illumination, they all appeared to be the same. I vaguely recalled that the barrel had been in the middle of a row and between rows. That wasn't much help.

Looking up and down the rows, I noted with dismay that there were a lot of barrels and if I had to check each one, it would take a while. No help for it so figured I'd best get started.

In fact, there were ten rows of forty-five barrels each. Fifty less than I'd guessed, so that reduced the number right off. That bit of good news failed to improve my spirits any as I began at the second row. All I had to do was push against the bottom of each barrel at floor level to see if there was a small amount of play that might indicate it would pop out.

The second and third rows yielded nothing and I was midway through the fourth row when one of the bottoms shook as I pushed against it. Trying to contain my excitement, I ran the flashlight beam all around the bottom in an attempt to locate a catch or hook of some kind. If one was there, it was invisible. I started to push against it with my fingers when I felt the moisture on the wood. False alarm. A bit of wine was leaking out and the barrel would need repair, but it wasn't the one I was seeking.

I continued on checking another two rows before I once again felt the give in the bottom of a barrel just a little off the middle of the row. Nothing was obvious in the pass of the flashlight so I used my fingers to explore the ridge around the bottom until I felt something. It was only a small bump on the cask, but if you pushed on it, the door slid about half an inch. Very ingenious design by whoever made this cask.

Holding my breath, I carefully pushed on the false bottom and it popped out to reveal a larger space than I'd remembered. It was still only four inches deep, but I'd misjudge the radius of the fifty-gallon wine barrel. And there, in the middle, leaning against the real bottom, was, not a journal, but a notebook.

My hands were shaking with excitement as I removed the notebook and opened the cover. The handwriting was Philip's and on the first page, it boldly proclaimed that this was a complete record of the events and transactions of Claremont Vineyards beginning in nineteen sixty-two. As I turned to the next page, I was shocked to see my name inscribed across the top in his bold, hasty handwriting. Kneeling and leaning against my heels, I began to read his message to me.

"If you are reading this, then I am probably dead. I have expected and prepared for it. In this log, you will find several possibilities for my murderer. At least four people began to realize that I knew too much. Which of these four is responsible, I can't say, but more than likely it was accomplished expertly and proving it will be impossible. I'm not asking you to prove it. I only want you to be aware of what's been happening here. I'm afraid some of what you will read will hurt because it affects your life in San Francisco, but you need to know. So, my dear sister, read, be warned and be careful..."

A chill shot through me. How could what had occurred here possibly affect my life in San Francisco? My hands trembled, shaking the book and I didn't want to read it. I didn't want to know anything that would destroy my world, my life, for me, then I remembered it had already been destroyed. I glanced around, listening for any noise in the winery and aware that it would be daylight soon. I didn't want anyone to find me here. I would read the book back at the house in my own room so closing it, I slid the false bottom back into place and began to rise to my feet.

I froze as I heard a sound, the scraping of a door sliding against the concrete. Someone was coming! As I switched off the flashlight, I eased my way to the back of the corner of the last of the long rows of wine barrels. Afraid of discovery, I crouched down taking shallow breaths, hoping I couldn't be seen or heard as I watched the approaching flashlight. Why would anyone else come into the room in darkness unless it was for the same reason I did? Then a voice called out, a voice I recognized and welcomed. Paul. He was the only voice that was safe here. The only one with no connection to this whole messy business. The only person I really felt I could trust.

I let out my breath and gasped with relief. "Here, Paul."

As I stepped out from behind the barrels, the flashlight bounced in my direction. "What are you doing, pet?" he asked as he came toward me. "I saw your lights on under the door and I thought I might speak to you. Try to smooth out that nasty scene. It was spoiling my sleep, I must tell you. When I found you weren't in your room, I came out looking for you. You shouldn't be out here alone in the middle of the night like this."

"How did you know I was here?"

"I noticed the door slightly ajar and figured you must have come inside. Why on earth did you come here?" He glanced around with obvious distaste apparent in his scrunched up nose.

"I was following a hunch."

At last, he noticed the notebook in my arms. "What's that? Have you found Philip's journal?" There was a strange excitement in his eyes. "Here, let me see it."

Clutching it a little tighter, I moved away from him. "I'd rather not. I don't want anyone to see it just yet."

With unexpected speed, his hand clamped down on my arm. I looked up into his face in surprise. In the darkness, little was discernible except the whites of his very wide eyes.

"I think you better give it to me," he stated in a very cold voice quite unlike anything I'd ever heard before.

I ran the tip of my tongue over my lips to moisten them as I tried to think. What connection did he have with Claremont Vineyards? Why was he so interested in Philip's journal? "Why do you want it?" I managed to ask. "I don't understand."

He grinned, his teeth looking fierce in the dim light of the flashlight, and he twisted my arm. "If you were to read that book, you'd know. But you won't ever read it now, so give it to me."

I wasn't so dumb that I didn't catch the implication. Obviously he didn't consider me much of an opponent either since he didn't have any kind of weapon out. Did he really think I would just hand it over without a fight? But he'd forgotten that when I had done an article on ways a girl could protect herself in the big city, I had taken the course the police department offered in basic self-defense. Judging the best I could, I twisted sharply, ground my elbow into his stomach, twisted again and swung my knee up into his groin.

There was a sharp intake of breath, a deep groan, and his grip on my arm slipped as he doubled over in surprise and pain. As the flashlight clattered to the floor, I tore loose and ran. I knew I had a little time, but not nearly enough, while he recovered. Already I could hear his curses and gasps behind me and it wouldn't be much longer before he gave chase. I had to get out of this storage room. It was too easy to trap someone in here. I had a better chance of evading him in the processing rooms, but how long could I avoid him? I had to think of another plan.

My tennis shoes made a faint flopping sound as I scurried across the concrete floor. On the wooden floors of the other rooms, they wouldn't make that much noise and it would be harder for Paul to follow me. Once I made it to the door and stepped through, I heard the still faint, but growing sounds of his pursuit.

Turning to the left, I loped toward what I hoped were the cooling vats. At this point, I was relying on my memory, which had only been slightly refreshed the day before. Where the door at the other end was ajar, there was a faint light, but not enough to illuminate my immediate area, so I continued in darkness. Stretching my left arm out, I hoped to touch any obstacles before I ran into them. When my fingers brushed the cold steel of the first tank, I quit running and moved as quietly as I could, feeling my way through the vats. I slid my hand along that vessel, locating the next and edged my way around it.

My knee connected with a piece of metal that protruded out, poking it right in that spot behind the kneecap that felt like a hammer hit it and I bit off the cry of pain that almost escaped my lips. My left hand dropped to my knee, rubbing at it and probing to make sure it was just a bruise, then I leaned against the vat, pressing my knee against the cold surface until the aching ceased enough to put my weight on it. My eyes were adjusting enough to the small amount of light filtering in to give more definition to the vats, controls and tubes that kept them chilled. I wondered if Paul was also gaining night vision.

A moment later I got the answer to that question as I saw a beam of light burst through the darkness from the aging room. I cursed in silence. He'd found his flashlight. Knowing I didn't dare use mine, I had to find a place to hide where his beam couldn't locate me. With very careful and silent steps, I made my way to the fermenting tanks. They, at least, wouldn't freeze me. I pressed my body tightly against the stainless steel tub and wriggled my way in the cramped space between two of them. It wouldn't be much cover if he directed his light between them, but at least I wasn't out in the open.

"Marti! You may as well come out. You know I'll find you eventually. All I want is the damn book." His voice still sounded unnaturally cold.

Although I remained silent, I had the horrible feeling that he knew exactly where I was. I tried to take very shallow, soundless breaths and to hold perfectly still. I turned my head toward the sound of his voice. It was not easy to see him, but I could tell the flashlight beam was directed away from me. In his right hand, something shiny and metallic flashed for a moment. Shocked, I realized it was a knife!

Dear Lord, what on earth could involve Paul here? I never even dreamed he had any connections with my father or brother. Where had he been the weekend Philip died? He told me he was in Sacramento and was detained after the interview with the senator, then decided to stay the night, but it could just as easily have been Claremont Vineyards, a place he swore he'd never seen before.

The flashlight swung toward me and I flattened back against the vat. Sweeping back and forth in slow motion, the light moved toward me. I wouldn't be able to hide from him much longer. I cursed myself for not wearing a dark scarf over my blonde hair. As I slid down the side of the vat, I tried to slide my dark sweater over my hair and I searched for any kind of a hiding place. I knew it was hopeless. There was no place I could squeeze my body and if I moved now, he would spot me right away. I slid my feet under one of the cold tubes attached to the tank in the hope it would help hide them. It may have worked, at least for the moment, as the light moved on to the next tank.

"Marti!" Paul's voice was sharper. "Don't be a fool! I know you're in here so come out now!"

My options were limited, stay crouched where I was in this awkward position, try to make a run for it, or give Paul the notebook. The last one wasn't a real option, but I put it in my list to make me feel I had choices. Was there anything near me I could use as a weapon? Something that could stun him without getting me near that knife? Could I remove one of the control wheels and throw that? As I was considering this, another voice cut through the stillness.

"Over here, Thorpe!"

I saw the flashlight beam swing toward the door, then a row of lights burst into white brilliance as the newcomer flipped the switch. For a moment, I was blinded and, most certainly, so was Paul.

"It'll do you no good, Thorpe. Too many people know about you." I recognized Lee's voice now.

"He's got a knife!" I screamed and straightened up to exit from my hiding place. I could hear Paul's footsteps running in the direction of the door and Lee's moving away from it, coming closer. I slipped out from behind the vats and into the aisle created between the vats and the cooling tanks and began running toward the door and escape. I heard the scuffle as Lee and Paul met each other. By the time I drew even with them, they were both rolling on the floor, the knife gleaming dangerously between them.

Frantic, I looked around for a weapon I could use to help Lee but there was nothing small I could grab and my next thought was to go for help. Then I screamed again as the knife slashed at Lee and came up dripping red. Lee rolled away from Paul, blood beginning to spread on his shirt. In seconds, Paul was on his feet, advancing towards me in an uneven gait when Lee unexpectedly lunged at him and tackled him down again.

"Get out of here!" Lee yelled as he and Paul locked in battle again. Frightened for him, but thinking I could find a shovel or something to fight with outside, I obeyed him and rushed out the door... and into my father!

Chapter Twenty-One

*B*reathless and frightened, I sputtered, "Papa! Thank God! Paul's trying to kill Lee. I think he killed Philip!"

With that, I flung myself into the sanctuary of my father's arms, still clutching the precious notebook to my chest.

My father hesitated, then wrapped his arms around me, offering comfort and security. "It's okay, Martinique. You are safe."

"Didn't you hear me, Papa?" I pulled back and stared at him in confusion. "Paul is fighting with Lee. He has a knife and he's trying to kill Lee." I glanced back at the winery door, fearful that I might see Paul emerge. As my gaze returned to my father, I noticed that his eyes were fixed on the notebook in my arms.

"So you found it," he said, his voice barely audible as he spoke more to himself than to me. His eyes glittered with excitement and I realized that he, too, wanted the journal. He held out his hand. "Give it to me. I have a right to it."

My mouth fell open and I slowly shook my head. "No. Philip left it to me. It's in his own handwriting that I should have it." My voice trembled as I spoke. I could understand that he wanted this memento of his last son, but whatever Philip had written, he had given it to me. It would be up to me to read it, to judge, and to decide what to do about it.

"I'm not asking for it, Martinique," my father said, his voice gruff. "I'm demanding it."

As my eyes met his, a cold spear of shock, as painful as a knife twisting in my flesh, cut through me.

His eyes were cold, gray steel, his face was the mask of a stranger, lacking in love or compassion.

"You!" I gasped with the sudden realization of his part in all that had happened. "You and Paul! Together—"

His face cracked into a bitter smile. "No, daughter, Paul did not kill your brother... my son. He only helped me to dispose of the body. To make it look like an accident."

I froze. For a long moment, I thought I was going to be sick. My stomach lurched and dizziness touched me. I couldn't believe what I was hearing. "You? You killed him?" I almost choked on the words. "But you adored him! He was your last son. Why? Why would you do it?"

For a moment, sadness touched his face, then the wrinkled old skin hardened again. "He was lost to me. Corrupted! This cursed valley ruined him and turned him against me. He would have destroyed the vineyard. All I worked for, and my father before me, and his father before him. He would have ruined it all. I did the only thing I could do to stop him. I didn't want to kill him. It was an accident—" His voice trailed off and his eyes grew distant as if he was reliving the moment.

"If only he hadn't meddled," he began again. "It would not have happened. But he found out and I couldn't shut him up. Even then, I never meant to kill him. We quarreled and he told me he knew all about my businesses. I think he wanted to force me into giving him the vineyard, but I lost control. We were both angry, shouting at each other. He threatened me, so I grabbed for something to hit him with and my hands fell on a shovel. So Paul and I staged the accident. We had to make it look as if he had missed a turn. Paul drove the truck to the very edge of the pavement, and together we pushed it over with Philip sitting behind the wheel and we covered our tracks. You must understand. He was corrupted; he wanted to take it all from me."

I shuddered at my father's words, knowing that I already knew too much. I could visualize the horrible pictures, could see them arguing, my father in a rage, grabbing at the chain around Philip's throat, perhaps trying to choke him or scare him. Maybe he even wanted to shake him as he had when we were children. And Philip probably felt he had power over my father at last and possibly he even laughed as he turned from the tired old man. Still angry, Papa reached, hands falling on the shovel, and slammed it against his head. No, I didn't need any more details.

In the brief time that I'd pieced it together, I realized that my only hope for safety would be to delay him until help arrived. And if help didn't arrive? Well, I refused to think about that. A more immediate problem presented itself in the scuffling noises that came from the winery behind me. Lee and Paul were still fighting, but that wouldn't last much longer. If the wrong one was victorious, I was in a vulnerable position.

"How was he corrupted?" I asked to keep my father talking. I began backing cautiously away, the movement slow and careful. If I could just inch my way to his left side where I would have a clear path—

It was like a storm breaking in the old man's face and I halted in terror as he shouted. "He wanted more machines! He would have turned this place into an all metal monster—forfeiting the old ways, the good ways. He no longer cared about the quality of the wine, only the quantity and how cheaply it could be produced. Finally, he even schemed to get it from me. He didn't know I knew, but I did. I knew he was behind the Kellogs plot to buy it and I knew about his affair with that—that Mexican hussy!"

He was mad, I thought, as I gaped at him in astonishment. But he'd known all along and how much did he know about what I did? Was someone following me?

As if he read my thoughts, he said, "No, I am not insane. I only wanted to stop your brother from adding more machinery, from trying to modernize everything at the cost of the family tradition. First it was stainless steel vats and bigger crushing machines, then he wanted automatic grape pickers—where would it end?"

"But these machines were brought in," I pointed to the building that housed the huge brewing vats. "They haven't changed the quality of the wine. Philip only wanted to increase production to keep in step with the times."

His eyes narrowed and his face became a fierce mask of anger. "So I was right about you! You would do the same as your brother. I would give you all my life's work and you would destroy it as your brother would."

Realizing I'd made a mistake defending Philip, I tried to steer him another way. "No, Papa! I don't even want the vineyard! Forget about it. But I don't understand. How does Paul fit into this? What connection does the editor of a news magazine have with the vineyard?"

Even though his face remained rigid, his eyes seemed to find amusement in that. "Who do you think financed his magazine?"

In disbelief, I gasped and barely managed to speak. "Oh, no.. not you?"

"With the stipulation he hired my daughter. Of course, I wanted to be sure you were taken care of, my child. I knew you'd set your sights on a journalistic career, but even the best need help, and you didn't want my influence so—"

"So you bought a magazine for me! You couldn't let me do it on my own. Even then you had to control my life! And I thought Paul Thorpe called me because he really thought my writing was good. Oh, I was gullible! I should have known that the few byline articles I'd done for the paper weren't enough to warrant the attention Paul paid to me."

I stepped further away from him, crossed my arms and spoke with bitterness sharpening my tongue. "All this time I thought I was a good journalist, I was just the owner's daughter. You never understood me. You never gave me credit for my ability."

My father looked shocked at my tirade, likely thinking that I was being unreasonable. I was just his little girl having a tantrum. I paused for a breath, then another thought struck me. "I suppose Paul's romantic advances were part of the deal. You even bought him for me. I can just hear it— 'Keep her happy, Paul. Make love to her and I'll keep the money flowing.' My God, I can't believe it. My whole life is a lie." I was shattered by this new knowledge and all the implications.

"You never appreciated me, Martinique. But no matter. It is over now. No one will inherit the vineyard. I will destroy it myself first. Now give me that book you hold." He reached again for the notebook.

In defiance, I stepped back another step. Self-preservation might have dictated that I keep my mouth shut, but no, I had to deny it. "No! This book will convict you and Paul! Philip meant it for me and I intend to keep it."

He leered at me, a horrible grin that reminded me of a demon's mask. "As you wish. If you do not choose to hand it over, that is all right. However you look at it, you are dead, my poor, tragic daughter, and I will have it anyway." He came at me then.

Only my small size and speed, plus the few extra steps I'd taken away from him, saved me from being grabbed as I darted from his reach. Screaming Lee's name as loudly as I could, I bolted toward the open fields and the rows of grapes. I feared how his battle with Paul was going, but I had no time to dwell on it. My own death sentence had just been pronounced and Lee's peril only flashed through my mind as I scrambled across the soft-soiled rows.

The sun was fully up, hiding behind white clouds and the grapevines were coated with a light dew, presenting a lovely morning to die. I could feel the moisture brush against my hands as I dashed past the vines. Although my father had much longer legs, he was old and I had youth and a lot of motivation on my side, so I managed to stay ahead of him. It was clear he was far more mobile than I had thought he was.

I tried to plan ahead. When I reached the end of the fields, I could climb the fence and run to the Kellog house—if I could hold up! At least it would not be any easier for my father.

I wasn't one to exhibit a great deal of confidence in God, but as I ran I found myself praying to Him for help. Unconsciously, one hand went to the small gold cross around my throat and clutched it tightly. The other hand still grasped the notebook as if it held life itself.

A thick, low-hanging grape branch grabbed at my jeans, caught, and I tugged hard to get it loose. With a ripping sound, my jeans gave way, tearing a line across at my left knee, then I was running again. Here and there, huge roots thrust dangerously from the ground. Glancing down constantly, I tried to avoid them, keenly aware that I couldn't risk a fall now. I would never recover in time.

Off to my left, I heard a voice shouting, but I couldn't make out the words. A quick look revealed a male figure running at a diagonal toward me, his features unidentifiable from this distance. Jacques? His words came back sharply to me; his words of warning. Although he tried to tell me to leave, he didn't tell me enough. Did he know all of this or was it only suspicion? It didn't matter—I was stubborn enough that I wouldn't have gone home without the journal anyway.

Behind me, I could hear the thrashing of my father through the vines and I could feel the thumping of the ground from our footfalls across the plowed furrows. Risking a glance over my shoulder, I was alarmed that he was scarcely more than a few yards from me. Far too close; I needed to pick up my pace. My only chance was to outrun him.

But the quick look had revealed another figure pursuing us from the direction of the winery. Whether it was Lee or Paul, I couldn't tell and I didn't dare speculate.

The glance back cost me as my foot caught something, a root sticking up, and I stumbled. Unable to keep my balance, I flung my arms wide to try to break the fall. The notebook slipped from my hand and landed several feet ahead as I went down to one knee and both arms, then pushed up to regain my footing. Hoping to scoop it up without losing much time I veered toward the notebook. As I bent to grab it, I heard a curse and a scramble of breaking wood behind me. I spun around to see my father, recovering from his own collision with a branch, far too close to me. Desperate, I looked for something to defend with and my eyes lighted on one of the wooden stakes supporting a grape vine.

Finding strength in my fear, I grasped the heavy stake then yanked and twisted it until it pulled out of the ground. My father was close enough that I could hear him gasping. Over-excited by this, he was having trouble breathing. Thinking only of slowing him down long enough for help to arrive, I straightened and brought the stake around like a baseball bat to try to hit my father as he lunged forward to grab me.

He threw up an arm to block the blow, but it struck his shoulder hard enough for him to lose his balance on the uneven row and he stumbled. I turned away and started to run again when I heard the sound of wood cracking as it broke. This was followed by a scream of agony that sliced through the air like a howling winter wind.

Terrified, I tripped and fell to my knees when I tried to twist back around. In horror, my eyes locked on the view of my father impaled on the broken wooden stake that had supported a now-crushed grapevine. His wide open, vacant eyes stared ahead, frozen in pain and shock. He was dead; the stake had gone through his chest, angled from below the sternum into his heart.

Finding my voice at last, I screamed, a horrible cry that sounded like a wounded animal poured from my throat. On hands and knees, I crawled to him, my eyes riveted on the stream of crimson running down the several inches of exposed stake and soaking into the ground. Although the memories blurred, I think I was still screaming as tears poured down my face.

How long I knelt beside him I couldn't say, but someone's hands grabbed me and turned me into his arms. I recognized Lee's body, heard his voice, and I buried my face against his shoulder. The tears, almost under control, broke again like a flood and I sobbed in shock and grief as he held me, rocked me from side to side, and stroked my hair while he murmured soothing words.

Other voices began to chatter around me, but I didn't pay any attention. My mind refused to function, that gruesome sight of my impaled father remaining as the only clear image in it. I heard Lee say, "I'll take that, Jacques." A few moments later, I felt, rather than saw, his arm reaching for something then the notebook was pressed into my hands.

"Hang on to that," Lee said in a whisper and he lifted me to my feet, holding my head pressed closely against him so that I need not see what was still so clear in my mind. On weak knees, I stumbled, with his support, toward the house. I became aware of Jacques' presence, as well as Elaine and Hector, hovering near my father's body.

My mind finally beginning to work, I pulled back a little to peer up at Lee. "Paul?" I asked in a hoarse voice, then noticed his bloodstained shirt. "You're hurt!"

"It's nothing, honey. Just a nick. And Paul is all right. I only knocked him out. My dad is with him. He'll come to trial, don't worry." He forced a smile at me, but his face was tired and pale.

"How did you know, Lee? If you hadn't come—"

"Did you think we didn't keep an eye on you? Jacques and I were looking after you." He frowned, a dark, concerned look in his brown eyes. "But we were almost too late. Jacques phoned me as soon as he knew you'd gone out and Paul had followed you. Then he called the sheriff. I don't think he expected your father to go after you also. I know I didn't. Evidently, your father saw me going to the winery and came down to personally take care of you. I didn't think he was up to it, but he had more strength than he let on. Now, I have to ask, what are you going to do about that notebook? It's Phil's journal, isn't it?"

I still pressed it to my chest. "He left it to me. I don't know yet what I'll do, but I need to read it. I don't think I want to hand it over to the sheriff. I think it might hurt more people than just my father and Paul."

He nodded in approval. "We'll work on that. The sheriff will probably be here in about fifteen minutes. Do you trust me? Then let me have the book and I'll put it somewhere safe."

Without reservation, I handed it to him. It would be safe, I knew that. Lee, my friend and protector, would take care of it for me.

Madame Boucher came rushing out to meet us and I was ushered into her kitchen. Lee left with her fawning over me like a mother over a wayward child. She brought me a cup of coffee and one sip told me it was strongly laced with brandy. But it served its purpose; it warmed me and numbed my mind. "My poor father..." I managed to say to her, but she shushed me and pulled out the First Aid kit to bandage my scrapes.

As she took care of me, I replayed those last minutes in my mind and realized in grief and a bit of fear that he was dead because of me. I hit him in self-defense, but much like how he killed Philip, it was an accident. I never intended for him to die. Still, I wondered how did his mind get so twisted?

* * * * *

When Sheriff Eberman arrived, he found me much calmer and efficiently helping Emily Boucher bandage Lee's injury. Lee was right—it was only a nick, nasty-looking, but clean. The knife had sliced between his ribs but if its position had been over an inch or so more, it might have been very serious.

On the table lay a notebook, its pale blue cover lightly coated with streaks of dust. I told my story exactly as it happened, even about finding the notebook. Except I didn't tell him I found Philip's journal, only an old notebook in the wine cask. The sheriff picked up the book and opened it. I watched his face as he flipped through a few pages.

"Why do you suppose anyone would want a collection of poetry, Ms. Claremont?" he asked, as he set it back on the table.

"I believe they thought it was something else. My father seemed to believe it was a journal. I only know that the note I had from my brother hinted at something concealed in a hiding place. It wasn't that one since that notebook was my poetry collection. I'd forgotten I'd put it there for safekeeping when I thought it was valuable. I was young and naïve back then."

The sheriff's big head bobbed up and down. "Uh-huh. Well, at least that gives me a motive for the break-ins, even if the alleged journal hasn't been found. The description I have for the second burglar fits Paul Thorpe, who also seems to like using knives. I don't guess it will be too hard to prove he was in Sonoma one day before he showed up here. You know, that journal might tell us a whole lot, but I don't suppose we'll find it?"

"I don't know where it is," I said, being straight forward and honest. Where Lee had put it, he hadn't told me and I hadn't asked. He had come back with a collection of poetry he'd dug out of my closet to replace the book I'd found. "My brother and I had a lot of hiding places when we were children. I really can't remember them all and his note didn't give me any clues, but you can read it for yourself."

Eberman looked askance. I was sure he didn't believe me. He already had the note in the evidence he'd gathered since he arrived. "Well, if you happen to remember and you find it, you will bring it to me, won't you?"

"Yes. Of course," I replied, feeling only slightly guilty about the lie. It would depend on what the book said. I was not going to hurt innocent people. I didn't think Philip intended that when he began keeping his records.

With both Lee and Jacques as witnesses to the events and my father's pursuit of me that culminated with his accidental death, the sheriff wasn't arresting me. He advised me I was still "under investigation" and to not leave the area until he told me otherwise. "Did you have any suspicions that your father might have killed your brother, Ms. Claremont?"

"None. It was a total shock when he told me what happened." I had already told Eberman everything about what was said and Paul's part in it. I think he thought that after my visit to him a couple of days earlier, I might have suspected my father, but the sad truth was that it caught me by surprise.

After the sheriff left to continue his investigation outside, I exhaled with relief. Paul was already on his way into town in the custody of the deputy. He would be booked and jailed. I gazed out the window where a dozen or so people swarmed over the fields, investigators, police lab men and reporters. The ambulance bearing my father's body had departed only minutes before the press began arriving.

Both Lee and Jacques deterred the reporters as best they could, telling them I had suffered a severe shock, which was true, and was not available for comment. No, they had nothing to contribute either. Hector and Elaine had disappeared even before the sheriff arrived. As far as anyone knew, they were never there.

The next few days were going to be difficult. Again the tears welled in my eyes. "You'd better rest," Lee said with concern when he came in to check on me. His hand touched my arm, rubbing it with affection and worry.

"You're right," I agreed. I was exhausted and Madame had given me another tea laced with brandy "for medicinal purposes". He half-carried me up the stairs and we climbed without haste. My only thoughts now were of my bed and sleep.

Chapter Twenty-Two

When I opened my eyes again, it was dark and the soft light of the moon rising slipped through the curtains into my bedroom. For a long while, I stayed in bed without moving or thinking, watching the moon glide on its path into the sky. I was afraid to think, afraid to allow the floodgates of my mind open and wash my consciousness with all the painful memories of the past few days. The hour was still early, about eight, I guessed, but the house seemed strangely silent. The fear that I'd been left alone in the house was what brought me fully awake. Pulling my summer robe on, I made my way downstairs, flipping on every light I encountered along the way.

I still blocked the painful thoughts that pressed for freedom, but they were there, materializing in mental pictures. The evil look on my father's face. The glitter of Paul's knife in the dimly illuminated winery. The wooden stake with the flow of red washing down it. My own part in his death. To shut them out, I tried to think of other things. Still each thought led back to them somehow. Even the magazine was connected to the events of the day. The whole thing was a fake. My life was an illusion. The only reality was here in the nightmare I'd live through these past hours.

As I stepped into the living room, the welcoming glow from a fire burning greeted me and before it, lounging with his long legs stretched across an Ottoman, a drink in his hand, sat Lee. Seeing me, he rose, set his drink down and came forward to take my hands in his.

"Are you all right, darling?"

I nodded, then in spite of myself, pressed against his chest and wept quiet tears. He folded his arms around me, enduring my emotional moment with patience, although, I later realized, it must have been painful having me pressed against his injured side. For myself, I took comfort in the strong, steady arms cradling me and in the feel of the rough cloth of his chambray shirt against my cheek. Only when I became aware of the large, moist spots I was making on his shirt did I manage to stop my tears and apologize for my outburst.

His smile was warm and loving, nourishing my soul. "It's all right, honey. Are you feeling better?"

I managed a weak smile. Although I was better, there was still too much sorrow. "Yeah, I am. Where is everyone?"

"The Bouchers went into Sonoma to arrange the details of the funeral in the afternoon and are probably enjoying dinner and an evening in town," he said. He settled me on the sofa and draped an arm around my shoulders. "Elaine and Hector are staying in Napa tonight. So, you're stuck with me. How about something to eat?"

"I don't think so. I'm really not very hungry. I don't think I could eat."

"You should try. How about a nice bowl of potato soup made especially for you?" he coaxed.

I looked at him, amazement apparent in my expression. "You made it?"

He laughed. "I never claimed that! No, Madame Boucher made it although I did help her peel the potatoes. She left me instructions to be sure you eat so be a good girl and let me bring you a bowl. Otherwise, I'll be in the doghouse."

With a chuckle, I agreed. I couldn't have Lee in Madame's bad graces. I slid further back into the sofa as he left the room. From the fireplace, the crackling of the burning logs and glowing embers in the center gave a pleasing warmth and comfort. I watched them, happy to bask in the peculiar oblivion they offered, the illusionary suspension in time.

Returning with a serving tray, Lee set it up before me and placed the tray on top. Steam rose from the white china soup tureen as he ladled soup into a bowl, then poured a cup of coffee for each of us. "I did make the coffee." A small plate with freshly baked sourdough bread and butter rounded out my meal.

He sat silently in the chair by the fireplace while I ate. After the first few spoonfuls of the creamy, thick soup, I admitted I was hungry and ate several spoonfuls before pausing. A lot had happened since I had last eaten, I thought when I realized that it had been over twenty-four hours earlier.

Between the hot soup and the strong coffee, I regained my composure and, pushing the tray aside, faced Lee. Now I could allow my thoughts to trickle out. I could begin to face them. "Paul... What's going to happen to him?"

Lee's face was grim. "He's been arrested and charged with murder and assault. The murder charge may not stick if what he says is true."

"And what does he say?" I knew the answer already, but I wanted to hear it as it would be printed in the newspapers.

Delaying his answer, Lee rose to pour himself another coffee, offered to refill mine, then spoke. "He says your father killed your brother, but it was an accident. He says he only helped to make it look like Phil had a car wreck." He spoke slowly, with difficulty, and I understood how hard it must be for him to tell me. He didn't know I already knew the truth.

"Did he go into detail?"

"It's in the newspapers. 'Murder in the Vineyards' is the headline. Even the San Francisco papers are carrying it."

"Sensational deaths are big news," I said, my voice sounding bitter. How well I knew that. "They increase the circulation. People love to read about gory deaths, especially when the people involved are prominent, as my father was, and Paul is quite a celebrity also. He is telling the truth, though. My father told me a few minutes before...before..." I swallowed hard against the sob that choked me.

With tact, Lee changed the subject or rather returned to the original one. "There is still the assault on you, Marti. Paul would have killed you for that notebook."

"Even yesterday, I wouldn't have believed that. But then, I wouldn't have believed my father killed Philip and would have killed me. It was so unexpected. Philip's death may have been an accident, but Papa actually planned to kill me. How could he change so much, Lee?"

"I don't know, honey. I guess pressures build up and a man begins to feel desperate. He gets an idea in his head that dominates and everything else is secondary to that idea."

"Do you think he was insane?"

"To a degree, yes. Maybe that will tell you more." He motioned toward the notebook on the coffee table—Philip's journal.

"Have you read it?" I asked.

"No. I read the first page, Marti. Phil meant it for you and I respect his wishes. If there's anything in there you want me to know, you'll tell me yourself. Otherwise, I'm sure you'll do what's best for everyone concerned."

"It's caused so much pain and sorrow..."

He cut in. "It's just a record of what was happening here already. But it did almost cause your death. The rest would have happened anyway." He stood up, gazed into the fire as he thought, then sat next to me. "Would you rather stay at our house for a few days than here?"

"No. I'll be all right here. The Bouchers will be here and you're just a phone call away. Besides, there's no one left to harm me."

"Then I'll leave you for now. I think you need some time to yourself." He kissed me goodnight and started for the door.

"Lee," I called. I wanted to bring him back, ask him to stay. I was afraid to be here alone, but he was right. Instead, I asked, "Will the Bouchers be back soon?"

Understanding, he nodded. "You won't be alone long, so take advantage of it while you can. Don't forget, I am just a phone call away. Goodnight."

After he'd gone, I stared at the notebook on the coffee table with hatred. So much grief and my father's death for a plain blue notebook. Did I really want to know what was in it?

Eventually, I rose, poured myself a glass of wine and set it down on the coffee table. Slipping away from the present, I recalled the past when I was a child. One happy memory followed another as I remembered my father. Tears began to trickle down my cheeks as I thought of the good man, the good father. How had he changed so? What had brought him to the desperation of this morning? Uneasily, I looked at the notebook again. Were the answers in it? I had no choice except to read it for it was the last place I had any hope of answering my questions.

As I reached for it, my hands shook with apprehension, but I lifted it into my lap, took a sip of wine and settled back. Turning to the first page, I read Philip's message to me again.

"... So, my dear sister, read, be warned and be careful..."

I did as he instructed, my eyes riveted to the pages filled with the bold, dark handwriting. It was as he'd said, a journal with the phrasing so exactly the same as Philip talked that it was easy to hear his voice saying the words. For the next couple of hours, I wandered through people's lives—my father, Elaine and Hector, Paul, Consuelo, and Lee. Through that book, I saw them exactly as Philip had seen them.

Consuelo was a loving entry— "she's the most beautiful woman I've ever known. Not just outward beauty, but with great depth and intelligence. I'd like to marry her, to spend all the rest of my days with her, but I don't dare with Pop still alive. Can we wait until we are free of his grip on us? It hurts her and I feel like such a coward. I can't say how much it tears at me, but she doesn't complain. I think she knows even more than I can express how much the vineyard means to me."

Then later, "Consuelo is studying to be a lawyer and I have told her I would do all I can to help her. She is good to me and for me. I wish I could do more. Would Pop truly disown me if I were to marry her?" He poured out his love in other entries that read much the same, each ending with the same anguished expression of doubt and fear of my father.

My eyes fell on another passage. "Elaine has been looking pale and tired these past few weeks. I asked her before what was wrong, but she didn't want to tell me. This morning, she broke down and confessed that she was carrying Manuel's child. What a shock! I would never have imagined her with one of the workers. She said she didn't love him; she only wanted to find out what she had missed all these years. She told me she didn't want the baby so I agreed to loan her the money out of my own account for the abortion. When the harvesting is over at the end of the month, I'll let Manuel go even though he's been a good worker in the past. I can't allow him to remain after this where Elaine can see him constantly. If it weren't for the obvious questions that would be asked, I'd let him go now. But it will give me an opening for Hector."

Well, that explains Manuel, I thought, feeling like a voyeur into Elaine's life. Still, I began to see my half-sister in a different light as I realized how lonely her life must have been. What was it that Lee had said? He didn't think Elaine would get that involved with Manuel? Philip hadn't even told Lee. He'd kept her secret. Even more surprising was the obviously close relationship my brother had developed with our half-sister.

I skimmed ahead a few pages until Lee's name caught my attention. Exactly as he had described them to me, Philip detailed the arrangements for buying the vineyard. At this point, he only had suspicions that our father was having financial problems and might be willing to sell. He had already ceased to allow Philip any control in the vineyard and my brother was making a desperate attempt to gain what was rightfully his. A few days later, he wrote about the failure of his plan and the now strained relations with the Kellogs, then added:

"Pop has instructed me to stay clear of the Kellogg family as if he really expects me to follow his instructions. Of course, I can't be too open about it as long as Pop threatens to change his will. I still don't understand everything, but I am positive there are financial problems involved. I've tried to talk to Pop about using automatic grape pickers, but he refuses to listen. Just as he refuses to listen to the logic behind increasing wages and bettering working conditions. He's always been there before, but something has happened to change that. If only I could see the ledgers, I'm sure I could discover the reason. He won't let me near them, though. He won't even discuss the vineyard with me anymore. Even Jacques has noticed a change in Pop and he, too, is being left out of the running of the vineyard."

He talked about Hector and Elaine also, expressing surprise that they liked each other but seeming genuinely pleased at Elaine's newfound happiness. He even said that Elaine had decided to keep the baby. Maybe that explained the loose clothes she wore and I was glad to read it.

A dark shadow was cast upon this a few pages later when he reported his findings about Hector. Evidently, Hector had been involved in quite a few activities prior to becoming "Chavez's right arm", activities that weren't always legal or for the public good. He'd been a key factor in more than one Chicano riot in Los Angeles and was one of the instigators of the student rebellions at Berkeley. Philip added that he recorded this information as a safeguard.

However, it was in the final pages of the journal that Philip unraveled the mystery. I paused, refilled my wine glass for the third time, and resumed reading. It was dated May 12 at 11:30 AM—the day of his death.

"Pop isn't himself. He seems obsessed by his own ideas. I can't talk to him anymore. Every time I've mentioned getting new or additional equipment, he's gone into a rage. At last, I begin to understand. Pop and Jacques went into town this morning which gave me the chance I've been waiting for to try to get into the safe. He had the combination in the secret compartment in his desk. I guess he forgot I knew about it. Anyway, it was there and I opened the safe and went through the books. The vineyard and winery are in deep financial trouble, but I couldn't understand it at first as they seemed to be making money. When I examined them further, I discovered that Pop has taken money from the winery since nineteen-fifty-nine to finance that magazine where Marti works. Evidently, he planned for her to become a writer for this magazine as soon as she graduated.

"I don't blame him for wanting to look after my sister's future although Marti might have something else to say about his apparent lack of confidence in her abilities. Still, he never should have taken money from the winery to do it. According to the agreement he had with Pop, Paul Thorpe was to keep Marti working for his magazine until she voluntarily left. In return, Pop would allow Thorpe to buy the magazine once it began making a profit. As near as I could tell, that has just started to happen. Pop took out a sizeable loan when Klein was here to even have operating costs for the winery for this coming year.

"Yes, now I understand why he refused to consider my ideas, why he wouldn't allow me to see his books and why he was so against increasing wages. He even convinced himself that there was no need for new equipment. Well, I will face him with it when he returns. I will not let him destroy my vineyard before I have my chance with it.

"I have to tell Marti about it also. She has a right to know how her life has been manipulated. But I can't write her about it or call her. She will have to come here. I'll write asking her to come, then I can tell her to her face. Meanwhile, there are other things to do."

The next entry was dated the same day at 3:45 p.m. "Elaine and I quarreled again about my firing Manuel. She'll give me no peace even though I did it for her sake. She seems happy with Hector, so why does she continue to harass me about Manuel? She says I had no right to fire him. Women! Who can understand them? Lee interrupted our fight—thank God! I wanted to tell him about my explorations this morning, but he didn't have time for a drink and I didn't feel I could go into much detail in privacy here. I'll have to get him to meet me later. Then Pop came back. I told him I knew what he was doing with the vineyard. He took it very calmly, not denying it. He said he would talk to me later this evening."

That was the last entry. Apparently, he'd gone to the shed later where my father killed him. Tears burned my tired eyes as I slammed the book shut.

It was a lot to digest, much of it very painful to me. Even though I realized that my father's interference into my life was because he loved me, it didn't make it any easier to know that I hadn't really made it on my own. That had always meant so much to me that it was like watching a dream shatter. I couldn't thank Philip for that. Sure, he meant well with his desire to inform me, but I would have been happier not knowing. I also realized now that my father, not being able to admit that he, himself, was destroying the vineyard, shifted the blame to Philip. And if my brother hadn't pried, none of this might have happened, not even his death. No, I couldn't blame him. Wouldn't I have done the same thing if the situation had been reversed?

Setting the book on the sofa, I rose and poured another glass of wine, then crossed to the window and gazed out toward the acres of vineyards that had meant so much to both my father and my brother. It was my family's legacy and was now mine unless my father had already changed his will again. Then there was the magazine. Technically, my father had owned it, although Paul always claimed it was his. But if Paul was convicted of the charges against him, what would happen to the magazine?

I turned back to the sofa and the journal on it. How safe would that book be with me? There might still be some who sought it for the information they feared might be in it. I was certain I didn't want to turn it over to the sheriff. This was an area where no secrets were kept, so even if Eberman did agree to reveal only the parts incriminating my father and Paul, the rest would still get out.

Besides, I still thought enough of Paul not to let the price of his ambition be published. Enough would come out without going into details.

Picking up the book again, I suddenly felt sorry for those people whose lives were documented in the worst way. No wonder any one of them might have wanted to kill Philip. Slowly, page by page, I tore them from the book and tossed them into the leaping flames of the hearth. There would be no more damage from it now.

As I turned from the fireplace, I was overcome by deep depression. Dropping to the couch, I let my grief find release in a fresh flood of tears. I didn't stop crying until I heard the front door open, then I forced myself to sit up and I wiped my eyes with a tissue. It was nearly midnight and Jacques and his wife were plainly surprised to see me up, but Emilie Boucher took charge as she as always did. I vaguely recalled asking them to please stay by me, to remain at the vineyard, as Madame urged me up to my room with soft-spoken assurances.

Chapter Twenty-Three

*F*eeling numb, I watched as the rich brown earth claimed the last of my family, my father. He would rest eternally and, I hoped, peacefully alongside his sons and wives–my mother, my brother, and the whole family I never knew except by stories and photographs. Leaning against Lee, who gripped my arm in a tight lock, I didn't fight the tears that streamed down my face and stained his suit. People spoke to me and I replied in automatic mode, neither hearing what they said nor what I answered. The words were routine anyway, the same ones my father had said a week earlier. I cried for the memory of the father I'd known and loved and tried, for the time being at least, to forget the person he'd become.

As we turned from the grave site, I looked around me. It was a warm, clear day hinting at the hot summer just around the corner—a day created for swimming, picnicking and rejoicing in life, not facing the darkness of death and the end of all that I knew. "Dust to dust." The words echoed in my mind as if in a cavern. The end of the Claremont name and possibly the end of Claremont vineyards.

Although we asked for a private funeral, a number of spectators had turned out anyway; those peculiar people who seemed to find a perverse enjoyment in watching other people's grief. I was fortunate that Jacques and Lee ran interference for me and we escaped to the waiting limousine.

Elaine hadn't returned to the house since Papa's death, but she was at the funeral. She had watched the proceedings in silence, her face a mask that revealed neither gladness nor sorrow. It was impossible to tell what she thought. When I'd gazed at her, I realized

I would have to make my peace with her. We were all the family either of us had now. However, she didn't return to the house after the services. She and Hector slipped away before I could speak to her, but I knew she would be present at the reading of the will. I resolved I would talk with her then. Although I doubted we would ever be close, there could at least be understanding and unity.

* * * * *

$\mathcal{T}$wo days later, I sat down to go through the vineyard's books. Financially, my father's affairs were even more complex than I'd imagined and as near as I could tell, more dismal. I knew there would be debts, but I hadn't anticipated the extent of them. As I went through the books noting where he juggled money from one account to another, I realized I was totally muddled. My head ached from trying to calculate exactly how much in debt the winery was. I finally gave up, and shoving myself away from the desk, went downstairs for a stroll around the grounds.

In the afternoon warmth, my hair clung to the back of my neck. Yes, it would be a hot summer, perfect for ripening grapes. As I leaned against a peach tree, I thought about the work ahead of me. I would have Jacques to help... and Lee. No, I couldn't and shouldn't count on Lee. He had his own vineyard to manage.

Lee— His name flitted back into my mind like a word of enchantment. I didn't want to think about him, but I couldn't stop myself. I loved him. I was sure of that, but I was still unsure of marriage. Not that I didn't want to marry him. It was just that I still had something to prove to myself, some unfinished business with my life before I could become his wife. I had to know that I could truly take care of me. I sighed. That brought me back to the vineyard.

A small yellow and brown butterfly danced in uneven flight across my vision and landed on a leaf. Oh, to be a butterfly and wing away on a summer breeze without a thought or care, I mused, pleased for the diversion. Felling weary, I pressed my head against the back of my hand that still caressed the tree. I'd been a butterfly escaping my life too much already. It was time to stay and face it. My soul-searching was terminated by a shout and a wave as Jacques called from the back door of the house. The lawyer was here.

Simon Lavant was a bony-built man of small stature, who was in his late fifties, I judged. As he sifted through his papers, his wire-rim glasses slid precariously to the end of his long narrow nose. He spoke rapidly, barely taking time to inhale.

"Well, Miss Claremont, if you want my advice, I'll tell you. This winery has financial problems. I'm sure you figured that out; it doesn't take a genius. Now, there are a couple of ways out. Number one, you could talk to the bank about your father's loan, checking the practicality of assuming it and weigh the possibility of paying it off without sinking further into debt. Number two, you could sell this whole business—house, land, everything, as well as the magazine, which has to go anyway—pay off the debts, settle the terms of the will and have a nice little nest egg left for yourself. That would be my honest recommendation. Number three, you could sell the winery, equipment, machinery and backlog of wine for enough to settle the outstanding debts, then run this as another grape farm without the expense and headaches of brewing wine. At least you would hold on to the land that way. But there is a catch. That would settle the debts more or less, but not the terms of the will. You would have to have everyone's agreement to do that.

"The magazine has to go," he continued. "What the hell your father got into that for I can't understand. It is clear that he didn't ask for my advice. Plus there's twenty-five thousand dollars in stock purchases which will sell for a little under twenty thousand on the current market."

"Why do you think he bought the stock?" I asked. I was still bewildered by the full scope of the disaster.

"I can't say for sure, but my guess is he bought the magazine for

God knows what reasons, then when it failed to pay its way after the first year, he began trying to invest his money in various stocks hoping to make a sizable profit on them. The stocks were high risk and so far, they haven't paid off. You'd probably better check with the broker before you decide about them." He glanced pointedly at his watch. "Two-twenty-five. Will the reading be in the library?"

I confirmed it and waited while he gathered his papers together.

The few beneficiaries of the will were waiting for us, Jacques and Emily Boucher and Elaine. My eyes met Elaine's for a moment then I looked away. Her face appeared exhausted and her eyes were worried. As soon as I took my seat Lavant began.

While he read the will, I studied the others. Jacques and Emily gravely watch the lawyer. Elaine stared at the floor, seeming almost indifferent at the disposition of the will. Only the fidgeting of her hands, one plucking away at the button on her sweater, gave her away. Small wonder she was worried. What thoughts were on her mind now? What was she really qualified to do? She'd made the vineyard her life for several years now and I didn't think she had the training to do anything else. Did she expect me to throw her out without a second thought? For that matter, what did she think of me now that it was all over?

I turned my attention back to Lavant. The will was simply stated and although we'd talked earlier, this was the first time I heard the full details. Five thousand dollars each was to be given to Emily and Jacques for their long and devoted services and the wish that they would remain to serve the new owner as well; ten thousand dollars to Elaine as a firm base to build on, the least you can do for a daughter not of his own flesh; and the remainder, all real estate and property at Claremont Vineyards, including the debts, to me, his only surviving direct heir. It was a generous will considering the state of finances. Lavant went on to explain that the estate was floundering financially and that he and I were trying to settle it to the best advantage.

I'd watched Elaine's face when he'd read the small inheritance my father had designated for her. Her face revealed little, but her mouth was downturned in disappointment. Given Papa's feelings about her, I thought she was lucky to get anything. It might help my negotiations, though. After he concluded, I approached Elaine. "Would you please wait? I'd like to talk to you alone."

She darted a suspicious look at me, then nodded. I turned to the Bouchers and confirmed again my desire to have them remain as long as I owned the vineyard. Finally, I thanked the lawyer, assuring him I would indeed contact him in a day or two with my decision regarding the estate.

At last, I closed the door behind him and swung around to face Elaine. She was staring out the window, deep in thoughts of her own. I suspected she was trying to figure how far the money, after taxes, would get her and what she would do next. Before I spoke, I cleared my throat with a little nervous cough. This was not going to be easy.

"Elaine, I know we've had our differences in the past and we are both stubborn, so this isn't easy for either of us, but we've got to try to work together."

She was watching me now, her suspicious eyes narrowed into a frown, but she didn't interrupt. At least, I would have my say.

"The terms of the will are hardly fair considering how much you cared about this place. But it's more awkward than that." I told her the whole story then, being as honest as I could. From the steady gaze as she listened, I concluded that none of it surprised her. I ended with the options the lawyer had given me and his recommendation.

"And what do you intend to do, Marti?"

"That's why I wanted to talk to you. I want to keep the vineyard intact. It won't be easy, but with the sale of the magazine and the assumption of the loan, it should be possible. Of course, the catch is that I can manage the cash for you and the Bouchers only if I sell the machinery. I feel confident Jacques and his wife will wait on their portion. For them, it's more like a continuing investment here. This has been their lives as much as ours. I need your cooperation, too. And not just with the money," I added quickly. "I need your help running the place. I don't know that much about it. You do. Your money and knowledge would buy your share of it. Will you do it, Ellie?" The name from our childhood slipped out in this moment of genuine affection for her.

Elaine half-smiled. "And if I say no?"

At first, I gazed at a spot on the floor but forced myself to meet her eyes. "Then I'll sell the brewing equipment and attempt to become a grape grower."

"What guarantee would I have?"

"A contract. It would state the terms clearly and it would guarantee your percentage of ownership based on your monetary investment and the know-how you'd contribute." I waited, hoping that she would say yes or at least consider it.

"I don't know, Marti. My inheritance would be a good down payment on land of my own, a place where Hector and I could start our own lives together."

"But it wouldn't be Claremont Vineyards." I dangled it and I knew how that would entice her.

"No, it wouldn't." Her face screwed up as she thought about it. She had reservations and I couldn't blame her. "But do you really think we could work together? And what about Hector? Where would he fit in?"

"Where do you want him to fit in? You know his qualifications better than I do. All I'll say is that you're both welcome here. This is a big house and there's room for all of us. I know I came off pretty arrogant in the past, but I'm asking for your help now and I'm willing to try if you are."

"One last question. Why? Why don't you just sell the whole place? You could get another writing job and you would have enough money to enjoy life. Why struggle with the vineyard?"

"Let's just say I have something to prove to myself. To be honest, I believe I always wanted the vineyard. I just didn't admit it until these past few days when it became a possibility. You've known that you wanted it much longer. It can be ours now, but it's up to you. I won't beg."

"I'm sure you won't." She flashed a brief smile at me. "I'll have to think about it and talk it over with Hector."

"Of course. By the way, I'm happy for you, Ellie. Lee told me you were marrying Hector."

She smiled at that. "He's a good guy. I think you'd like him." She picked up her purse. "I'll let you know what we decide tomorrow. All right?"

I nodded as I saw her to the door.

After she'd gone, I sat for a while longer and mulled over our conversation. I was almost sure she'd do it. It would be a big adjustment for us, but it would work. I felt confident about it.

I ambled back outside and followed the familiar path toward my garden. In spite of all that had happened, there was hope and peace within me. Through the eucalyptus branches, I could see the rows of grapes standing tall and proud in the sun, each a green fountain of leaves falling to the ground. A light breeze ruffled my hair and clothes. Throwing out my arms, I spun around like a child, then sprinted down the path. As I swung into the garden, I halted sharply.

His tall, lean figure sat at the edge of the duck pond and my heart leapt with joy. I controlled myself, determined not to go running to him. Not yet.

He stood and extended his hands to me. "I knew you'd come."

"Yes, Lee. I came." I took his hands and we embraced, his kiss sending my blood pulsing.

"What are you going to do?" he asked.

I told him, leaving out nothing. "Now I've got to return to San Francisco, clear up my affairs there, make arrangements to keep the magazine going until I can sell it, get my dog and other belongings. Then I'll begin rebuilding."

"And you and me?" His voice was hesitant and I could sense the uncertainty in it.

That was harder. "Give me a year to prove myself. I know it's not fair after all you've been through, but it's important to me—to us. I love you so much, but I have to feel I can do this or it will eat at me."

With a deliberate nod, he wrapped his arms around me in a cocoon of love and kissed me with tenderness. His voice in my ear was soft. "At least, you're next door again. I'll wait, honey. I'll wait."

I squeezed him as I kissed him back with a fierce passion that screamed my desire. Yes, he would wait for me and I would make it work for both of us. I was sure now that I had the strength and love to do it.

*****

Did you enjoy reading *Bitter Vintage*?

If you enjoyed the book, I would really appreciate it if you would consider leaving your honest review at the store where you purchased it. Reviews are important to both the writers and other readers. Whether short or long, they are awesome. Thank you for reading.

About this Book

BITTER VINTAGE is set in Northern California in the Napa-Sonoma region in the mid-1960's when there was considerable unrest and civil rights causes swirling around the farm workers, both American citizens and those from Mexico, concerning low wages and threatened deportation. When I revised the book, I chose to leave it in this setting against the events of the time, even though they don't strongly affect the story.

While all of my characters are fictional, as are the valley and vineyards in Sonoma where it takes place, the history of the region is a woven thread in this fiction. Cesar Chavez was a real person, who championed the field workers and formed the National Farm Workers Association in 1962. With the Agricultural Workers Organizing Committee, the two groups made their first strike against California grape growers in 1965.

Claremont Vineyards and the San Martino Valley don't actually exist, but are a fictional representation of the wine making industry in the 1960's. California wines were just beginning to get recognized for their quality and in a few more years would begin to win international competitions. I've tucked the valley in neatly between Napa and Sonoma where some of the most wonderful vineyards I had the pleasure of visiting and sampling products are located.

At the time this book was written, Point Reyes was a beautiful, unspoiled seashore area with very few visitors. Drake's Bay was breath-taking and I, like Marti, imagined the Golden Hind in that bay. The last time I was there, it was very crowded, so if it sounds fanciful to say that Marti and Lee were on a deserted beach near San Francisco, it was possible in 1965.

About the Authors

Riona Kelly hails from the southwestern United States where she was raised until 21, then she migrated to California. She lived there several years before moving back east all the way to Las Vegas, Nevada and eventually moving north to the foothills of the Sierra Nevada Mountains. She enjoys painting, drawing, music and living an uncomplicated life while serving the needs of her feline companions. She's a fan of figure skating and has skated herself. Writing is a passion so like it or not, there will be more books.

Riona's early influences came from fantasy, science fiction, and suspense romance. She devoured books by Mary Stewart, Helen MacInnes, Morgan Llewellyn, Sharon K. Penman, and others whose writing influences her style.

You may learn more or contact the author through their her page at www.pynhavyn.com/rionakelly

OTHER BOOKS BY THIS AUTHOR:

Echoes of the Past

A picture perfect morning. A dead woman washed onto the beach.

Kathleen Donaghue's summer research trip to Wales turns upside down in that horrible moment when she finds the body. Without warning, the intrigue surrounding the victim sucks her into an eddy of unanswered questions. Who was she? How did she come to be washed ashore? Was it murder?

Signature of a Soul

Accepting her father's decree that her aunt will escort her summer trip, seventeen-year-old Michelle fears it will dash her hopes for a romantic adventure aboard. Free-spirited Lindy, a well-known artist, is pleased to chaperone her niece, but she has her own misgivings about the trip. Until they meet a dashing young Spanish street artist and a British movie location scout, setting off romantic sparks.

Charmed by Roberto, the artist, Michelle is drawn into the beauty of his coastal city while her aunt is fascinated with Colin, the well-traveled and handsome Brit, who invites her to accompany him on a location scout. While the younger couple dines out, someone steals a few paintings, including a commissioned work, from Roberto's home studio.

Why would a thief take the seemingly low-value paintings? Intrigued, Lindy and Michelle are unwittingly drawn into a dangerous quest for answers.

Read an excerpt from **ECHOES OF THE PAST**

Chapter One

"... on waves of the summer sea..."

I loved this coastline, felt a familiarity with it that filled my very soul as if this were my true home and had been since the beginning of time. The beach stretched out in a broad horseshoe, the northern end barely visible in the light fog while the southern end disappeared totally from my view. At my feet, the chill waters of the Irish Sea gently lapped up to anoint my bare toes, welcoming me back.

Behind me, sand dunes rose tall, crowned with long grasses, while in the distance, the stark outline of Harlech Castle perched like a giant eagle on the cliff looking out towards the sea.

As I gazed towards the northern hook of land, I noticed something bulky deposited on the beach. Often the waves brought in debris and now and then, something that had died. I turned and strode towards it, my bare feet slapping on the wet sand as I walked.

Getting closer, I made out a shape that looked like a sleeping person, folded into a circle as the sea had pushed the limbs towards the middle. I broke into a run, a sense of urgency driving my legs to get there as quickly as possible.

Before I reached her, I could tell it was a woman. Wet dark hair twisted around her head, covering her face and draping over her breasts. No movement disturbed her body, and I hurried more, adrenaline kicking up at the need to reach her.

I fell to my knees to see if she still breathed, leaned close to her face, and shoved the cold wet hair aside. Her skin had turned a light blue, her lips a purplish shade and no air seemed to come from either her mouth or her nose. Her face and body looked swollen, and I could see where her skin stretched on her arms. No movement lifted her chest. Nothing to indicate she still breathed.

As the realization set in, I jerked back and caught my breath sharply. Jumping to my feet, I stepped back several paces and shuddered as I continued to gape at the body.

Dead. She was dead. Beyond any help.

Hand shaking, I reached for the phone in my back pocket to call for emergency services. I fought to maintain a calm voice as I explained what I'd found. The telling somehow made it more real, and I choked on the words.

Holy crap, I'd just found a body.

Another shiver of shock ran through me.

The emergency operator kept an even, professional tone as she took the information, a factor that helped me to hold my emotions in check while I spoke with her. At the end, she told me not to touch anything else and to wait until the police arrived.

I nodded as if she could see me.

"Miss? Did you hear me?" she prompted.

"Huh? Oh, yes. Yes, I'll wait here." As I ended the call, I added "hurry" under my breath.

Still shaking, I settled myself on a sand dune drawing my knees up and resting my arms on them. Only a few yards back from the body, this perch afforded a clear view. Not that anyone was likely to come by at this hour of the morning. The breeze from the sea blew gently as I pondered what had happened to the woman. It hadn't been stormy during the night, so how had she ended up washed ashore? Who was the poor girl?

I'd risen early to come down to the beach to take photos of the sunrise over Snowden as it cast its rays down the slopes and touched the castle. Afterward, I'd turned to the sea, grabbing images as the light danced on the rolling waves. Then I'd tucked my small camera into my shirt pocket and gazed with affinity at the bay before I'd spotted her.

Now, as I waited, fidgeting nervously at my fingernails, I kept glancing at the body and wishing I hadn't been the one to find it. Needing to do something, I strolled back and decided to take a few photographs before the police arrived.

Why? I wasn't sure. Maybe a morbid streak in me demanded it. Or, perversely, I needed proof that this had happened. Although I told myself, it would be a good thing to do in case someone came along and tried to interfere. Like anyone would.

As I squatted down to get a picture of her face, I noticed her right hand clutched a locket with something etched into it. A Claddagh design, I noted as I glimpsed enough of the pair of hands holding a heart. I knew it as my father had given my mother one a few years earlier. Touched, I wondered if a lover or husband had given it to her. Sadness washed over me, and I blinked away threatening tears.

Snapping another photo, I straightened and looked towards the road where I noticed a car had stopped and two men wearing bright yellow vests climbed out. The police had arrived. I walked back towards the public access road to meet them.

They greeted me with a half-wave as they drew near enough to shout.

"Kathleen Donaghue?" the taller one called out.

I stopped walking and nodded my head as I shouted back, "Yes, that's me."

They hastened their footsteps a little, coming up to me in short order.

"You say you found a body on the beach?" the same man asked as the other, younger-looking man followed behind and observed.

Both wore white police caps with a checkered band, bearing a badge on top, over their matching almost black hair. The older sported a beard, which might have been the only thing that prevented them from looking like brothers.

"Yes." I pointed towards the body lying where I'd found it although I noticed a man approaching from the other side of the bay.

"Until now, no one else has been on the beach," I added.

The younger man took a quick glance that way and set off at a swift pace. Seeing the officer, the advancing fellow turned and retreated. The constable picked up his pace, waving and calling to the man.

The officer with me introduced himself as PC Hughes and asked, "No one else has been around then? Just you."

"That's correct."

He kept walking towards the body as I fell into step beside him.

"Tell me how you found the victim." Hughes' voice was calm and all business.

Routine for him maybe but I was undeniably nervous. "I'm staying at the hotel across the road, up on that little bluff, and I came down this morning to get a sunrise photo over Snowden. After I got the shot, I turned towards the beach and noticed the big lump that ended up being a body. I called as soon as I found her."

"I see. No one dumped it?" he asked, glancing at me, his dark eyes sizing me up. "You're American, yes?"

"I am. No, I didn't see anyone. She's soaked and there's seaweed on her, so I think she washed up on the shore during the night." Cripes, I didn't think about anyone dumping her on the beach. For that matter, they could have dropped her from a boat. That would make this a homicide. Well, damn.

"What brings you to Harlech, Miss?" he asked then as we approached the body.

"I'm here on summer break. I'm a teacher, and I'm doing some research. I like this area of Wales."

He raised an eyebrow then turned his attention to the victim. The other officer had already started to set up the perimeter for the scene.

"I'm going back for tape and cones," he told Hughes. "I'll call for the team."

Hughes nodded and walked around the body, looking at the footprints—mine—and then gazing out to the sea. Nothing showed on the beach. Anything that might have been there had already washed away.

"Your footprints?" he asked.

"Yes, and my knee marks where I knelt when I first found her and thought she might still be alive."

"Okay," he said with a note of disappointment. "Is there anything else you can tell me?"

"Not really. I just found her was all, then waited here until you arrived." I crossed my arms over my chest protectively and gazed down at the unfortunate woman.

"You're staying at the Thornhill Hotel, right? If we have any other questions, I'll find you there?"

"Yes, sir."

"How long?"

"Pardon?" I queried, uncertain what he was asking.

"How long will you be there?"

"Oh. Another month, at least." I wet my lips and managed a tight little smile.

"Right. Research. You're free to go now. Thank you for calling us." Done with me, he turned to the real business.

Casting one last glance at the woman, I turned away and headed back to the dune where I'd left my sandals. The woman had looked about my age, not quite thirty, and fit. Somberly, I wondered if I'd learn any more about her and what had happened or if she was just an unfortunate accident victim.

I slipped my shoes on and started to climb back over the sand to the public beach access path. The coastal highway was, perhaps, a half mile back from water in a pleasant walk.

My hotel, a charming bed and breakfast inn, was just across the highway, partway up the side of a bluff. Facing the sea, much the same as Harlech Castle, it had a similar view although my room looked towards the castle and the town.

As I climbed the steep steps, I passed numerous clumps of dewberry vines whose prickly thorns gave the Thornhill name to the hotel. Once I reached the front garden, I paused to look back towards the road along the beach where an additional police car and an ambulance-like vehicle parked behind the first. On the beach, more little dots of people scurried towards the others. Shoulders slumping, I tackled the subsequent six stairs into the hotel with the somber thoughts of the dead woman dampening my natural buoyancy.

Even though it was June and the start of the usual summer season, the place was almost empty. Poor weather along the coast and a lack of American tourists this year made the hospitality business a tad slow, or so the hotel's owner had informed me. In fact, other than myself, there were only two couples registered.

In my four days here, I had established my own table in the small dining room, so I went directly to it, not waiting for Mrs. Linton to acknowledge me. I liked the table's location as it afforded a splendid view to the northeast, the castle, and the mountains. I had barely settled myself in when Mrs. Linton hurried over with the pot of tea. She had discovered my passion for breakfast tea on the first day of my stay and never bothered to ask anymore.

"Did you have a nice walk, love?" Her accent was decidedly English. Neither she nor Mr. Linton were Welsh but had bought the little hotel three years earlier as an opportunity to get away from the big city life.

"Yes, thank you," I replied, reluctant to tell her anything about the body on the beach. I didn't lie; it had been a pleasant walk up to a point.

She peered out the window a frown wrinkling her forehead. "It looks like a bit of a hubbub down on the beach. Police cars and the mortuary ambulance. Someone must have drowned, poor soul. Did you see anything, Miss Donaghue?"

"Something washed ashore during the night. I guess it was a body. The police were checking it out when I left." I hoped I sounded innocent enough.

She clucked her tongue a couple of times. "A shame, but it happens every once in a while. I guess we'll hear about it on the news later. English breakfast this morning or would you prefer something lighter?"

"Just toast sounds good, please." I didn't think I could face a full breakfast right now.

"Certainly," she replied and turned to go to the kitchen, spotting the young couple who walked in on the way.

"Good morning, Mr. and Mrs. James," she called and motioned them towards a table closer to the front of the room.

The petite blond girl looked barely sixteen with a fresh pixie-face devoid of makeup while her husband wasn't much older, in spite of the barely-there mustache that graced his upper lip. A slight bump below his bride's waist suggested the reason for the early marriage.

Turning my eyes away, I pulled out my camera and thumbed through the morning's photos. The daybreak photos looked stunning, at least in the size of my viewer, and I was eager to see them on my laptop. When I got to the beach photos of the dead girl, my mood sobered again, and a shiver raced through my spine, tingling down my arms in a chill. Sometimes my imagination is too vivid, and in my mind, I could see the poor thing drowning, caught in the tide, and pulled out into the sea.

I reached for my tea, savoring the warmth and comfort of the beverage as I shoved the images away. It was done. Sympathy wouldn't help the woman any.

My toast arrived, and I turned my attention to eating and planning the afternoon's excursion. Mrs. Linton stopped back by again to inquire if I needed anything else.

"My nephew is about your age," she added slyly. "He'll be coming up from Kent this weekend. I think you would like him, love."

I managed a half-hearted smile. This was the third person she'd mentioned to me since I'd arrived four days earlier. First, the gardener; she'd brought a nice twenty-two-year-old fellow with a stutter to meet me while I sat on the patio in the back garden reading. He'd looked like he wanted to run away when she'd introduced him. The second was a thirty-something man, who owned a grocery store in the town. He'd been delivering an order to the hotel and clearly had no interest in being detained to meet an out-of-towner.

Now, it was her nephew. Did she think I needed a companion while I was here? Perhaps she was trying to match me up with someone for the Saturday evening festival at the church. At any rate, I hardly needed her help.

"That's good news for you, Mrs. Linton," I replied. "I'm sure you'll have a lovely visit with him. Will he be here long?"

"Just three days," she answered. "You'll have to meet Eddie when he gets here. You know, someone to chat with while you're visiting." She cast a reassuring smile at me before she flitted away to check on her other guests.

After I finished my tea, I rose and retreated to my room for a quick shower to wash off the sand and sea salt from my skin. As I dressed in a pastel-colored summer dress with loose sleeves, I still chuckled over her efforts to find me a companion. As it happened, I had a date of my own.

www.ingramcontent.com/pod-product-compliance
Lightning Source LLC
Chambersburg PA
CBHW020557180626
46810CB00007B/2543